I0549310

The Shadow of the Moon Rider

By

Joan Byrd

Deep Indigo Books
Published by Indigo Sea Press
Winston-Salem

Deep Indigo Books
Indigo Sea Press
PO Box 26701
Winston-Salem, NC 27114

First Deep Indigo Books edition published
February, 2020
Deep Indigo Books, Moon Sailor and all production design are trademarks of Indigo Sea Press, used under license.

For information regarding bulk purchases of this book, digital purchase and special discounts, please contact the publisher at indigoseapress@gmail.com

Cover illustration by Joan Byrd
Cover design by Pan Morelli
Manufactured in the United States of America
ISBN 978-1-63066-499-2

*Once in a lifetime you are given one powerful book of
fiction to write! It fills the imagination with a powerful
character who will change the literary world forever!
In creating this beautiful love story, packed with action,
in the 70s, my constant friend, my niece and little buddy,
was there to walk this journey with me as we were swept
into this story of Marcia Karnstein, my beautiful heroine,
and the mysterious Moon Rider!*

*I dedicate this book to Daphine "Dene" Murrell
and the many times we "read" this story over and over!*

—Joan Byrd

Chapter One

The sun shone brightly through the small arched window as Marcia's angry brown eyes pierced down at the vast courtyard of Karnstein Manor. She loved it here at Melbourne and her heart ached at the thoughts of leaving. If it weren't for that heedless Krantz Hamish, she wouldn't be running away, she thought, as she slammed her fist down on the stone mantel.

"Calm down, my lady. Would you wake up the entire house?" Elizabet Harmon walked quickly from the closet, balancing a blue cotton dress in her hands.

"I would indeed!" Marcia snapped "Why should I be the only one around here to suffer? Is it not my own father who insist I marry that impossible man?"

"Aye, my lady, but your father is doing what he thinks best." The lady's maid blinked nervously when Marcia twirled around.

"Best! Whose side are you on, Elizabet?" Marcia stormed across the room. "And do you think marring the raven is the best? You, of all people, should be fighting this unheard-of-marriage!"

"My lady, me thinks perhaps the raven would not be so terrible once you became his wife." The devoted woman held out the dress toward the startled young face. "Best get yourself dressed in your gown."

Marcia's hand flew toward the gown and sent it to the floor as she narrowed her eyes at her old nurse and friend. "And if it were you, would you marry the great black raven?"

"Me, marry the handsome Duke?" Elizabet's stomach jiggled as she laughed. "I would marry any man who saw fit to ask."

"This is no time to jest, Lizzie! I 'will not' marry Krantz Hamish and that is final! He is a villain, a liar, and a vicious man!" The beautiful young woman's trim fingers swooped the gown up off the marble floor. "I stayed up all the night thinking and have come up with a plan that will save myself."

"A plan, my lady? What is the plan child? Can you not share it with your old faithful nurse?" The middle-age woman brushed down her white apron nervously.

1

"First, you must promise me that what I tell you will be kept to yourself and naught will drive it from you." Marcia looked down into her nurse's eyes.

"Sweet child, you know you have always been my first concern. Naught will make me speak of what you are about to share with me in secret. Nay, not even his royal majesty, our own King Henry!" Elizabet smiled loving up at the relieved girl.

"As you well know, my father will leave today for Tilbury. There he will meet with Sir Krantz and give him my hand in marriage in exchange for great riches. It would appear, my dear father has lost quite a substantial amount of his own wealth in bad investments and the need to gamble." Marcia titled her head with pride. "Dear father plans to restore Karnstein Manor when I am 'sold' off to the raven, which goes to show how very little my father knows that evil man!"

"Aye! He is a bit of a snuffling serpent. Not at all a good match for my beautiful pompous young lady." Elizabet's fat hand smoothed down Marica's ruffled uncombed hair.

"I thought you were all for my marring the black hearted man." Marcia noticed a twinkle in the older woman's eyes through the vanity mirror as she brushed her ward's long chestnut hair smooth. "Oh, you be a teasing with my feelings again! Never mind. I'm just glad you are on my side instead of father's." She kissed Elizabet's chubby cheek as she stood up and climbed inside her blue dress. "Whilst father is in Tilbury collecting only false promises, guess where we shall be?"

"On our way to London, I suppose, to spend some time with your aunt." Elizabet heard the young woman laughed as she walked over to the small arched window that looked out over the courtyard below. With small quick steps, the nurse hurried to her side. "That, is it, is it not? Your father said you were to go there to have his sister, your Aunt Coreen, help you buy your wedding garments."

"That, my dear sweet nurse, is where my poor father thinks we shall be off to." Marica walked over in front of the vanity and smiled at her refection. "Whilst all the time you and I shall be on our way to Canterbury."

"Canterbury?" the nurse asked, startled.

2

"Aye!" Marica twirled around, laughing then took her companion by the shoulders. "Lizzie, we are to tell no one where we are going! Cook, house maids, Elsa and Kathlyn, your lovely friends, not a soul, understand? When we reach Canterbury, we shall call each other by different names. Absolutely nobody must know our true identity."

"We are running away?" the worried woman twisted her hands.

"We are indeed, dear friend and the only thing I shall truly miss is Karnstein." She looked down once again in the courtyard. Everything she had ever known was right here at her loving home, but she must leave if she hoped to escape the evil clutches of Sir Krantz Hamish. "This night, we must pack our things and be prepared to set out for Canterbury as soon as father has departed to Tilbury. Our small staff will assume we are heading for London."

"But my lady, do we dare to set out on our own, just the two of us?" Elizabet's eyebrows twitched nervously. "It will be tomfoolery, two women alone. How will we fend for ourselves?"

"Lizzie, where is your spirit?" Marcia chuckled. "After all, this is 1659 and things are beginning to change somewhat." Marcia noticed the anxious look still on her old nurse's face. Reaching over, she gently patted her soft cheek. "Stay here if you choose. I will go alone, on my own."

"Now, what a thing is that to say to your faithful old nurse? Did not I cuddle you as a wee babe, hold you up as you toddled about and was it not I who watched you grow into the fine lady that you have become."

"Aye, 'twas you Lizzie." Marica watched her personal maid closely as she walked about, fretting.

"And did you not say, just this second, that I could stay behind and leave you to go all by yourself into Canterbury, a town you know naught about?"

"Aye, dear friend. I thought, by your reactions, you chose not to go." Marcia pulled a large traveling bag from under her high bed as the nurse ran over to assist, her voice growing high with excitement.

"Did I say that, did I now?"

3

"Nay Lizzie, not in your word but what I read in your demeaner. I just though" Marica laughed as the high-strung woman tapped her lips loudly.

"You thought? Now would I let you race off to Canterbury and have all the excitement all by yourself?" the short-stout woman gave a chuckle.

"Nay, I knew you would come along." Marica gave the heavy lady a tight hug as she reminded her "Now, remember Lizzie, not one word of this to anyone."

"Me lips are sealed, my lady." Elizabet Harmon walked over to the adjacent room and opened her chamber door. "I shall go fetch me garments and placed them in my bag so to be ready for our new adventure!"

Marcia sang softly to herself as she made her way slowly down the wide-curving staircase. Henry Karnstein stood to admire her beauty as she descended gracefully to his waiting presence. The handsome middleman aged smiled broadly at his daughter, extending her his hand.

"My dear Marcia, it does my heart good to see you so happy."

"Does it father? My joy does not descend from your recent news, Father." She walked past him, ignoring his proffered hand.

"What's this? Does not the news that I have chosen you a husband bring you joy?" Henry's voice grew heavy.

Marcia twirled around to face him. "Nay, Father!" her voice returned just as bitter. "Your poor choice does me a great misjustice!"

"Do my ears deceive me?" his eyes held his daughter's. "Poor choice? Is not Krantz Hamish one of the wealthiest men in England? Has he not waxed into one of England's greatest defenders! He is of royal blood, made Duke of Tilbury after his older brother was mysteriously murdered."

"Murdered no doubt by the black hearted devil! England would be well to be rid of him!" Marcia's voice shook with anger. "He is a lying thief, that raven and I shall have no part of him!"

"Have no part, you say!" Henry Karnstein stared over at his daughter, fire shooting from his eyes. "You do as I say, girl! You will marry Hamish and there will be naught else said about it!"

4

"Nay! Not for all the crown heads in England! I WILL NOT marry that dark raven!" Marcia stomped her foot.

"SILENCE!" Lord Karnstein's voice rang through the manor. "I will hear no more nonsense! The wedding is set! I leave today for Tilbury to discuss the final details to your betrothed." The angry father turned quickly to face Elizabet, who stood staring at the little scene from the bottom step. "If you wish to retain your position Miss Harmon, take care that you get my daughter to her Aunt Dorinda Coreen Karnstein in London!"

"Aye, my Lord." She bowed nervously.

"See that you get finished within a few weeks and return to Melbourne with speed." He rang for his page. "Fetch my horse and see to it my bags are made secure."

Elizabet watched the young page hurry from the door and jumped when Lord Karnstein stepped in front of her and stared down.

"Well woman, what holds you here?"

"We shall take leave at once, my Lord." The nurse swallowed and grabbed for Marica's hand. "We shall indeed make haste to London and finish quickly with the lady's finery."

"Good!" He walked over to the door and glanced back to see Marica staring angrily at him. "See to it that my saucy daughter tries none of her childish tricks!"

Elizabet smiled sheepishly. "Aye, my Lord, I will watch the girl closely."

"See to it!" Henry Karnstein walked quickly from the room as Marcia squeezed her companions' hand and whispered

"Let us make with haste as father wills." She smiled down, her face lit with mischief. "Can we help, that by being women, we lose our way and in up in Canterbury?"

Chapter Two

The quite little village of Canterbury lay sleepily beyond a long row of sycamore trees. From either side one could see long stretches of wooded ground or wasteland. The streets were narrow and steep and the noise of cartwheels rumbled and echoed along the cobblestones.

Agar Bellingham watched a male sparrow making its way across the church yard. His thoughts twirled in front of him as his mind wandered back to Collinwood and the task that lay ahead of him this night. His thoughts were disturbed when he heard the young voice of his companion.

"Father Bellingham, didn't you hear me?"

His attention fell quickly to the small child at his feet. "I'm sorry, Nora. My mind was afar." His tall frame bent to pat her blonde head. "What was it you said, child?"

"I said I saw that same sparrow here yesterday. He has a little steak of yellow running through his brown wings." Her bright blue eyes glistened. "Do you suppose he lives in yonder tree?"

"Could well be." The handsome young priest swooped the small girl up in his arms. "I cannot think of a better spot in all of Canterbury to live than right here."

"Not anywhere, Father?" Nora ran her small hand through his blonde locks. "What about Collinwood?"

"Ah, yes, Collinwood. Now there's the most beautiful place in England!" Agar's long legs carried him through the white gate and down the cobblestone streets of the village.

The young child waved at shop keepers she knew, sitting high on the young priest's shoulders, as her eyes danced with delight. "Do you think I shall ever see Collinwood. Father? I should like that very much."

"Aye, I am sure of it!" He tilted his head up to give her a handsome smile as he made sure he had a tight grip on the happy child.

"You know what I shall like best of all, Father Bellingham?"

"Tell me Nora, what is on your small heart?" he paused to listen to his little friend.

"To be able to take your hand and walk all the way to Collinwood with you." Nora looked down sadly at her crippled legs, dangling loosely around her good friend's strong shoulders. "Will that just have to stay a dream, Father?"

"Nay, my lovely little friend. Miracles are known to happen, from time to time." He patted her small hands that looped around his neck for support. "But, if, perchance, you could take to walking Nora, don't you think Collinwood is a little far for walking on foot?"

"Oh, nay, dearest friend! We could make a day out of it!" Nora's eyes opened wide with excitement. "Start out early, then we could carry a lunch and rest along the way!"

"Nora, Nora!" Agar laughed "Such a little girl with grand ideals!" Reaching the girl's cottage, the young priest handed her over to Madam Banistry, Nora's mother and made his way back up the hill to the church.

His thoughts began to wonder again to the nights events as his feet fell into a steady rhythm on the cobblestones. Without warning, from out of nowhere a small cart was approaching him swiftly. Agar made a dive for safety as the young woman pulled the reins tightly on the high-spirited mare.

Marcia jumped down quickly off the cart and ran over to where the priest lay.

"Is he hurt, my lady?" Elizabet called nervously from the cart as she held on to the reins. "Lordy me, that is all we need, to hurt a holy man and soon as we arrive to Canterbury!"

"I think not." Marcia touched his arm lightly and Agar rolled over to stare up at her. "Father, are there any broken bones?"

"Nay madam, ye just scared the saints out of me!" Agar stood up and began brushing off his black robes. "This is not a racetrack, you know."

"It's Maggie, my very spirited mare, she's feeling much too good today, I'm afraid." Marcia reached over to help brush the dust off the handsome stranger's back. "We are really terribly sorry."

"Tell me, do you try to run down a priest every day?" he picked up the small bible that had fallen from his pocket and crammed it back in as he looked the pretty young woman over.

"Oh, heaven no, Father! Just every other day!" Marcia laughed as she noticed a beautiful smile stretch across his handsome face.

"I take it you are new in Canterbury, are you not?"

"Aye, as a matter of fact, we are." Marcia noticed he glanced up inside the cart to see who this fascinating creature was traveling with and was happy to see no presence of a man, just a heavy-set lady, looking alarmed. Smiling to herself, Marcia walked back over to the cart. "My aunt and I have been traveling here all the way from Cambridge."

"That's quite soon distance for two women traveling alone." Agar stroked the mare's neck before rubbing her smooth nose. "Did you meet with no trouble along the way?"

"Nay, none. The Lord saw us safely here." She couldn't help but stare at the handsome face. "It was quite a pleasant trip actually."

"Will you be living in Canterbury?" The attraction he felt for the stranger frightened Agar. He had noticed his heart took up speed when she had first looked down at him with her incredible eyes.

"Aye, for a time. We thought we might see how we like it here." Marcia pulled herself away from the priest and the sudden feelings she was having for him. She turned to get back on the cart and felt the priest slip his strong hands around her tiny waist and lifted her up with ease. "That's most kind of you sir."

"Men who are not gentlemen are not worthy to receive a woman's beautiful smile, such as you have." Agar's broad smile made Marcia's heartbeat heavily in her throat as she watched him step away from the cart when she took the reins from Elizabet. "See to it that you keep a tight hold on those reins. We do want your stay here to be a joyful one, don't we?"

"We do indeed, Father." Elizabet chuckled out loud. "Seems strange that I should be calling a young man like you, Father, when to know it, I be old enough to be ye mother."

Agar smiled at the cheerful woman. "My mother? You certainly could have fool me madam." His attention fell once again on Marcia. Feeling her face flush hot, she quickly looked down at her hands, for fear he would think her bold for staring at him for

8

so long. Her faithful nurse was overcome with the compliment toward her as she nodded her head politely and said

"Well now, isn't that charming. Me thinks we best be going while ye thinks such a nice thought about me." Elizabet patted Marica's knees. "Are you ready, my dear one?"

"Aye." Marcia looked down at the priest and noticed his blue eyes still held hers steadily. "I hope we shall be good friends."

"I should hope we already are. Take care now." Agar watched the cart moved out of sight, down the streets of Canterbury. Slowly, he started back up the path that led to the church on the hill. He caught sight of a moving object making its way swiftly toward him. Agar smiled, as he focused his attention of the red hair blowing wildly above the green bushes that lined the churchyard.

"Master, I have been looking all over for ye!" Amby Steen brushed his hand through his thick locks. "Why can't ye ever stay put?"

"My dear friend, my work sometimes carries me beyond the church gate." Agar laughed as he put his arm around his friend's shoulders. "You, of all people, should know that."

"Aye, I know well the work you do beyond the church gate." Amy shook his head. "He who walks on thin ice usually gets wet!"

"Aye!" Agar pulled a vessel from the altar and pour out two mugs of wine. "Drink up my friend, and tell me the news that brought you in search of me."

"Word was brought to us that Enoch has paid another visit to the widow Parker. This time he got away with quite a large bundle." Amby finished the wine and set down his empty mug.

"When will Enoch learn he cannot possibly get away with his dishonest behavior?" Agar stood up and pulled the burse over the vessel and mugs.

"A job for the Moon Rider?" Amby waited for Agar to respond.

"Aye, Amby. At the first glimpse of the moon, the Moon Rider will bring the role of evil back around to good!"

"Aye!" Amby chuckled "To Collinwood?"

"To Collinwood!" Agar led the way down the steep steps to the back entrance of the church. Within minutes both men were on

9

their horses and headed through the forest to Collinwood.

Marcia looked around at the simple surroundings of the small village flat. She noticed a picturesque flower box adorning the small window facing the street and walked over to find it giving off a fresh clean fragrance. Gazing from the window, Marcia noticed the village was made up with a row of houses, some three or four stories high with workshops on their ground floors. The upper floors jutted out over the street so far that in smaller lanes, the houses almost touched.

"Well, my lady, tis not much, is it?"

"On the contrary, Lizzie, I think it is quite a lovely place." Marica began pulling her clothes from the traveling bag. "I shall search for employment tomorrow."

"Employment? You, my lady?" Elizabet nervously dropped the parcel from her hands causing Marcia to laugh.

"Aye, and why not? We cannot expect to live on what we brought with us for long, now can we?"

"Nay, I suppose not, but employment." The nurse stared helplessly at the young woman. "It's not fitting for a lady, with your high up-bringing, to take on a position in the workplace. Your father would..."

Marcia looked up and narrowed her eyes at her trusted friend. "Lizzie, will you restrain yourself from talking about my father! I care not to hear his name whilst we are in Canterbury!" she walked over to the door and slung it open. "I am sure there is something around Canterbury that a lady can do that is respectable."

"Then let me get the position, my lady." Elizabet walked over next to Marcia and peeked out around her. Marcia kissed the older woman's cheek, then gave her a loving hug.

"I'll not hear of it, Lizzie! Now how would it look to these folks of Canterbury, if the lazy niece, years younger, stays home while the poor old auntie takes on a job, hum?"

"What they gossip about, makes no matter, my lady. I know what you be and I would feel much better if..." Before the nurse could continue, Marcia touched her lips lightly.

"Shish! No more talk Lizzie. Just busy yourself with fixing this place up a bit. See if there is a privy in the back somewhere.

There's plenty of daylight left. I think I will pop off down the street and look for work this evening."

Elizabet glanced out and noticed the streetlight had not been lit yet, but the sun was slowly sinking in the evening sky. "Darling girl, it's getting late for popping about." She tied the apron around her big middle. "Strange towns are no place to be wondering about in the gloom."

"My dear Lizzie, you worry much too much about me." Marcia patted the bun on the back of the nurse's head. "I promise to be back long before dark."

"If you wait till the morrow, I can go about with you."

"Look, Lizzie, if I see that I am having no luck, I will come straight home." She raced out the door before the worried woman could say a word more.

Chapter Three

The moon rose over the towering walls of Collinwood as the great shadow of a huge horse and its rider rode swiftly from the gates. Within minutes, the Moon Rider and his companions rode silently up to the steps of Sir Henry Enoch's residence. The tall grey stone structure rose grotesquely in the moonlit night and laughter and merriment could be heard clearly just within. The Moon Rider gave his silent signal and his men quickly obeyed his command.

"We outdone ourselves this time, Sir Henry!" one of his bearded companions laughed loudly. "We must have rid the widow of most of her wealth!"

"Ah, 'tis true, and the overly smart Moon Rider has no clue it was us." Sir Henry held up his mug, a sign for his servant to bring wine. "Bring more drink, and more for my guest! This is a time for much celebrating!"

"And you, Larky, what will you do with your share?" One man slapped the skinny lad, at his side, on the shoulder.

"I'm gonna hop off to Canterbury and pick me out a big busted woman and fill up her cup!" He laughed, half-drunk with wine. "It was so easy robbing that old bat!"

"And the killing, was that easy too, me boy?" Sir Henry laughed.

"Killing? What…what killing?" he stuttered.

"When you killed the old woman. Have you forgotten already, sonny boy?" Sir Henry's smile faded from his face.

"Killed? But I…I…" the young lad rose on wobbly legs.

"Are you telling me that you did not kill the woman? I gave the order, no witnesses! You fool!" Sir Henry jumped when the candles blew out, leaving them in the dark. He and his nervous guest looked quickly over to the dark figure crashing through the heavy door.

"Great Scots, it's the Moon Rider!" Henry eyes grew in round saucers as he yelled "Man yourselves!"

"Aye, man yourselves indeed, and I shall proudly reward you

12

with slashed throats!" The Moon Rider's voice rang through the air. "Now, if you behave, and give back the riches you stole from the widow Parker, I might spare your lives."

"And, not a word to the police captain?" Enoch swallowed.

"And let your crime go unreported? Nay, 'tis not likely." The tall black figure motioned for his men to enter. They came from all directions, as though they were seeping from the walls. "Gather the widow's riches and bind these villains. We shall take them on a little visit to Canterbury."

"Listen, Moon Rider, you are a reasonable man. Let us be and you may share in half our riches." Enoch forced a laugh. "No one will be the wiser."

"When will you ever learn, Enoch? Have I not told you a thousand times over? He who tries to hide evil never wins, because God, who has made all, sees all!" Moon Rider slapped Henry Enoch on the back. "Perhaps after a little time behind the dark walls of the dungeon, you will come about to my reasoning."

"You scalawag!" Enoch barked. "Someday, I will get even with you, Moon Rider! Someday, somehow, you will slip up, and I will be there to put a sword through your bloody heart!"

"Take him from my sight!" Moon Rider walked quickly to his horse and led the way through the darkened forest.

Marcia kicked at a loose stone as she made her way back to her flat by the street oil lights. She had thought finding a job would be easy, but the sky had begun to grow dark and still she had nothing. She paused just outside a small shop when she heard a woman and man arguing with one another.

"I told you Hillary, do not get involved with the customers!"

"And I told you, Joe is not just a customer, you louse!" The woman's voice came loud through the closed door.

"How would you like to find another position, huh?" the man's voice rose to meet her volume.

"You know what you can do with this lousy position, eat it!" She shouted then stormed out the wide door, past Marcia and down the cobblestone street, mumbling loudly to herself.

Following the woman to the door, the bald-headed man shook his fist at her, unaware that he was being observed carefully by the beautiful young woman standing next to him. Watching his worker disappear around the corner, he mumbled softly

"Hateful bitch!"

"I am certain the young lady will think it over, once she calms herself down, and be back to work tomorrow to do her job." Marcia smiled, knowing she had taken the stranger by surprise.

"What's this?" for a brief moment he had been startled by her sudden presence, then looked around her to find her completely alone. "Miss, it's not safe for a lady to be out on the streets of Canterbury at night. Have you no mummy to look after you?"

"I assure you, sir, I am in no need for someone to look after me. I am quite capable of taking care of myself." she smiled gaily. "I have just moved here with my dear aunt, good sir and to tell the truth, I have been looking for a position to help bring some income in to see us through. It grew dark on me, so I was heading back to our flat when I heard all the commotion inside your business. If the girl I saw leaving here so briskly won't be returning to her job, perchance you could take me on in her place."

"Now, how do you like this one?" he laughed as though he were speaking to a third party. "Ye will take on a position you know absolutely nothing about?"

"Indeed, I would! That is, if the job is honest. I would never do anything that wasn't." Marcia pulled herself up as tall as she could. "I am quite capable of doing almost anything."

"Aye, me girl, I just bet you are!" he chuckled as he patted her head as though he was talking to a young child. "Come by tomorrow at teatime and we will discuss a position. But for now, you better run on alone home before your sweet aunt starts worrying about your where-about."

"Oh, thank you! You won't be disappointed, I promise!" Marcia put out her hand, not to be kissed as was tradition but for a business handshake. The business owner stared for several moments at her soft extended hand before shaking it, knowing this was no ordinary lady. She was a well brought up young woman from a distinguish family.

"Young lady, tell your aunt to come alone with you for tea. She may wish to hear about your new position too."

"My good sir, I am quite capable of finding a position on my own. I need not have her approval." Marcia was tired of being treated like a child by this man with the friendly face.

"Never-the-less, I should like to meet your aunt anyway." He laughed and waved her away. "On your way now, it grows late."

"Aye, I shall see you tomorrow and bring my aunt." Marcia turned and started back to the flat when she suddenly heard cries just down the street. She paused momentarily and recognize the sound of a woman screaming for help. Marcia lifted up her long skirt to give her legs more freedom to run, like she had done often as an only child, playing in the back hills behind her manor house. She dashed quickly down the cobblestones to where the screams came from. Stopping briefly to catch her breath, Marcia noticed the scene below her.

The calm daytime streets had turned a fiery orange as the torches waved back and forth from the horsemen's hands. Raiders had invaded Canterbury, looting, making rude passes at the women and taunting their weak men. Marcia watched in the shadows, unknowing what move to make. The wrong move would put her in the same situation as the other town women. Her attention was drawn to a house across the street from where the commotion was going on. A single rider was pulling a woman from the house. She held tightly to her torn dress as he laughingly thrust his hand inside to her breast. The blood began to boil in Marcia's veins as her fist went into a tight ball. Her eyes fell down to a screaming child clutching to the man's legs as he pulled the frightened woman to his horse. Holding tight to his foot, the small girl was dragged over the cobblestones.

"Let go of my leg, brat! You won't be going along with us!" He shook his foot, but the little girl held on as she screamed out

"You let my mummy go! He will get you, all you mean villains! He's coming, I just know it!"

"Shut it up, kid!" the angry man bent over and pulled the child free from him, then slapped her back out of the way. "Now, get lost!"

Marcia could not hold still any longer. She raced across the street and dived on the man's back. Startled by her actions, the man dropped his rape victim to grab the hands choking off his air as he managed to say, "What the...bloody hell?" He struggled

15

wildly to pull her free, but not soon enough. Marcia sank her teeth into his thick neck causing him to curse loudly. He yelled "You little hell cat! Damn you, woman!"

"You, beastly demon!" Marcia yelled in his ear. "Who gives you the right to take helpless women from their homes and kick around innocent children?"

"Let him have it, lady!" The little girl pulled herself over to her mother.

At the sound of horse's hoofs pounding their way along the cobblestones, the raiders darted in all directions as the little girl shouted with total joy.

"It's him! The Moon Rider! He came! He really came!"

"The Moon Rider?" Marcia turned to see who had everyone so excited, giving the angry man the chance he needed to be rid of her. The villain grabbed her off his back and slung her on the ground, before climbing on his horse and taking off down the road.

Dark eyes looked from the mask of the Moon Rider's hood. He gritted his teeth as he made his way quickly to where Marcia lay. He stared down at her briefly, then made off after the man who had mistreated her. Marcia managed to sit up and watched the mysterious masked man overtake the bad man, then sprang quickly off his saddle upon the man, pulling him to the ground.

"Draw thy sword, you villain and pay for your wickedness!" the Moon Rider shouted. "Draw, I say!"

"I will not stand a chance against you!" No more, cocky, the bandit backed away nervously.

"You should have thought of that before you decided to touch that woman!" he shifted the sword from one hand to the other. "Draw, I say! Draw and take your punishment like a man!"

"Please, good sir." Marcia took hold of his sleeve and the women standing nearby gasped at her actions. Rider's dark eyes looked down at her hand clutching his black sleeve and then stared in her luminous eyes. "What you do is brave and gallant, but surely it is not your intent to slay this man."

"Wench, this man has treated you without care, has he not? Would you that I turn him loose without punishment?"

"I think his fear of you is punishment enough. It is obvious he is no match for you." Marcia noticed how well the black clothes clung to his manly body. "I think he has learned a lesson and I think not that he will do any more wrong in Canterbury."

"Then, it is obvious you are a poor judge of people. Fair one." His eyes burned down on her from under the mask.

Suddenly Marcia felt this man was a pompous, ostentatious person as she threw back her head with pride. "On the contrary, I am a very good judge of people! Take you for instant! It is quite obvious you enjoy putting on a show with your vain appearance and think you are above everyone else!"

"And you, sassy wench, are obviously ill-bread, rude, ungrateful and impolite!" His voice remained calm and deliberate.

"Name calling fits you well, Sir Knight!" she mocked "But if you had observed, you should have noticed that I was defending myself without your help."

"Aye, that I did. A well, high spirited wench. That is my favorite choice!" Rider laughed. "But there is one thing you must learn, woman, never take your attention away from the enemy. It is bad strategy."

"Sir Knight, had it not been for your dramatic entrance into the village, I would not have looked around." Marcia narrowed her eyes at him when he gave a smug laugh. "Why does thou laugh in such a manner?"

"So, it was my good looks that drove you to look and loose your hold." He laughed out at her expression. "I am truly flattered."

"You, sir, are indeed conceited! I fancy not your manners or your appearance!" Marcia jumped when the Moon Rider brushed her aside and slashed through the arm of the bandit whose sword was raise for an attack. Marcia gasped down at the moaning man, holding his bleeding arm. "He…he…"

"Aye!" The Moon Rider waved some of his men over. "take this man and lock him with the rest!" His attention fell on the beautiful girl staring up at him. "You see, it pays to be on guard at all times. That villain thought I had my attention drawn away from him by your undying charm, fair one."

"I could do well without any attention from the looks of you, Sir Knight!" Marcia arched her eyebrow and turned to leave when he grabbed her arm. Her eyes blazed into his as she spoke bravely.

"If you would be so kind as to remove your hand!"

"In time." His finger moved along her arm. "Wench, before long, you will welcome my touch, long for it."

"How dare you speak to me thus!" Marcia tried to pull free, but found it hopeless. He held her tightly, a smile on his lips as he watched her struggle. "Let me go, you…you beast!"

"Aye, for the time." Rider's eyes burned down into hers. "Soon I will ride in between your thighs and you will enjoy it!"

"Why you…" he released her arm and climbed up on the black stallion while Marcia stared up at him.

"Until next we meet, wench, adieu." The Moon Rider blew her a kiss and was gone in a flash.

Marcia felt all the stares she was receiving from the village people and knew they had been silently watching and listening to the conversation between her and the masked man. Without hesitation, she gathered up her skirt and dashed off for the small flat.

Chapter Four

Marcia and Elizabet made their way into the little shop that Marcia had discovered the previous night. They both recognized at once that the place was a tavern. Elizabet lend over and whispered in her wards ear.

"My lady, you cannot work here! It is no place for a lady like yourself."

"Look Lizzie, I'm sure I can handle it well enough. I look as capable as the last lady who worked here!" Marcia nodded for her old nurse to stay quiet when she saw the bald-headed man approach them from the back room. "Good day, sir. We came together as you suggested. I hope we are not too early."

"Nay, the tea is prepared." The owner looked from the older woman to the younger. Putting his hand up to his chin, he studied them both carefully. "Nope, I do not see it!"

"If you would be so kind as to tell us what it is you do not see." Marcia could not make up her mind if she like this man or not and what it would be like working for him.

"I mean to make no offence to either of you lovely ladies, but for kin, you two look nothing alike." The tavern keeper chuckled when the women smiled. "I mean, I see absolutely no family resemblance."

"Nay, I dare say you will not. There is none." Elizabeth laughed out. "Me dear niece looks exactly like her dear departed mother. She did not get any of myself or my brother, that would be her father. Nay, none of our traits, I grant ye."

"Come on up into my rooms. The tea is laid out along with some custard and teacakes." He led them up a narrow staircase to a small living room, furnished sparsely with an old sofa and matching chairs. "It's nothing fancy, mind you, but it is some of the best tea in England."

Marcia graciously took the china cup, filled with the wonderful brew, and stirred in one sugar and cream. Taking a sip, she declared "Aye, you are right, it is very good." Marcia sipped a while on the steaming tea before eating the creamy custard with a teacake. "Mumm, this is very good too. Did you make this wonderful food?"

"I pride myself on being one of the best cooks in all of Canterbury." The friendly man laughed as he licked some custard from his fingers.

"Well, I will not be saying you are the best until I've had the chance to sample some of the other cooks in the village." Elizabet reached for another teacake and custard as she pushed her empty cup his way for a refill. "But, I can warn ye fairly, you have to work pretty hard to beat my cooking."

"Your cooking?" He smiled down at her round belly across from him. "Aye, I'll be taking your word for it, madam."

Marcia tried to hide her smile as she waved away a second cup. "Could we discuss the position now please. I'm sorry, but I don't know your name."

"George Holmes, at your service." He took a third custard and mumbled through each bite. "And your name my dear, what is it?"

"Cia, Cia Stone." Marcia smiled over at her trusted friend. "My aunt is Lisa."

"Cia and Lisa Stone." George Holmes gulped down the remainder of his second cup of tea and wiped his face before continuing. "This position may be pretty hard for a young girl like yourself to handle."

"I am sure I can manage it, Mr. Holmes. Just tell me what I will be doing." Marcia was getting irritated by this man referring to her as a child. "Now, this is a tavern, is it not?"

"Aye lassie, and one of the best and busiest in Canterbury. We have a decent clientele and not much trouble with the chaps that come in. The rougher bunch gives Harry's their business, what with their barmaids being prostitutes and harlots."

"Mr. Holmes, what sort of job would my la...lovely niece be a doing in your fine establishment?" Elizabet cleared her throat, the ideal of her ward working around a lot of men drinking.

"I run a respectable place here, madam. Her job would be to wait on the customers and do a little bit of dancing." George waved his hand over his head. "You know, to help entertain the gents while they partake in beverages."

"Entertain the gents!" Elizabet stared angrily over at George

20

Holmes. "I don't think I like the sound of that."

"Please Lisa, let me handle this." Marcia was growing impatient with her two companions. "Just what sort of dancing did you have in mind, George?"

"You know Cia, just move your shapely hips around a little to the slow music of Yancy Weatherspoon playing the harpsichord. Something to give the chaps a little enjoyment before they return home to their boring wives." George noticed the angry stares he was receiving from his two visitors and pulled at his neck collar. "Well anyway, it is a part of the position, take it or leave it. There's plenty of women waiting to get this position, what with the good pay and tips from happy customers."

"I'll take it!" Marcia stood up. "When do I start?"

"My lady?" Elizabet looked aghast.

"Please, Aunt Lisa, I said I can handle this."

"Tonight Cia, you can start tonight." George Holmes pulled a box from under the table and handed it to the beautiful woman. "You can wear this. All my girls dress the same."

Marcia took the box and headed down the steps and out the door, George following close behind.

"Thank you, George. I will see you tonight." Her attention fell on the young priest she had met the previous day, making his way down the street. She felt her heart race just at the sight of him. "George, who is that yonder?"

The tavern keeper looked down the cobblestone street and saw the fish merchant, out in front of his store, two men chatting under the shade trees and the priest, from the Holy Catholic Church on the hill.

"I see four men down the street Cia, which one do you question?"

"Yon priest. What is his name?" Marcia's attention held fast to the handsome clergyman with extraordinary blue eyes. "I ran into him yesterday and fell to get his name." as she thought to herself "Literally ran into him!"

"His name is Agar Bellingham. He is the young priest who has the chapel on the hill at the edge of town."

"What do you know of him?" Marcia could not draw her eyes away as she watched him waved and speak to those passing by.

21

"Not much, I'm afraid, lassie. He is a strange one. The church sent him here about four months ago." George scratched his bald head. "He seems to be a pretty fine fellow though. Really helps out in the town's problems."

"Agar Bellingham." Marcia repeated his name softly. "I think I shall go over and pay the priest my good day."

"And I think we best be off to home, me girl." Elizabet pulled at Marcia's arm. "I am sure the young priest is much too busy to pass the time of day with the likes of us."

"Then you go home, Lisa. I shall go over alone." Marcia gave her old friend a light push. "I shan't be long." She walked quickly across the street, leaving her companion mumbling to herself. The young man had squatted down to examine a broken bench and started repairing the wobbly legs when Marcia stepped up next to him. "Good day to you, Father Bellingham."

Agar's eyes moved up the shapely figure standing above him. His bright smile stretched across his handsome face. "Mistress Stone, I believe." Agar stood up and towered over the beautiful woman.

"Aye, that is correct, but how did you know my name?" Marcia stared into his blue eyes in total confusion. "I do not recall telling you my name yesterday."

"Nay, you did not." He laughed softly. "You must forgive me, but I made a few inquiries."

"May I ask why?" her eyes fell to his lips. They were so perfectly shaped and she had only seen lips like this once before, lips that she felt a desire to kiss. Those below the edge of a mask, those mocking lips that spoke so boldly to her.

"It is not every day I get nearly ran down by an angel." Agar brushed his blonde hair from his eyes. "Such a fair angel."

"You are too kind Father Bellingham." Marcia glanced down at her hands, thinking to herself, "What manner of speech is this for a priest? Could he possibly be having the same sort of feeling I have for him?"

"I try to learn about every new stranger in town. It wasn't too many months ago when I too, was a stranger to Canterbury." Agar motioned for her to sit down. "It is safe now. The legs are quite stable."

22

"It would appear you have done a splendid job with this bench, although the neighboring bench looks a bit sick." She pointed to the broken leg on the bench next to her and received only a smile from his handsome face. "I did hear you had just arrived a short time before my aunt and I." By his smile, she suddenly wished she had not offered that information as she tried to smile. "I mean…I…"

"Looks as though I'm not the only one who has been asking questions." Agar laughed.

"Nay, I just thought I should like to do something to make up for nearly running you down yesterday." Marcia moved nervously about as she tried to laugh. "I couldn't very well do it without knowing anything about you, could I?"

"Nay, I suppose not." Agar turned to the other bench and started repairing it. "Did I not see you across the street at George Holmes Tavern?"

"Aye, that you did." She tried not to stare down at the handsome face, but found it difficult to look away. "Do you know George well, Father Bellingham?"

"A very nice man, George Holmes. He seems to do a remarkable business for himself." Agar turned the bench upright. "There, all finished."

"A priest and a carpenter." Marcia smiled up warmly. "What other hidden talents do you have?"

"Ah, in time, dear Cia, you may well find out." Agar picked up his tools and placed them back inside his wooden crate. "Did you know George before you came to Canterbury?"

"Nay, I just met the gentleman last eve. It was getting late and I had almost given up hope of finding a position when I came across this little scene between George and one of his bar maidens."

"Bar maidens? Are you saying that you got a position working for George?" A deep cloud covered the young priest's face.

"Aye! I start work tonight." Marcia boasted. "I was quite fortunate to find the position."

"Find another!" Agar started walking up the hill toward the church as Marcia raced quickly behind him trying to keep up with his long strives.

"Find another what?" she called out of breath.

"Position! That is no place for a lady to work!" the priest kept his eyes straight ahead on the rising steeple of the church.

"Father Bellingham, I am sure that working as a bar maiden is not all that bad." She forced a laugh. "I can see being a priest you probably have naught to do with drinking men, but George says his tavern is indeed dignified."

"And your aunt, how does she take to your working at a tavern with a lot of drunk chaps?" He stopped and his eyes fell on her perfect face. "She cannot possibly approve of your working there!"

"Aunt Lisa knows as well as I that we need the money." Marcia looked down to avoid his burning stare. "If I find the work is more than I can handle, then I shall find another."

"I can assure you Cia, it will be." His strong hand pushed the white gate open and looked down to see her hand on his robe sleeve.

"Father Bellingham, I am perfectly capable of handling men, any kind of man, sober or drunk." She wished she hadn't sounded so bold. Why had she suddenly felt the need to defend herself. First, with the masked man called the Moon Rider, and now, this young priest that set her body on fire.

"Aye, from what I heard of your little adventure last night, I assumed that you could handle yourself." His eyes suddenly held a twinkle and she stepped back.

"Last night?" Marcia swallowed. "I was not aware that you were there last night."

"To my regret, I was not." Agar motioned her through the gate. "I was away in the country, visiting a sick woman, a devout member of my church."

Marcia seemed to feel relieved that the young priest had not been a part of the previous night's events. Would he have stood back like the other men from the village, afraid to fight the invaders? Perhaps his faith and priesthood would have prevented Agar from being a fighting man.

"I hear you stood up to the great Moon Rider." His tone was somewhat mocking but she assumed he did not care for the masked man.

24

"I care not for the conceited arrogant man!" Marcia felt the warmness of the afternoon sun fade when she walked into the cool opened church, made of smooth stones and stain glass windows.

"Then I take it the Moon Rider has one less fan." Agar laughed, then motioned her to sit down as he made his way inside another small room. He called out "It must have really put him down."

"He could use a little putting down." Marcia glanced up when she noticed him carrying a tray decked with goblets and small game pies. "Oh, Father, you really should not have gone to so much trouble. I never meant to barge in as a guest."

"Tis no trouble. I was already prepared with my own meal; I only wish to share it with my new friend." Agar handed her the tray before returning for a pitcher of ale. "It's not every day that I have the opportunity to have such a lovely dinner guest."

"As I recall, it was I who was going to do something for you." Marcia bit down into one of the pies, then licked her lips. "Mumm, I have discovered another one of your talents."

"Cia, you will find out that my talent for cooking is very limited. In my spare time, I like to shoot for my own game and I've learned baking them in pies is simple, yet a complete meal in itself." Agar smiled as he poured the refreshing ale out in their vessels. Their eyes met as he said softly "I shall hold you to your invitation, Cia."

"I shall like doing for you, Agar." Her eyes fell to the glass in her hands. "I really must hurry and be on my way. I told my aunt I would not be long. I'm sure she is beginning to worry."

"Aye, but do eat first." His eyes studied her closely. The warm yellow dress expressed her rounded bosom and he could not help but notice how her breast started to heave up and down when she said his name. Agar found it difficult to look away as he searched for something to say. "I have planned a picnic this Sunday with some children in my parish and I was wondering if you might like to come and help me?"

"Aye!" Marcia answered with excitement, then quickly looked away, feeling embarrassed. "I mean, if you need me, you know I would love to help with the children."

"It will not be all work, I assure you, Cia. The children are a delight and fun to be with. They all require lots of love and attention."

"I can see these children must be very special to you." Their eyes met again.

"Very special, as are you." Agar gathered her hand in his and helped her up. "Our picnic will start around noon, right after the church service."

"I shall be here." Marcia walked over to the open door and glanced around to find him still staring at her. "Thank you for the cool drinks and pies. They were quite good."

"My pleasure." Agar's smile was warm and Marcia realized that if she did not leave at once, she might say something foolish. Turning, she made her way quickly from the church and across the lawn to the gate. She dared not turn around to look, but if she had, she would have noticed the loving eyes that watched her until she was out of sight.

Chapter Five

Marcia stared down at her new image as she got herself ready for her first night's work at Holmes Tavern. It was obvious to her that the dress was made to emphasize the bosom. When she heard Elizabet coming up the steps to her room, she reached for one of her shawls and draped it quickly over her, hiding her tavern uniform.

"Are ye ready yet, my lady? Let's have a look at your work clothes." The old nurse stared at Marcia as she hung her bag around her neck.

"Aye, I am ready and must hurry so that I am not late on my first night! Mustn't get on George's bad side even before I wait on the first customer." Marcia started for the door when her old friend grabbed her by the arm. "What is it Lizzie? I really haven't the time to waste."

"What are ye hiding under that shawl, my lady?"

"I hide naught." Marcia forced a weak laugh. "What sort of silly nonsense is this you speak? I wear a plain simple peasant dress, nothing more."

"Then, take away your wrap so that I may see for myself your simple peasant dress." Elizabet folded her arms in the manner she always used whenever she meant business. "Well, young lady, I am waiting!"

"Very well, Lizzie, but you must realize that it is a little different than what you are used to seeing." Marcia slowly removed the shawl and bit her lip when the nurse gave a loud gasp.

"Holy Saint Peter! You cannot be a roaming about Canterbury dressed like a common wench!" Her fat fingers twisted her white apron bib. "Marcia, 'tis not fitting for a lady of your fine upbringing to be seen in such disgraceful attire!"

"Have you forgotten, dear Lizzie, as long as we are in Canterbury, you and I are just common folk." She put the wrap back around her bare shoulders. "As far as the good citizens of this town are concerned, we're just an average aunt and her niece, struggling to make a respectable living for ourselves."

27

Elizabet snorted and waved her hand over at the beautiful girl. "And this is what you call respectable?"

"It is Lizzie! It is not what adorns your body that is important; it is what you do, how you act. I intend to behave as much like a lady in this dress than in any other. Now please, Lizzie, worry not about me!"

"And the dancing to entice those menfolk, is that behaving like a proper lady?" she gasped.

"I will hear naught else about it, Lizzie! Is that quite clear?" Marcia opened the door, Elizabet close behind her.

"But, my lady…" Marcia touched her finger lightly to the depressed woman's lips.

"I shall be alright, Lizzie. You can trust me." Marcia kissed the top of Elizabet's head and dashed out the door as her worried companion shook her head then she watched the head-strong girl disappear in the growing darkness.

Marcia moved from table to table, waiting on the large group of loud men. She knew well the habits of men after they had a few drinks. The beautiful dutiful daughter had waited on her father and his men many times and knew how uncontrollable they could become. One of the louder men called from his corner table.

"Hey, barmaid, come here!" Marcia walked slowly over to the table and stared down into the red eyes of the drunk. He smiled up as his fingers ran up her arm. "Hey, sweetie, why don't you and I go someplace quiet and we can…"

"If you want another drink to finish you off, I will bring it! If it's trash you wish to talk about, you are wasting my time!" Marcia started to leave when the drunk grabbed her wrist. "Let me go now or I shall have to hurt you!"

Laughter came from the men sitting close enough to hear their conversation. One of the older gentlemen held up his mug of beer and shouted, "My bet is on the little lady!"

"What are you trying to do, woman, make me look foolish?" the drunken young man stood up on his wobbly legs. "Answer me!"

"You, sir, are making yourself look foolish. Now, why don't you go home and sleep it off." Marcia pulled at her arm, but the drunken man held on tight. "Alright, I warned you!" Marcia brought up her knee quickly and sent the man screaming in pain to the floor. Laughter and clapping from the other customers filled the tavern as Marcia stomped back angrily to the bar. George had laughed along with the other men, but he quickly tried to hide his amusement when the irate girl stared up at him.

"Way to go Cia. I have never had a girl who could handle the men on their own." George reached across the bar to pat her back. "Now, run along to the back and get ready for the entertainment."

"But, George, could you not perhaps get one of the other girls to dance tonight. I have not had time to practice or observe the others dance and I really think I should before going in front of an audience." Marcia felt sure she was fighting a losing battle with her boss, but she would try nevertheless. "You do understand, don't you George?"

"Cia, these men would not know if you had been practicing a year or a minute. Just move with the music and believe me, they will love you." George and Marcia glanced up when the tavern door opened and four rough looking men walked in and found a table, all four set of eyes noticing the beautiful woman at the bar. "Run along now and get ready. I've got some customers to wait on."

Marcia moved quickly to the back room. She felt sure that at least one of the new arrivals would cause her trouble. She knew it the moment he entered the tavern. Although all four men observed her when they arrived, this one man who had found her immediately and held her in his gaze until she disappeared behind the door to the back room. Taking a deep breath, Marcia slowly opened the door and peered through the crack. The stranger was talking freely to George, and Marcia felt her heart drop when her boss looked over toward the backroom. A chill ran through her veins as she made her way across the room to where she would be dancing. When George noticed her waiting, he smiled and clapped his hands loudly to get every man's attention.

"Gentlemen, you know for entertainment we bring you nothing but the best here at George's. So, sit back, sip on your drinks and watch the spellbinding dance of our own Cia!"

"Nothing but the best." Marcia mumbled to herself as she began moving slowly to the slow keys. Within seconds, she had caught the rhythm and from the outburst of whistles and applause as she danced, it was obvious she was doing a marvelous job. Marcia tried to focus on the flickering candles, but she could still feel the piercing stare from the stranger. Her eyes wondered over toward his table and her heart felt sick by his small gestures.

The music seemed endless and Marcia felt herself growing dizzy from the heat and pipe smoke. With one last turn, the dance was over and she felt relieved to hear the loud clapping and shouts for more. She thought as she walked off the small stage "They like me and that should make George happy he hired me." Looking his way, Marcia found George grinning his approval.

"Cia Stone, you certainly know how to move your body. I could almost feel it." Marcia hadn't noticed the stranger moving over next to her. His fingers clutched the back of her neck as he spoke softly "You really make a man feel like he is ready to begin."

"My dear sir, I am afraid I really don't understand what you are referring to. If you will excuse me, I have a job to do and I haven't the time for talk." Marcia started to walk away when he grabbed her around the waist.

"Look sweetie, your job is to keep the customers satisfied, right?" he laughed softly under his breath. "And I pay good money when I'm treated good."

"Look mister, my task is to serve drinks to you chaps and dance ever so often!" she suddenly did not fear this overbearing man, she just felt disgust for him. "My position does not require me to permit animals to touch me just because they feel the whim! Do I make myself clear?"

"Too clear, little lady!" the man gritted his teeth. "I take it you are saying I'm not good enough for you, right?"

"If you want me to be frank, sir, that is correct!" Marcia's eyes grew cold. "Now, if you do not mind, just step to one side, I must get to work!"

"Aye, little lady." His eyes flashed fire as his hand swept across her breast.

Marcia's right hand flew around and burned across the stranger's cheek. He grabbed both wrist tightly and stared down into her eyes angrily. George rushed over when he saw that Marcia was having a little more trouble getting rid of this one.

"What is going on, chap?"

Ignoring George, a smug grin fell on his lips as he moved in close to Marcia's face. "Sweetheart, nobody slaps big Murphy without paying for it! What I have in mind for you, will be pure pleasure for me. You might decide to like it too."

"Take your hands off me, you bloody bastard!" she tried to free herself from his iron grip, causing George to step in closer.

"You heard the lady! My girls just serve drinks and dance for men's enjoyment! Nothing more! If you are going to get rough, you can just get out of my place!" Marcia had never seen George so angry and she suddenly felt close to him. "Now, big Murphy, and if you leave peacefully, I won't be fetching the police captain!"

"Oh, I'll leave! I'll leave alright!" the mean eyes remained on Marcia as he spoke. "I never intended to take the little lady here." His hand took hold of her face and with a smirk he whispered. "I will get you, little lady! Do you hear me? I'll get you soon, real soon! Canterbury, or all of England for that matter, is not big enough to hide in. When big Murphy gets it in his mind he wants something, he does not sleep until he gets it!"

"Oh, really!" Marcia caught him off guard and came up with her knee, sending big Murphy to the floor. "Do not lose any sleep over me, you pig!"

With the help of his three friends, the angry man stood up, eyes ablaze with anger. "Little lady, I promise, I will get you! Sooner or later, you will be mine!" Big Murphy turned angrily and limped out the door.

Chapter Six

The bells rang out from the chapel on the hill as Marcia and Elizabet made their way up the cobblestone path. Marcia had taken extra care getting herself dressed, for she knew she would be spending most of the Sabbath with Agar. Her secret joy set her heart to spending as she made her way up the hill.

"It makes me glad to see that going to church is so joyful for you, my lady." The heavy nurse held up her dress slightly as she walked up the steep hill. "Or, is it something else that has made you so happy, Marcia?"

"Oh, Lizzie darling, cannot I just be happy?" Marcia felt her heart race when she reached the chapel's double doors. "It is such a beautiful sunny Sabbath and I feel wonderful and free!"

Elizabet dipped her fingers into the bowl of holy water, bowed slightly and crossed herself as she spoke softly, "Father, Son, and Holy Ghost." And waited for her ward to go through the ritual as she whispered, "I am happy then that the fact for all your joy is not from your helping out that nice young priest."

Marcia stared down at her old friend. "And, what if it were, Lizzie?"

Elizabet stared at the feisty young woman as she walked past her and took a seat in the chapel were others had started to gather. The anxious nurse scurried up the isle behind her and slid in next to her, then leaned over to whisper.

"My lady, if you are thinking what I think you are thinking, then I suggest you reconsider your path forward!"

"My dear Lizzie, you are talking in circles." Marcia spoke softly as she smiled at the stranger beside her, who seem to be listening, so she drew in to her nurse's ear. "Now, get yourself quiet. The service has already begun." Marcia watched Agar as he walked from the back and into the pulpit. Her heart pounded in her chest and she could feel herself growing weak with warm desire.

Agar's eyes swept over the large crowd, trying to pick out the woman with the long chestnut hair. Once he found her, hair piled beautifully on top with ringlets flowing around her magnificent face, he never drew his attention away from her for the remainder of the worship service.

"As you well know, following services today, the children are invited to stay for a special treat." Agar had a way of speaking that enticed all the ladies present. His manner was so charming and gallant, one might see him more as a prince or a knight, not a humble priest, a man devoted only to the church. "I assure you mothers, your precious children will be in good hands. Mine, Mistress Cia Stone's, and the best hands of all, the hands of the Almighty God! You may come by to pick up your children around three o'clock this eve."

Elizabet had kept her eye on her ward throughout the service and noticed Marcia had not taken her eyes off of the young handsome priest. If she had been observing him as well, she would have found his attention was on Marcia and their eyes were locked as one for the entire service. The old nurse's heart grew heavy, fearing what emotions her young maiden might feel regarding Father Bellingham. After the service, Marcia stood up and smiled down at her faithful companion for twenty years. She immediately read the worry on the dear old face.

"Lizzie, you must not bother yourself with me today. I shan't have any way of knowing when I will be home." Marcia tried to sound calm and as normal as possible, although the fact that being alone with Agar set her pulse to racing. "It is such a lovely day, why don't you spend the day with Madam Roster. I know what a good friend she has become to you since we arrived in Canterbury."

"I did hear the priest tell the mothers to pick up their children at three. I can only assume that you will be leaving at that same time, Marcia." Elizabet waited a moment for a reply and received only a smile. "The children will be leaving and the party was for them, was it not? There is no reason that would keep you there after that set time."

"Lizzie, you, of all people, know watching young children takes every second of your time and children can be messy. I cannot just run off and leave the good father with all that mess to clean up, now, can I?" Marcia forced a bright laugh. "You know how messy children can be, Lizzie. Did not I have you constantly cleaning up after me when I was a child?

"Aye, and I also know when there is something different going on in that mind of yours, Marcia." Elizabet whispered loudly. "It is not normal for a lady to have romantic feelings for a priest. It just is not right!"

"Oh, why not, for heaven sakes?" Marcia stared down at her nurse, feeling somewhat annoyed with her for guessing Marcia's true feelings. "He is a man! A man like any other and can be capable of loving a woman! I think it is foolish that a man like Agar should not love a woman!"

"My dear girl, the plain fact is, he is a priest, sworn to devote his entire life to God and His church!"

"Perhaps at the time he entered into priesthood, he never dreamed of meeting someone in which to fall in love with! Like it or not, Lizzie, Agar Bellingham is a man!" Marcia saw the handsome priest walking their way. "He comes! Not another word, Lizzie! We shall discuss this later, if there is anything to discuss."

"My lady…" Marcia touched her lightly on the lips.

"I promise to behave myself today. Act like the perfect lady, prim and proper. Only if he makes the first move will I show my true feelings and do something rash." Marcia smiled up into Agar's handsome eyes as he came to a stop in front of her. "Father Bellingham, you are a very good spokesman. Lisa and I were just this moment discussing how good you were."

"I am truly flattered." His smile was so radiant, Marcia just knew he could hear her heart pounding away in her chest. His attention fell on Elizabet as he took her chubby hand, causing her to blush. "My dear lady, I do not know how long I shall be keeping your niece today, so look for her whenever you see her."

"I have been trying to convince my Aunt Lisa to spend the day with her new friend, Madam Roster. It would be a perfect opportunity for them to get together." Marcia tried not to look up into the handsome face, for fear he too, could read her enter feelings. Agar continued to give Elizabet his attention as he stated

"Madam Roster is a fine woman, Madam Stone. Cia is right. The both of you will enjoy each other's company and Rosemary Roster knows a great deal about the history of Canterbury. Just have a day of it and do not worry about your niece." Agar's eyes were drawn to Marcia's beautiful face and he spoke softly. "I promise to take good care of her today."

"It is the children that you need to be looking after Father, remember?" Elizabet felt sure there was something in the way the young priest was looking at Marcia, so she quickly added "Although, someone must always be watching our Cia."

"Aunt Lisa, you make me sound like a child!" Marcia walked past her old nurse and whispered. "Please Lizzie, go home!"

Agar simply chuckled at the notion. "Why must someone watch Cia, madam? Is she a naughty girl?"

"Not naughty, in so many words. Cia is a perfect lady, a good devout Christian, pure as the first fallen snow. It is that position she has taken. It will get her into trouble, I grant you, before the month is out."

"Why? What do you mean?" Agar's eyes grew serious. "What has happened down at the tavern, Cia?"

"Nothing really, at least, nothing that I cannot handle. My aunt just chooses to worry needlessly about me, that is all." Marcia walked over to the door, hoping they would follow. She turned to find Agar and Elizabet talking quietly. Marcia felt sure her overly protective nurse would say something wrong so she interrupted their conversation. "Are you two going to converse all day while the children starve to death."

"I have not seen a day yet when a child would rather eat than play with their friends." Elizabet walked past Marcia. "Take care that you do not stay out too late dear."

"Just go and have a good day without worrying about me." Marcia forced a laugh, feeling Agar's serious eyes upon her. "Well, what tantalizing news did my dear aunt have to tell you to bring about all this seriousness?"

"I have heard of that big creep Murphy, Cia, and I do not think he is someone to laugh off so easily." Agar's voice took a change of authority. "Just how long ago did your dispute with Murphy take place?"

"Oh, that aunt of mine! She really is the carrier of good tidings!" Marcia had tried to put the event with Murphy out of her mind, but bad dreams kept bringing his face back to haunt her. "It is nothing really. He was drunk and I am sure he did not remember a thing that happened the next day."

"Cia, it is obvious you do not know this man. Big Murphy is a thief and a murderer. A very clever one at that. He knows how to throw off his scent and the authorities cannot ever catch him in the act, so he gets away with it." Agar took her hand into his own and asked, "Has anyone been following you, watching you come and go?"

"Nay, I have seen no one. Agar, I cannot really think you are serious about…" he squeezed her hand lightly. "But, surely you don't…"

"Cia, I know this man. I know what he can do." Agar pulled her next to him and spoke just for her ears as the last parishioners were departing the chapel. "I have seen the results of some of his so call little games and they are not pretty, I grant you. Women raped and left for dead on the side of the road. Young girls, brutally beaten and cut because they would not surrender to his demands. The poisonous reptile!" For the first time, Marcia thought she saw genuine hate fill Agar's eyes as he boldly confessed "Cia, if he should touch you, I think I would be driven mad with hate!"

Marcia gently touched his sleeve as she said softly "Agar, do you care so?" with her caress and soft words, she noticed the hate melt away. "What happens to me, it would really matter to you, would it not?"

"Aye." Agar and Marcia stood silent, staring into each other's eyes and were lost for a brief moment until Nora's young voice called from the back yard.

"Father Bellingham, can we eat now please?"

"Eat! Of course, child, of course we shall eat." He said laughing, and looked around to find the other children running up to join them. "Alright, young ones, gather over by the old willow. Mistress Stone will go with you while I go and fetch the food."

"Would not you need some help with the food?" Cia did not want to be from his sight for one second.

"I have got all the help I need Cia, but thank you for your thoughtful offer." Agar squeezed her hand. "Just go stay with the children until I return. I shan't be long."

"Very well, Agar. I guess someone needs to watch the

children." Marcia smiled up into his blue eyes with passion, then made her way toward the small group of children, deliberately swaying her hips. She glanced back and caught him observing her, a smile on his handsome face. "Do hurry."

"Aye, I will." Agar had been regarding her every move with tender care, then turned to retrieve the picnic. He was happy to find his friend Amby Steen was almost finished preparing the picnic. He glanced up from his labors when Agar walked in the small hot room.

"There you are! I was beginning to think I needed to come and fetch you." Amby stared up from the game pies he had been stacking on large plates. "This picnic looks as though it will be somewhat different. Who is this woman that fascinates you so?"

"My dear friend, you are letting your imagination run wild as usual." Agar laughed and slapped his friend on the back. "Just put that food inside the basket and stop dreaming up fantasies."

Amy narrowed his eyes knowingly and began storing the food inside the basket. "Master, you cannot fool me. This one, she is different. I can see that."

"You see, my friend, what you want to see." Agar climbed down into the cool deep storage room and gathered some jars of juice. "Cia is a beautiful woman and I enjoy her company. She has a head on her shoulders and is a pleasure to know. There is really nothing to be made over it. She is strictly a good friend."

"I am a good friend, Agar. Nay, nothing to be made over! Except that you are supposed to be a priest, and a priest should not take any romantic interest in a woman, beautiful or otherwise." Amby took a tight hold on his friend's arm. "Agar, you find the wench to your liking, I know it."

"Very well, my inquisitive friend, I do find the girl to my liking." Agar's attention fell on Marcia's body as they walked from the church, their arms decked with food and drink. "Cia is very much to my liking."

"Master, he who hides in shadows, must not carry a torch!" Amby shook his head in defeat, knowing by the dreamy look in his friend's eyes, talking him out of any romantic plans with this woman was a waste of time. Amby knew when this special man walking next to him wanted something, he would not stop until it belonged to him. Stopping briefly, Amby looked over at the woman in question and indeed found her beauty striking. Stumbling on behind the young priest, he mumbled "It is no use. I waste my breath! The man is already stung by the wench's charm!"

Chapter Seven

Marcia smiled up from the cool grass. Amby quickly read the attraction was not only held by Agar, but also by that of this beautiful young woman. Agar returned her smile lovingly as he set the jars down next to her.

"Come children, we shall eat, then we will play games." Cia thought she noticed a hint of mischief in Agar's blue eyes as he spoke. "Would you be an angel, Cia, and pour the drinks?"

"Aye, I should like that very much." Marcia looked for the first time, at the stranger who had walked from the church behind Agar. She noticed what a strong yet gentle face he had and there was some sort of seriousness in his green eyes. "Hello, I don't believe we have met. I am Cia Stone."

"Aye, dear lady, Agar has told me." His serious lips broke into a smile. "Amby Steen, at your service."

"A true and loyal friend, he is too." Agar set a big bowl of fruit down, then glanced up at his trusted friend, still captivated by Marcia's charm. "Amby, be a good chap and pass out the game pies before they grow cold." Agar slipped down next to Marcia and stretched out his long legs. His eyes fell to the rising of her rounded bosom. So perfectly formed, he thought, and longed to reach over and slip his hand over those-tempting-breast. Agar could feel himself growing excited as thoughts of lying with Marcia circled through his mind.

"Aren't you going to eat, Father Bellingham?" Nora giggled softly from the other side. "Everything is going fast.

Marcia smiled over at the bright young girl, then turned and slowly moved her attention up Agar's trim body until her eyes landed on his. Marcia's heart fluttered, for she felt sure she read desire in his alluring blue eyes.

"Nora is right, Agar. You better have something." Without taking her eyes from his, she reached down into the fruit bowl and lifted out a luscious ripe pear, then held it out to him. His fingers slipped over hers as he took it slowly from her soft hand. Marcia smiled down nervously at her hands and thought quickly to change to a safer subject. "George tells me that you do a lot of work to help the citizens of Canterbury."

"Aye, but then, that is part of my work as a man of God, helping others." His eyes swept over the children, happily eating. "Take these children, for instance. Some of them have never had the love of a mother or a father. They have been passed from home to home, time depending on how long each family wishes to put up with an extra mouth to feed and give shelter to.

"Oh, Agar, how terribly sad!" Marcia looked around at the children's faces, trying to make out those not having a permanent home and family. She felt a sudden sting of pain for these big-eyed children, who seemed so happy and content and knew there were some who, she knew, was starved for love and affection. "Agar, is not there anything that can be done to help these children?"

"Aye, only the town people won't approve my ideal." Agar turned to look at the huge old chapel. "They let the vicar lead them blindly. If it had been his ideal first, he would have seen that his plan was carried out to the letter."

"And do you think that this vicar cares anything for the children at all, Agar?" Amby stood up and brushed off his pants. "Nay, I tell you! That man cares naught about anything but his crooked self!"

"Is it Vicar Hayworth you speak of?" Marcia remembered the obese vicar who had come to the flat the second day of their arrival to Canterbury. He had made the visit as a jester of faith, to welcome them to 'his' fair town. Even then, there was something about the heavy-jawed man she did not like.

"Aye, the same!" Amby let his discus for the man show. "There is only one vicar living in our town and that's one too many! The round belly, crook!"

"Amby, 'tis not wise to let your feelings show openly," Agar stood up next to his long-time friend. "If we dislike someone, it is well that we should try to like them."

"I could like the man, as long as he were somewhere other than Canterbury." Amby mumbled.

"Agar, what sort of ideal did you have in mind for these children?" Marcia stood up and knocked the loose grass from her skirt.

"I have been planning to build a home for the orphan children. Someplace they can call their own instead of being shoved around from home to home." Agar took her hand and led her around to the side of the church, then pointed to a lovely spot where a grove of trees stood. "That piece of ground over there has already been given for the project and I have found two old matrons, sisters in my parish, who wishes very much to look after the children in their new home."

"Oh Agar, how wonderful for the children!" Marcia looked out over the peaceful surroundings and pictured a small white cottage nestled in the grove of trees and a group of happy children running about. "I cannot see what reason the town people would not stand behind your loving ideal and began with it immediately."

"We told you." Amby gritted his teeth, feeling flustered. "It is that big ox, Hayworth! The fat vicar is only irritated that he did not get hold of the ideal first!"

"I cannot possibly see what difference it should make to the vicar as long as the project is carried out and the children have a home of their own." Marcia looked from Agar to Amby for an answer. "Why would the over-weight man not agree?" she heard the young priest laugh softly by her description of their enemy as Amby Steen sneered.

"Money, stacks and stacks of money that would be pouring in from the unsuspecting givers! You see, Miss Cia, our friend, the vicar, has a way of turning a profit from all the projects he is in charge of. They become a money-making scheme for his fat pockets!"

"You mean that the vicar is dishonest?" Marcia turned to Agar, who had been standing silently. "Is he, Agar?"

"Well, Cia, we have no proof as of yet, but we are more than certain that Vicar Hayworth has been involved in several dishonest deals."

"So why do you not tell the people of Canterbury what you suspect."

"Because Cia, the vicar has been here for many years and I for only a few months. Why should they choose to believe me rather than a trusted old friend?"

"He whose friend is a serpent is better off friendless." Amby motioned for the children, who sat picking on one another loudly. "Come, you little noise-makers! Let us go play tag!"

Agar and Marcia watched the children dash off excited with Amby. Marcia smiled at his red hair blowing wildly in the afternoon breeze. She turned to the handsome priest.

"I like your friend. He has a lot of spirit in him. Amby speaks in riddles, somewhat ambiguous."

"Aye! Too much at times." Agar glanced over at Nora, watching the other children at play, then sadly he looked at her useless legs. "Nora, would you like to go over closer to watch?" Agar watched the small girl reached down to touch her legs, a tear glistening her young eyes. He rose to his feet and gently touched the girl's curls. "I will let you ride on my back. What do you say?"

"I say…" Nora stared up lovingly at the young priest. "Yes! It would be a great pleasure to have such a high seat to watch the tag game." She laughed as he lifted her up on his strong shoulders. Agar smiled down warmly into Marcia's eyes, who had been observing his beautiful actions, and offered his hand. "Come along, angel, I promised your aunt I would watch you closely."

Marcia took his hand and squeezed it. "I shall stay close then. Very close."

At six o'clock, Agar walked Marcia up to her front door. Neither had said a word since leaving Amby back at the church fence. There had been brief moments when their eyes swept over each other and the moment Agar had touched her shoulder, letting his fingers glide down her arm and rest comfortably around her hand. Now, standing at the door, Agar let his finger run gently over Marcia's lips as he spoke softly.

"Thank you for helping me today. It was a delightful pleasure having you with me."

"I'm afraid I really did not do a lot." Marcia felt her lips tremble. "Would…would you like to come inside for a little while?"

"I really have to be going." Agar found it hard to keep his eyes from straying to her bosom as he continued "Thank you for asking. Perhaps, some other time, Cia."

"Aye, I would like that." Marcia let her hand rub lightly through his blonde hair as she spoke a little softer "I would like that very much, Agar."

42

Agar's fingers cupped around her beautiful face as his eyes searched hers hungrily. Slowly his head moved down to meet hers, his lips parting, ready to cover hers with passion. A call from across the street stopped him cold. Agar twirled around to face Elizabet.

"Pray tell, what is going on here?" the confused nurse looked from Marcia to Agar. "Well?"

"Mistress Cia had an eyelash in her eye, my dear lady. I was but trying to get it out." Agar looked down at Marcia and smiled. "I shall be seeing you very soon, I hope."

"Aye, very soon, Father Bellingham." Marcia watched him walk across the street and make his way up the hill to the church. From the corner of her eye, she could see her old friend observing her closely with uncertainty. "I say Lizzie, I am terrible grateful that Father Bellingham got that aggravating lash from my eye. It was certainly a discomfort."

"Aye, my lady, those eyelashes can hurt you pretty bad, and your pretty long ones especially." Elizabet chuckled, feeling relieved that the priest was really just removing the eyelash instead of getting personal with her ward. "I remember once when I was a wee girl and this blade of grass blew in my eye. It wasn't so big a piece, but to me, it felt as big as a tree." The jolly woman laughed as she recalled the incident, only Marcia wasn't listening. She walked over by the window and smiled up at the rising steeple, shining in the rays of the setting sun. Closing her eyes, she could picture Agar lowering his face with the intention of kissing her.

"There will be another time." She thought to herself as she could hear her nurse raving on about her childhood. "Agar will kiss me and I will welcome his kiss gladly." She laughed softly as her mind continued to dream. "And, he will make love to me!"

Chapter Eight

"I say that it is up to us ladies to see that Father Bellingham gets the chance to carry out his fine project!" Marcia's voice rang out in the night air where she had drawn a huge crowd of Canterbury women. "Many of you have heard, Father Bellingham wants to build a home for the homeless children in our fair town. The same children you keep taking in and pushing out, when you grow weary of watching after them!"

"How can we be sure the children will receive a proper up-bringing, with all of them stuck in one place together?" One woman shouted from the far corner.

"Just having their own home is a start. Learning to live together, share work and have fun together as a family, are just a few reasons. Ladies, most of you have children of your own. You must understand how much love a child requires. Two loving spinster sisters have volunteered to give their time and love to these children."

"Miss Stone, our men think that the vicar should lead the project if approved. Father Bellingham refuses to let him take over!"

"It was Father Bellingham's ideal ladies! I, for one, think he should be the one to carry it out!" Marcia's hand flew up. "We are talking about the lives of innocent children, ladies! Now, if you support the young priest instead of the older vicar…"

"Mistress Stone, what you are saying is fine and even possibly only fair, bur our men think this is the affair of the men of Canterbury and we women have no say so in the matter." Madam Holmes spoke up loudly. "George would not take kindly to my even being here tonight and he would kill me if he thought I gave him my opinion on the matter."

Marcia could not contain her laughter as she spoke loudly "Ladies, surely you are not afraid of your husbands! There is not any man who, when handled properly, could not be made to give in to your desires."

"It is easy for someone as young, pretty and single as yourself to speak so boldly about us controlling our husbands." The lady in the front looked around at the other wives, nodding in agreement. "If we refused their needs, they would just get it elsewhere at the red-light district or Henry's Tavern."

"Frankly, I find men like that discussing." Marcia noticed the angry stares from the wives, so she added. "Nothing personal against your weak men ladies. Men will be men."

"Mistress Stone, the vicar wants the job of handling the children and…" Marcia cut off the wife of her boss as she spoke up.

"Madam Holmes, the vicar wants only to help himself to the funds that you raise for the project. He cares naught about the poor little children."

"My lady, stay quiet." Elizabet bent in to whisper when she noticed the heavy vicar stepped from the shadows, then walk up between the women.

"Who has been putting such notions in your head, dear lady? Our dear Father Bellingham, perhaps?"

"Nay, Vicar Hayworth! The kind priest would say naught wrong about no man." Marcia stared angrily down from her platform at the stocky robed man. "I find it degrading for a man of the cloth to be hiding in shadows to ease drop on what we have been saying."

"My dear lady, I am afraid that someone has filled your innocent young head with bad rumors about me, and I can assure you, that I am nothing but honorable." He looked over the women gathered. "Just ask any one of these ladies and they will tell you of my high morals and standards." The vicar gave Marcia a big smile, but she noticed a certain malice in it. He turned once more to the women, suddenly quiet and nervous by his presence. "I think you ladies had better all return to your homes and families. We would not want this little protest to get back to your husbands, now would we?"

"I see you stoop to blackmail too, vicar. Frighten these poor women into not standing up for what they believe!" Marcia sneered. "But, then it figures. One of your kind always does anything to get what he wants!"

"My lady!" Elizabet took Marcia by the arm and pulled her

off the platform and started dragging the angry young woman away from the scene. "Please, say no more, my lady."

"Let me go Lizzie! I am not through with that snake!" Marcia and the others grew silent when they heard the sound of horses heading straight for them. The towns women started scattering in all directions, but the riders were suddenly upon them. The laughing men scrambled from their saddles and began grabbing the women.

A voice shouted from the center of the wild bunch of men. "Get only the younger ones, boys!"

Marcia grabbed her nurse as she whispered loudly "My God, Lizzie, it is that bloody beast from the tavern!"

"My lady, we must run fast!" Marcia held tight to Elizabet as she dragged her up the cobblestone street. She could hear the horse coming behind them and the heavy breathing from its rider. Marcia's heart sank when she felt Elizabet's hand slip from hers and fell down hard behind her. Marcia turned to help her dear companion when a rope bit into her flesh, pulling her to the ground next to her nurse. Her eyes blazed up into those of Big Murphy.

"So, we meet again, little lady." He climbed down from his horse and grabbed her wrist, pulling her to her feet. "Only this time, I am running the game. I am making the rules!"

Elizabet managed to get up and she grabbed his arm in protest. "Leave her be, you monster!"

"Take your bloody hands off me, you, old crow!" Murphy shouted as he laid a hand across the nurse's face, knocking her back down. "Try it again and I will cut your big fat throat!"

"Leave her alone!" Marcia shouted as she kicked his leg. He gritted his teeth and pulled the rope tighter, then threw her across his horse.

He smiled down at the worried nurse and sneered "I will be leaving you here, old hag! You have nothing to offer me or my boys!" Murphy laughed loudly then climbed up behind Marcia. "When I get through with your little girl here, she won't be worth a mug of beer!" Still laughing, Murphy waved for his men, and they left screaming and hollowing through the streets with their captives.

Elizabet scrambled to her feet and raced off quickly toward

the chapel. Her fist pounded heavily on the heavy double doors as her voice rang out loudly in the night air for the young priest. She was about to give up and leave when the doors flung open and green eyes stared down at her.

"What is it lady? What brings you all the way up here in the dark. I was heading out the back when I heard all your commotion!" Amby noticed the heavy woman trembling with fear as she tried to catch her breath. "What be ye trouble lady? Speak woman!"

"Where is the priest? Father Bellingham? I must speak to him!"

"He is not here. Perhaps if you tell me what is wrong, I can get a message to him." Amby noticed her eyes grow wild with fear as she said

"Not here! But he has to be!" Elizabet started to cry. "My poor Marcia! He has to help her! Those men, those horrible men took her!"

"Please madam, I can take the message to the priest, but please tell me what it is these men have done."

"They took her, I told you! They took several women from town, I am not sure how many!" she covered her eyes with her hands. "I knew she would get into trouble working at that horrible tavern! I knew it!"

"Working at a tavern?" Amby took around the woman's shoulders. "Did you say Marcia?"

Elizabet swallowed, recalling saying Marcia instead of Cia. She looked around nervously as Amby shook her.

"Lady, in God's name, tell me the girl's name! Tell me who those men were!"

"Cia Stone." The old nurse stared up into the green eyes. "I just know Father Bellingham will want to go after her and bring her back."

"Cia?" Amby's heart sank. "The men, did you recognize any of the men?"

"Mar, Cia said the one that got her was Murphy, the drunk from the tavern." Elizabet's eyes pleaded. "Please hurry and tell him before it is too late!"

"I am off!" Amby disappeared in the vast darkness of the

chapel as Elizabet sank to the stoop, her eyes burning with tears, the sound of horse hoofs pounding away from the chapel and into the forest.

Chapter Nine

"Rider, I say the vicar is working with someone, someone of higher rank." A tall gray-headed man stood at attention from the far end of the well-covered table. Dark eyes stared silently from behind the black mask. "I just do not think Vicar Hayworth alone is smart enough to pull off all his pranks."

"And you, just this minute, came up with that conclusion?" Rider's hand slipped around the silver goblet and lifted it to his lips. "The vicar is indeed a clever man and does not seem to give a damn about our young priest or his ideals."

"Then, I feel we should help Bellingham." A gentleman next to the end spoke up. "We seek to find those in need and help, do we not?"

"Aye, my friend, but the young priest has not come seeking our help. Perhaps he feels this is his job alone to perform, gentlemen." The masked man spoke softly as he watched Amby Steen making his way down the huge steps toward him as the man near the end spoke.

"Perhaps young Bellingham is a proud man and will not seek our help."

"Then his pride will be his sword. I will not step in unless I see all else is failing." Rider noticed the worried concern in the arrival's eyes. "What is it?"

"Men rode into Canterbury and stole some of the young women!" Amby's voice came between heavy breathes.

"Then, perhaps the men of Canterbury will find themselves some new women and count their lucky stars!" The masked man laughed, joined by all his men seated at the table. "A new woman is not so bad after putting up with a nagging wife who has grown fat."

"My lord will not jest when he hears who was among those taken captive!" Amby's green eyes burned down on the black-dressed man.

The Moon Rider pushed his chair back and stood to his feet, eyes on the red head. "Her name!"

"Cia, master. Cia is among those captured!" Amby grasped his friend by the arm. "It was Murphy!"

"By God, he will pay with his life!" the black figure raced up the stone steps, shouting over his shoulder. "Come men, saddle up! We shall go after these villains and bring our women back!"

"Aye!" the men shouted in unison as they raced after their leader.

Blue eyes searched over the camp of men and their captive women until they fell on the one he sought. Marcia was tied fast to a tree as Murphy taunted her, but the feisty girl kept yelling insults his way. A smile of approval came to the masked man lips as he watched her continue to unwillingly co-operate.

"Take your bloody hands off me!" Marcia spit in the angry man's face. "Are you a man, Murphy? Or must you tie up a woman to get what you desire?"

"I will show you what kind of man I am, little lady!" Murphy grind his teeth as his sharp knife cut through the tough rope. His fingers bit into her arms as he forced his lips down on hers. Clutching her bodice that outlined a perfect small waist, he yanked her up close, then ripped the front of her dress down, exposing her full round breast. Marcia fought back wildly as he began forcing himself on her.

The Moon Rider clinched his fist with hate and motioned for his men to prepare for advancing. With lighting speed, the masked man rode his black stallion up on a small hill, over-looking the enemy camp, where his shadow appeared to be directly in front of the moon. Loudly, he gave his war cry, the sign for his men to advance quickly from their hidden shadows.

Marcia's mind was suddenly filled with mixed emotions when she saw the great shadow silhouetted against the large moon. The black mask rider was upon them within seconds, his sword drawn for battle.

"Die, you villain!" the angry shout came from behind the mask.

"You shall not take this wench from me, Moon Rider!" Murphy flashed his sword. "She belongs to me! Do you hear me? She is mine!"

Rider smiled and lifted up his sword in front of the defiant man. "This will determine that, Murphy!"

Marcia screamed when the swords began clashing all around her. Within seconds, big Murphy lay still at the black figure's feet, blood oozing from the slash across his chest. Rider glanced over at her briefly, then continued to help his men with the remainder of the outlaws. Shortly, the swords fell silent and the only men left standing were those of the Moon Rider. He walked back over to were Marcia stood, still shocked from all the fighting and killing. Dropping his eyes on her exposed breast, he smiled. With all the excitement, she had forgotten to cover up herself.

"Tell me wench, do you always go about displaying your goods. Tis truly a pleasure for us men." A chuckle escaped his lips as she quickly pulled her torn dress over her breast and held it secure.

"It does you good to make fun of others in trouble!" Marcia's fingers trembled as she clutched tightly to her torn garment. "And a perfectly good dress ruined! You will, of course, be a gentleman and take us back to Canterbury."

"These ladies will be taken back to Canterbury, mistress Stone." Rider motioned toward the other women, silently watching their gallant hero and secretly wishing he had chosen them to find fascinating. "But you, my sassy little wench, will come with me."

"Nay! I go back with the others!" Marcia started to join the other women when the Moon Rider took a tight hold on her arm.

"Nay, you are going with me." His smile was mocking. "This time, I rescued you. That makes you mine."

"Dream on! I am not yours, nor do I wish to be!" Marcia tried to pull herself free, but his fingers were too strong, then he pulled her closer to him. She stared up in defiance. "I repeat, sir, let me be!"

"You go with me!" Rider's eyes burned down on her as he gave orders to his men. "Take these ladies home. I am going to Collinwood." He dragged Marcia over to his horse and slung her up in the saddle. Before she could blink or object, he was up in the saddle behind her.

"Sir Knight, I demand that you take me back this instant to

Canterbury!" Marcia could not understand what made her heart race when he folded his arm tightly around her waist. "If you do not, I will see to it that you pay for anything you do to me!"

"And who will do it to me, fair maiden, that priest of yours?" his mocking smile drove Marcia's fighting strength to full force as she reached back her hand to slap him across the face. Catching her hand, he laughed out. "Ah, 'tis this fire I see in those beautiful brown eyes of yours?"

"Agar could take you on and he would, if he knew what you were doing with me!" she shouted.

"He would never turn a finger to defend you against me. He knows he would fail at swordsmanship." The masked man laughed loudly. "A man hiding in women's skirts, is really no man at all."

"He wears a robe because he is a priest!"

"And he is a priest because he is a coward!" the masked man waved for his men to depart, then he turned his horse toward the forest when Marcia sank her teeth into his arm, causing him to lose his grip. She jumped from the saddle and started running. With a flash, Rider was off the big stallion and chasing close behind her. Within seconds, the Moon Rider caught Marcia and slung her to the ground, falling on top of her. She fought wildly until he managed to get her arms pinned down beside her. His eyes calmly burned down into hers until she finally stopped fighting and stared back into his. He brought his knee up and pinned down her right arm as his free hand lowered the torn dress from her bosom. Rider's hand gently moved over the rounded breast.

Marcia could feel the fire growing in her veins as her body grew limp. She could feel his hot breath on her neck as his lips made their way slowly down to her nipple. His tongue ran over it with passion as his breathing grew along with hers. Rider lifted his head and looked deeply in her eyes. With madding slowness, he let his finger glide over her full lips.

"Kiss me." Marcia whispered breathlessly.

A faint smile covered his lips as they parted gently over hers. Suddenly, realizing what she was doing, Marcia pushed him away, realizing he had released her arms. Rider stood up and pulled her to her feet, then his hand folded tightly over hers.

"Someday, you will give in to me, Cia Stone, someday soon."

Rider's eyes searched hers. "You will desire me as much as I do you. Your thoughts will turn to me and not that priest."

"You sir, are much too sure." Marcia pulled tightly at the torn dress, confused at her feeling for this arrogant man. "I will never desire you, never!"

"We shall see Cia." Rider led her back to his horse, who stood, patiently waiting for his master's return. After lifting her up in the saddle, he climbed behind her and let his hand rub gently through her long hair chestnut hair. His lips pressed down softly on top of her head as he spoke in her ear. "I will take you home for now so that you can think of me and long for me."

"You, sir, are quite conceited. I have no desires to dream about you." Marcia wished she didn't have the feelings she did whenever he touched her, but she would not be sharing that information with him. "Just take me home!"

"Aye, but remember, you belong to me now." Rider rode his horse swiftly until it stood in front of her rented flat. Sliding easily from the saddle, Rider lifted Marcia down. With expert skill, he removed his sword and waved it in front of her. "I promise, the next time I have you in my arms, I will not stop with a nuzzle or a kiss."

"Good-bye Moon Rider!" Marcia turned angrily to the door and slung it open. Glancing back, she could see the black figure disappear in the darkness. Her heartbeat rapidly as she remembered his burning lips upon hers and his hand upon her breast. "What is wrong with me?" Marcia thought as she made her way inside the door and slid the lock in place. She made her way quickly to her room and sat down in front of her mirror, staring at her flushed refection. "How can I be having the same feeling for this contemptible man as I do for Agar?" She jumped when her old nurse ran inside the room, almost shouting with joy.

"My lady! You…you are safe!" Elizabet grabbed Marcia in a bear hug. "Thank God! I just knew Father Bellingham would help bring you back!"

"Lizzie, it was not Agar who rescued me. It was that beast, the Moon Rider!"

"Well then, the man is a hero and should be commended all the same! You are safe Marcia, and that is what is important!" The nurse kissed her wards cheek and chucked. "I will turn back your covers and help you in your nightgown, child. You must be completely exhausted after that ordeal."

"Thank you, Lizzie, I will gladly except your kind offer to get me ready for bed." As her old nurse and friend turned down the bed covers, Marcia stared down at her torn dress. Once again, her thoughts turned to those mysterious eyes looking from the dark mask and his gentle hands moving slowly over her breast, causing her nipples to harden and her pulse to burn with desire. After climbing under the sheets and watching Elizabet take the candle out of her room and shut her in darkness, she let her mind wonder. Whether she wanted to admit it or not, she thought, she really did not want to leave Rider's arms.

Chapter Ten

Marcia moved lazily in her bed when she heard the soft knock on their front door. Listening carefully, she listened to Elizabet's heavy footsteps walking swiftly to the door and the early morning visitor. Marcia sat up, straining her ears to catch the conversation in the adjacent room between the two parties. Her heart began beating rapidly when she recognized Agar's voice. Without hesitation, Marcia jumped from under the warm cover and started getting dressed as she scrambled into her soft blue dress.

Elizabet opened the door slowly and peeked inside, finding Marcia awake and up. She chuckled. "I see you heard our morning visitor. I never saw you scramble about so fast."

"Where is he Lizzie?" Marcia whispered as she brushed through her hair quickly. "He did not leave, did he?"

"Nay child, he waits, just outside this door." Elizabet smiled as she poured some water in a white porcelain basin. "Now, wash your face when you have finished brushing those chestnut locks. He will be waiting for you. I've got the kittle on and have offered him hot tea while he waits. I shall leave a cup for you."

"Good, good!" Marcia grabbed her arm. "Lizzie, what does he want? I mean, did Agar tell you why he was here so early this morning?" She splashed some cold water in her face.

"Nay, just that he wanted you to help him do something." Elizabet wiped her hands on her apron and walked over to the door. "Now, hurry along. I will go and fetch that hot tea for the young priest."

"Go then and tell him I will be out soon." Marcia continued with haste, and with one last look at her reflection, she stepped out from her room.

Agar smiled as he stood to his feet, his eyes studying her body with approval. "Cia, I hope this was not the wrong thing to do, coming by like this without asking earlier." Agar's smile was so brilliant, she couldn't help but laugh softly.

"You may come by any time you like Agar." Marcia laughed again, seeing Elizabet's look of disapproval as she poured the tea.

"Lisa said you wanted my help doing something."

"Aye, that was my purpose for coming by so early." Agar took the offered cup and stirred some cream and sugar. "Thank you, madam, your tea is perfect." He watched her smile and walk out after serving Marcia. "I also wanted to be sure you were alright after last night. When I heard what happened to you, I…I was beside myself with worry. I have never been good with sword fighting and after becoming a priest, I made vows to never lift arms against another soul."

"It was a trying experience and that Murphy was out to rape me and would have if he had not been stopped." Marcia walked over to the window and looked out to find the cobblestone streets flooded with sunlight, a far cry from the previous night. "I suppose I should be thankful to that overly wonderful Moon Rider for saving my life, but his manners are really not to my liking."

"Why, what did he do?" Agar moved over next to her and turned her around to face him. "Did that man do something to you?"

"You do care what happens to me, don't you Agar?" Marcia could read the deep concern in his blue eyes. His hand slipped from her shoulder and cupped her hand.

"Did Rider try anything with you Cia?"

"What is done is done." Marcia closed her eyes, trying hard to block out the incident. "It is over with now and I would just as soon forget it ever happened."

"But, Cia, if Rider tried something with you, I want to know." Agar searched her eyes for the answer. "Did the man try to get intimate with you?"

"Please Agar, I would rather just forget it. What…What was it you wanted to do today?" Marcia forced a smile up at his serious face.

"Alright, I will let it go for now." Agar clutched the cross hanging around his neck. "He had better never try anything ever again, where you are concern."

Elizabet had been silently listening through a crack in the kitchen door and came walking out flustered. 'My God! What did that man do to you last night, Ma…Cia? You never said either man touched you, although I am quite certain that Murphy tried to before your rescue." The heavy nurse scratched her head when she realized "As a matter of fact, you never told me anything last night after coming back worn to a frazzle."

"Lisa, nothing bad happened last night so just forget the whole silly incident! I am still a virgin, if that is what you are fretting about!" Marcia gathered the empty teacups and handed them to the nurse, then took Agar's hand. "Let us make with haste before my darling aunt and I get into a non-ending conversation."

Agar smiled over at Elizabet, who was shaking her head as her fat fingers wrung at her apron, after setting down the cups. "Lisa, please stopped worrying about your head strong niece. I will take good care of her." Agar's voice was reassuring and it brought a smile back on Elizabet's face as she watched him follow behind Marcia, calling to her. "Alright, young lady, are you ready to work?"

Marcia tuned around laughing as she answered "That all depends, Father Bellingham. What kind of work do you have in mind?"

"No work involved, really. I just wanted a charming face to accompany me to Collinwood today."

"Collinwood?" Marcia's eyes grew wide, recalling the Moon Rider had mentioned that very place on the previous night. "Why...why are you going there, Agar?"

"Remember that parcel of land behind the church? The man who is supplying the land and most of the money for my home for children project, lives at Collinwood." Agar lifted Marcia's face. "Cia, why does Collinwood upset you?"

"Oh...it does not really. How could it? I have never seen the place." Marcia smiled and started up the hill toward the church. "It is a beautiful day to go for a ride in the country. Especially in the company of a young handsome priest with blue eyes." Staying a few steps ahead of him, she glanced around and gave him a warm smile. Agar let his fingers run over her forehead, then across her lips. Hearing a shout up ahead, they both looked up toward the church to see Amby Steen waving from the white gate.

"The carriage is waiting, Agar." Amby smiled down at Marcia, recalling the night before. "You look beautiful today, Cia."

57

"Thank you, Amby." Marcia smiled at him lovingly, admiring his royal blue shirt. "You look rather nice today yourself."

Agar cleared his throat and took Marcia by the hand and led her over to the waiting carriage. He placed his strong hands around her tiny waist and lifted her up to the seat. Amby climbed up on the other side and the three traveled from the churchyard onto the country road leading to Collinwood.

Marcia relaxed, feeling safe riding between Agar and his friend, Amby, although her thoughts swam ahead of her. Would the Moon Rider actually be at Collinwood? Why had he mention taking her to Collinwood to his men if it wasn't his home? Surely, he would have no reason to lie about that around her, not a man of his high ranking. Marcia jumped when she felt Agar's hand fall gently on her shoulder. He glanced down, laughing softly. "I did not mean to frighten you, Cia. Your mind seems to be miles away."

Miles away, how many more miles, she wondered, was this Collinwood? Her eyes met his in a smile. "Nay, I was just caught up in this beautiful scenery."

"Aye, it is a pleasant countryside; my favorite spot in the area." Agar glanced around at their surroundings. The peaceful, winding road moved lazily through a forest, then vast openings of rich green fields. "I come out here often, just so I can see it."

"Then, I suppose you and the owner of Collinwood know one another quite well." Marcia missed the exchange looks of humor between her two companions, as her attention was on what lay ahead.

"Aye! You could say that I know the gentleman quite well. Working with him on the children home project has brought us together on several occasions." Agar's tone held a hint of teasing, but Marcia did not catch it. Her thoughts were totally consumed with thoughts of the master of Collinwood. Who was he and what exactly did he look like? She had hoped that Agar would not grow suspicious from her many questions concerning this man.

"What sort of man is he anyway? Is he married with a home filled with lots of children?"

"The man is a very happy bachelor and has no interest in marriage at this time. Why? Do you wish to capture him into your heart so that all this magnificent estate can be yours one day?" Marcia noticed his voice sounded somewhat joking, but his intense stare was serious. "Or, are you giving up so fast on me?"

"Agar." Marcia studied his handsome face, trying to make out whether or not he was joking, but his eyes remained serious. "I was just inquiring on what sort of man I would be meeting today, that is all."

"Well, lady fair, the dear gentleman of Collinwood will probably be gone when we arrive." Amby leaned back in the seat and took a deep breath.

"Gone? Where?" Marcia looked down, wishing she could be less talkative. "I mean, does he not know you are planning a visit with him?"

"Aye lass, but anything to do with business he leaves to his head servant." Amby smiled down at the beautiful woman who had stolen his friend's heart. "In all honesty, the lord of Collinwood would much rather spend his time on a merry hunt or out chasing women."

"I cannot see why a man would devote all his time to pleasure." Marcia suddenly felt deprived that she would not be meeting the owner of this magnificent estate which in an odd since, she suddenly felt a strange part of. "It looks as though a man with his obvious high standings, could take more interest in the wrong doings going on in Canterbury."

"Well Cia, he actually does, in his own way." Agar kept his eyes on the road stretched out in front of him as he drove the two horses forward. "The lord of Collinwood just goes about things a little different than most men, that's all. Believe me, he does more than his fair share."

"Aye!" Amby laughed "He who follows his dreams of destiny, will deny his own life for the cause of love."

Marcia stared up at her red-head companion, unsure to his words as Agar laughed and patted her knee.

"My dear friend Amby speaks from within his self, riddles that have a hidden meaning." The young priest turned Marica forward so she could have her first glimpse of Collinwood Castle as it came into the clear view, sitting spaciously upon a rolling green hill. Its huge white turrets stretched upward into the vast blue sky and the massive white castle climbed up and out, making a visitor hold their breath beholding the enormous size of it. The only thing standing between them and the fairy tale castle was the massive iron gates connected to a ten-foot high stone wall. It was obvious to Marcia, all the visitors who might be lucky enough, would be allowed to pass through the strong gates and unwanted intruders would not be allowed to pass through. Agar's eyes lit up at the very sight of it as he spoke softly.

"There she sits, in all her radiant splendor! Collinwood Castle! How do you like her, Cia?"

"Oh Agar, it is the most beautiful place I have ever seen!" Marcia felt as though someone had knocked the wind from her. She had never seen a place to match the elegance that this castle held, not even her beloved Karnstein Manor. Her heart was pounding with excitement when Agar lifted her down from the carriage and she barely was aware of the attendant that ran up to hold the reigns while they climbed down. Her thoughts were wrapped up on Collinwood and she could not understand why this place had such an impact on her. It was all strange to Marcia, why a place she had never seen could make her feel like she was a part of it. As though it was reaching out and wanting her to know that she belonged here.

Marcia felt Agar take her hand as she walked between him and Amby through the gates and up the long stone walkway to the massive front doors that stood open for their arrival. Entering into the enormous hall with the winding steps gracefully dancing down in the center, Marcia looked around, eyes wide with wonder. Rich walnut chairs framed the walls and the spacious space cause a newcomer to glance up to the high vaulted ceiling overhead, dominated by a massive iron chandelier, filled with thirty oil lite candles. She glanced up into Agar's eyes, who was regarding her closely. He took her inside the adjacent sitting room, even larger and more elegant than the entrance hall.

"You will be alright in here, Cia, while I run take care of the business?"

"Of course, Agar. You shan't be long?" Marcia looked down and noticed her fingers were clutching tightly to his sleeve.

"Nay, Cia. I shan't be but a few minutes." His smile was

reassuring so she released his sleeve and returned a warm smile of her own. Agar gently stroked her soft hair. "Just relax and enjoy the splendor of this room."

Marcia gazed up into his handsome eyes, then looked around at her rich surroundings. A plush sofa sat stately in front of a massive stone fireplace that seem to climb right through the ceiling. Matching love seats rested on either side of the white sofa and several chairs lined three of the walls while a well stock library lined one entire wall. The huge arched windows let in the morning light and made the rich green velvet curtains glisten with riches.

"It is a lovely room Agar. I shall be indeed happy to wait in here." Marcia watched Agar walk quickly from the room, Amby close behind him, much like a little puppy, she thought with a smile. Slowly, she moved around in the big room, taking in every detail. As she let her eyes wonder over the row of books, Marcia's mind was on a certain masked man.

"Could this be where he lives?" walking over to the stone fireplace, her fingers ran gently over the heavy Cyprus mantel. From the large mirror over the mantel, Marcia could see the winding stone steps in the entrance hall. Stepping over to the open door, she looked up the long flight of stairs and saw another large hallway. "There must be rooms up there. Bedrooms, perhaps." She thought and moved closer to the steps and gazed up. "His room is probably up there. His room, his bed."

She sat down on the bottom step and placed her head in her hands as she whispered to herself. "What is wrong with me? It is Agar I care about, Agar I dream about, his making love to me, but yet…" Marcia stood up and moved slowly up the stone steps until she was standing in the open hallway. Looking around to make sure she was still alone, she whispered to herself. "Well, I have come this far. I might as well take a look around. Surely one little look cannot possibly hurt anything."

Her fingers clutched the first doorknob until it turned under a little pressure. Looking around, it was obvious to Marcia, the room definitely belonged to a woman. White ruffles laced the princess bed and the three arched windows. Everything in the room was tidy and in proper order, complete with a fancy vanity laden with a pure silver brush and comb set. A matching wardrobe sat stately in one corner, large enough to hold several beautiful dresses and the chest of drawers could hold any delicate feminine apparel. Marcia felt somewhat angry that there might be another woman in his life. On the other hand, she assured herself, it could very well be a mother or a sister who had this beautiful room.

Marcia backed slowly out the door and closed it quietly before continuing her way down the long hallway until she stood frozen, in front of a solid black door. Swallowing the fear that invaded her heart, she took hold of the doorknob and turned it. Marcia stood in the doorway, giving her eyes a chance to grow accustom to the dark room. Leaving the door open for light, she stepped inside and looked around. The entire room was done in black. The bed, the walls, the floor, and the curtains, that hung closed, dropping to the floor. Afraid she might get caught, she closed the door and made her way across the room to one of the windows. As she reached up to pull the curtain back, a hand grabbed hers and placed another over her mouth. Marcia's heart sank with total fear as she tried to fight off her attacker.

"What have I caught here, creeping around in my room?" The voice was well-remembered and Marcia suddenly felt ashamed and embarrassed to be discovered snooping around. His fingers loosened from her mouth, but he kept a tight hold on her hand. "What have you to say for yourself?"

"I...I should not be...up here like this, I know." She stammered.

"Perhaps, your body longs for mine, Marcia." He said mockingly.

"Marcia? Why...why did you call me that?"

"Because, that is your name, is it not, Marcia?" His hand moved to her hip and he caressed it. "Did you long to come to my bed?"

"How dare you say such a thing to me?" she forced herself to try and free her arm from his tight grip. "I had no intentions of seeing you! Agar said you would be gone! I take him at his good word!"

"Agar?" the dark figure laughed. "What have we here? You address this priest by his first name?"

"And why not? The way I feel for him, I find it perfectly

natural to call him by his Christian name." Marcia wished that Agar would come looking for her and rescue her from this illogical person. "Now, if you would be a gentleman and kindly let me go, I should like to rejoin him."

"Would you really?" he laughed softly. "Why, for heaven's sake? He cannot give you what a woman like you needs. You need a real man, Marcia." His fingers gently brushed over her face. "A man like me." His lips parted tenderly over hers.

Marcia could not control her arms from moving around his neck and giving in to his kiss. His hands moved slowly over her breast as his kisses continued to burn on her lips with passion. Breathing heavy next to her ear, he whispered

"You will love me, Marcia, not him. A priest cannot give you the love you demand, but I can and I will."

Marcia tried to pull away, suddenly torn between the desires she felt raging inside her for this man and the deep love she felt for Agar. "He can give me love. All the love I need." Her voice did not sound natural to Marcia, for her breathing was heavy and her flesh felt fiery hot. "Just let me go, please."

"Your words are pleading to go, but your heart, your body, they want to stay, Marcia." His lips brushed through her hair. "Give in, dear one. You know you want to."

"Oh, God! Yes!" she whispered, as his lips melted over hers. Her thoughts went to Agar. He was probably wondering where she was. Waiting for her in that big room. She had promised to wait for him, Agar, her love. But yet, she was here, longing for this man's arms, his lips, his perfect body. Marcia pulled away, taking a big breath. "I cannot! Agar is waiting. I must go before he comes looking for me!"

"What?" His voice fell breathlessly on her neck as he closed his eyes in aggravation. "It will not hurt him to wait! I need you, damn it!"

"And I need you, but I cannot give myself to you now! Not now!" Marcia wished the darkness did not hide his face from her as she moved her fingers through his long thick hair. "Tonight, come to me tonight! I will wait up for you."

He laid his head on her breast and breathed out slowly. "Very well, Marcia, but I shan't be stopped tonight, by anyone."

"You won't, I promise." Marcia felt her heart flutter as he led her over to the door. "Mine is the room on the back. I will leave the window unlatched. Just come in quietly."

"Aye! You can be sure that I will be there." His lips found hers again as his arms swept her up in a loving embrace. Being careful to remain in the shadows, he opened the door for her. "Go quickly now, before I change my mind."

Marcia raced down the steps and stopped just short of running into Amby. He looked at her with curiosity, unsure of what to say. He noticed the blush on her cheeks as he offered his hand for the last two steps.

"My lady, I have been looking everywhere for you. Where have you been?"

"A…just looking around. I am afraid I was tempted to explore this magnificent castle." She swallowed, hoping she had convinced Agar's dear friend. "Where is Agar? Surely the business meeting is over by now?"

"Agar? Well, he…" Amby stammered. "Agar is off somewhere looking for you. We sort of spit up to search for your where-about. The business meeting was over almost fifteen minutes ago."

"I see." Marcia tried to smile normally, but felt sure it came out awkward. "Well, why don't you find him and let him know I will be waiting down here in the entrance hall, so that we may be on our way."

"I would like to find him." Amby mumbled to himself as he looked around to decide where to start first. "I would like to know what is going on around here." He spoke under his breath and was relieved when the young priest came walking swiftly around the corner, panting for breath.

"Well, there you are Cia. Where on earth have you been?"

"Oh, just about, doing a little exploring." Marcia pretended to brush down her dress when she stood up to avoid looking into his eyes. "You seem to be out of breath Agar. I hope I did not make you run all over this castle with worry."

"Perhaps a little." Agar took her hand. "I did promise your aunt that I would look after you."

"Aye, I suppose you did." She followed him from the airy

64

castle, feeling at ease in the afternoon sun. "Did you get your business over with?"

"My business? Aye, the meeting went very well. Even better than I expected." Agar headed the horses from Collinwood Castle. "Did you find anything of interest while you were exploring the castle?"

"What?" Marcia blushed and tried to smile. "It is a very unusual place, truly fascinating."

Agar and Amby exchanged glances before Agar said softly "Is it?" then smiled to himself.

Chapter Eleven

Marcia avoided looking directly at Agar, for fear he would read her guilt. She walked slowly up to her front door, secretly wishing that Agar would grab her in his arms and kiss her longing lips, show her the man she knew lay deep within his priestly robes. Remembering the way Agar had looked at her and his concern regarding the Moon Rider, perhaps it wasn't as deep as she thought. Could his outpouring of words, wanting to know how far the masked man had gone with her, could it have been jealousy? She pondered.

"You certainly have been quiet since we left Collinwood." Agar's soft voice broke into her thoughts. "Are you sure something did not happen to you back there?"

"Happen? Of course not, Agar." Marcia forced a laugh. "I guess the grand castle has left me spellbound and the ride home was so peaceful and relaxing, I am letting it linger a while longer until I will be greeted by my cheerful aunt who will insist on hearing every single detail of my days adventure." Marcia finally looked up and saw him observing her closely, so she gave him a beautiful smile. "To be honest, Agar, I just feel light and breezy. You do that for me, did you know that? Being with you makes me feel beautiful all inside."

"Does it now?" his fingers gently stroked her face. "I too have beautiful feeling for you, Cia. Is it wrong that I should feel the way I do?"

"Nay, I think not. You are a man. I am a woman. It is very human that we should care for each other." Taking his hand, Marcia lifted it to her lips and kissed it, then looked up seriously, longing to know how he truly felt. "Would you kiss me, Agar?"

"Kiss you?" his eyes wondered to her lips. "But, Cia, I…"

"What is wrong? Do you not want to kiss me?" Marcia's eyes sought his pleadingly. "Agar?"

"Aye." His fingers brushed lightly over her full lips." I have often dream about kissing these lips. Sometimes, my dreams get deeper and I wake up longing for you, Cia."

"Then, kiss me my love. Anything that I have is yours."
Marcia felt her body tremble as Agar parted his lips over hers
tenderly. This is where she belonged, she thought, as Agars
flaming kisses continued to burn her lips. But why had the Moon
Rider's kisses affected her the same way. Could she possibly be in
love with two, different men.

Agar pulled himself away, breathing heavily. With longing,
he wrapped his fingers around her soft hand. "I must go, dearest
Cia, before I weaken more."

"Could you not love me without feeling that it was wrong, my
darling Agar?" Marcia's free hand reached up and tenderly
touched his handsome face.

"I do love you Cia." His reply came soft and sincere. "I never
knew my life would be so confused. Before I met you, I was
perfectly happy and content with my life as a priest. But, now,
sweet, beautiful Cia, I dream of lying in your arms. My thoughts
are constantly consumed with you."

"And mine of you, Agar." Marcia closed her eyes and smiled,
happy with his last statement. "Surely our God would not wish to
stand in the way of our love."

Agar looked up toward the sky, as though he were looking for
the answer. For an endless minute, he stared, never saying a word
Finally his attention fell on Marcia, who realized she had been
holding her breath in anticipation.

"I must think things out, Cia. I must pray about this shadow
that has passed over and swept me away." Agar, had grown calm,
his breathing had settled down to normal as he kissed her lips
lightly. "I must leave now, dearest Cia."

"When shall I see you again?" Marcia hated for this moment
to arrive, the moment for fair wells.

"Soon, my darling." Agar let his hand slide from hers and
within seconds, the young priest had disappeared up the
cobblestone path to the church.

Marcia walked dreamingly into her room, her mind caught up
in Agar's admission of his love for her. She had been happy to find
the note from her devoted nurse, telling her she had a busy day
with her friend and was worn to a frazzle, thus she would be
turning in early. Should she need her, kindly wake her up, if not,

she would welcome the much-needed rest. It had been a perfect day, she thought smiling, being with Agar. Her attention went to the window facing the back of their flat. The same window she had promised to have unlocked. Her heart became troubled as worry overtook her happiness. She could not possibly make love to this conceited man with the most incredible mysterious eyes. She loved Agar and had she not just confessed her love to him? Yet, in the heat of the moment, she had told Rider she wanted him to make love to her and it was she who had promised the window would indeed be unlocked for him. Marcia sat down at the small vanity and stared at her reflection in the mirror.

"Dear Lord, what a mess I have gotten myself in." she spoke softly to herself, not wishing to arouse her house mate. Through the glass she could see the window and felt a slight moment of reprieve. "Perchance he will be unable to come or have a change of heart. But if he does, I will simply tell him, in a polite manner, my mind has changed." Marcia walked over to the window and nervously undone the lock. Then moved over to her bed and sat down. "For his coming so far, I will let him in, but only to explain why I cannot bed with him."

Marcia had found a good book and had read ten chapters when she heard the mantel clock strike twelve. It had been several hours since she came in her room and she felt she had waited long enough. Yawning, she slipped the dress over her head and pulled a silk white nightgown over her head. She walked over to the window and peered out into the vast darkness. There were no sounds in the village streets, so a single rider could have been heard from a long distance. Marcia concluded the Rider had changed his mind.

"It is late. He shan't be coming tonight." She slid the lock back into place, carefully blew out the candles and climbed into her bed. Her mind twirled around her, filled with the day's events, the passionate kisses from both Agar and the Moon Rider, and how she had the same feelings for both men, who were nothing alike. Sleep finally overtook her as she drifted off but was suddenly awaken when a hand clasped down over her mouth. Marcia tried to shake the sleep from her eyes and collect her senses as to what was happening.

"Why did you not leave the window unlatched for me, Marcia? You promised you would." The voice came soft in her ear and her heart began to beat uncontrollably.

"It grew late. I thought you were not coming, so I latched it back." She whispered, not wanting Elizabet to hear, "How did you get in?"

"I forced the latch; It is not so hard." Marcia finally grew accustomed to the darkness so she could make out her intruder clearly. His black clothing made it hard to see him, but the nearness of his face brought out his mysterious eyes and his perfect lips. Not to get sucked into his charm, Marcia coldly remarked.

"I am sure you have had many experiences breaking into lady's windows!"

"Nay, yours is the first. All my lady friends happily leave their windows open." Rider's voice was mocking. Marcia's angry expression was clearly aggravated and this met with the Rider's approval. "Why does it bother you that I have other women?"

"I assure you, it bothers me not!" Marcia lifted her head with stubborn pride. "You might as well go to one of those stupid willing bitches, for I intend to do naught with you!"

"Nay, my raucous lady, you shall indeed make love to me. You will not escape my arms this night." The masked man remained calm and this upset Marcia even more. She began to grow uneasy with his steel determination.

"I have no desire to make love with you, you...you overbearing mutton-head!" Marcia tried to pull free from his tight grip. He laughed softly, making Marcia's temper flare up higher still. "Your conceit is growing with superabundance!"

"Marcia, you know you want me to make love to you." He whispered, as his lips brushed through her hair. "You desire me as much as I do you. Admit it."

"Nay! Please stop!" her pulse beat wildly as fire burned through her veins, from his very touch.

Rider's hand cupped her face as his lips folded passionately over hers. Marcia could feel her body growing weak as the Rider slid his body next to her. Pressing up against her, she could feel the huge swell inside his black pants. Her breathing grew heavy as his hand slipped the gown down below her breast and gathered them up in his hands. Slowly his kisses moved down her neck until they rested on one breast as he gently circled the harden nipple with his warm tongue.

"Marcia, my darling Marcia." His hot breath was next to her bare skin as he managed with expert skill to remove the rest of their clothes

Desire swept through Marcia like a raging forest fire. Just feeling his naked body next to hers, made keeping her hands to herself impossible as she moved them uncontrollably. Their bodies were in a tight embrace as his lips moved wildly over her body. Feeling the need for more, Marcia whispered breathlessly.

"Take me! Take me, Rider!" He knew she wanted him as much as he did her and Rider was more than ready to oblige the lady. Marcia could feel the breakthrough, the sting of her purity slipping away under his forceful pushing. The pain subsided quickly for Marcia as she made every effort to please him with her first attempt of lovemaking. His movements increased in speed as she moved with perfect rhythm under him.

"Oh, Marcia!" His tongue engulfed her ear. "You are so good for me!"

"Oh! Rider! Rider!" Marcia felt the fiery desires of ecstasy sweeping her away. It struck! It hit the target! It was all hers as she breathed out a satisfied sigh. "Sweet, my darling." She whispered as his hands pulled her to him even tighter as his pleasure struck with rapturous joy.

The Moon Rider held Marcia close, both temporarily in a trance-like immobility. Then ever so slowly, his hand moved along her curved hips as his voice came soft to her ears.

"It is me you want, Marcia. It is me you need. He could never give you the satisfaction that I can. He has his church, my dearest. Even if he gave in and made love to you, his thoughts would go back to the church. His guilt would drive you both apart and it will leave you heartbroken." Rider's hand moved tenderly to her face. "We belong together, you and I. You need a man, my love. A real man."

"Agar is a real man, Rider. Why are you always demeaning him?" Marcia did not feel frightened of the masked man any longer, only safe and protected in his strong embrace. "You are jealous, are you not?"

"Nay, such nonsense!" He burst out. "I only want you to open your eyes and see the truth as it is." His fingers moved slowly over her full lips. "You enjoyed yourself with me just now, Marcia, did you not?"

"Oh, I suppose it was alright." She teased. "I am certain Agar could do just as good, perhaps better."

With anger, the Moon Rider stood up and pulled his pants over his bare skin. Looking down on her, his eyes flashed fire from behind the black mask. After getting into his white shirt and black leather boots, he sat down on the edge of the bed.

"Then persuade that priest to bed with you. I can assure you, my misguided lover, his lack of knowledge will convince you that I am the best lover."

"What makes you think that Agar is inexperienced? And just in case he has never made love to a woman before, I know he will catch on fast." Marcia knew she had the upper hand when Rider gritted his teeth.

"What, pray tell, makes you so damn sure he will catch on fast?"

"A woman can tell just by the way a man walks and is shaped." Marcia laughed softly when he growled. "Agar moves quite well, you know."

"Nay, I would not know! Suddenly you have become an expert on sex, Marcia. One good lesson from the right partner and you are all knowledge." Rider covered her mouth with his hand to block out her mocking laughter. "Silence woman! I find naught funny!"

"Then let it go, Rider. I will convince Agar to make love to me and prove you wrong." Marcia pulled the covers around her neck to hide her breast from his wondering eyes. "By the way, you never did tell me how you learned my name. Who told you?"

"Old women's tongues wag when they are excited and frightened. In their haste to seek help, they forget what they are doing and spit out truths without realizing it."

"Elizabet!" Marcia let out a soft sigh. "I might have known. No other knew my true identity."

71

"Elizabet, is it? Your 'aunt' has been lying about her name too." The man behind the mask stared questioningly.

"You tricked me, pest!" Marcia sat up, keeping a tight hold on the covers. "I would apricate it very much if you would not go about spreading this little information."

"Whatever the lady says." The Moon Rider tilted his head in a knightly manner. "Tell me Marcia, why change your names? Running away from something?"

"I'd rather not say. Elizabet and I, just wanted to start a new life." Marcia looked over toward the window to avoid eye contact with her mysterious lover. "Just let it go at that, please."

"For now, my lady, but only because it has grown late." His hand turned her face toward him. "I must depart, dearest Marcia. I will return whenever I have a desire for you."

"I would rather not be on your list of women, Rider, if you do not mind. I will be second to no one!" Marcia spit out each word.

"Touching." The Moon Rider arched his brow and said with a smirk "Like I said woman, whenever I desire you, I will indeed bed you! You are mine, whether you like it or not! But I am sure you do. So, get that in your pretty little stubborn mind!"

Marcia tried to pull away when he reached for her. His fingers clutched her face as his lips melted over hers with passion. "Fare well, my headstrong beauty." He walked swiftly to the window and pushed it open. "Until next my eyes behold you, adieu."

When the window closed and snapped shut, Marcia climbed from her warm covers and pressed her face against the windowpane. Looking out into the empty courtyard behind the row of flats, she could see no signs of the man in black. He had already disappeared into the darkness.

Chapter Twelve

Henry Karnstein stared angrily down into the large courtyard of his estate. News had been brought to him about his daughter not arriving at his sister's flat in London. His fist slammed against the wide windowpane, causing the solid oak to crack.'

"Damn that stubborn girl! Had she not the proper upbringing, I might understand her callous actions! But her saintly mother, Josephine, God rest her soul, would certainly be ashamed of her childish behavior!"

"Henry, you are getting yourself in a state for naught." Dorinda Karnstein, Henry's spinster sister, had traveled from London when Marcia and Elizabet failed to show up. Worried something might have happened to them on the road, she made the journey to Melbourne to inform her brother. She reached up and patted his arm. "You have sent your men in search of her and Elizabet and I am sure they will find her soon. She could not have gotten far."

"Marcia? Ah, on the contrary. My ambitious young daughter would go to the other end of the earth to have things her way!" The owner of Karnstein Manor walked over to the stone fireplace and picked up the iron poker and jabbed away at an imaginary fire. "I cannot understand what is wrong with the girl!"

"Henry, perhaps Marcia wishes to make up her own mind about finding a husband. I have had occasions to speak to your beautiful daughter on my visits here and she has made plan that she seeks love, and with the right partner. You have a very smart and wise daughter, Henry." Dorinda sat down on the soft cushioned sofa and picked up her glass of Madeira. "Marcia is dreaming about love. That is a young girls fancy, you know."

"Poppycock! What does a young girl know about love? I say Marcia will fall in love with Krantz after she gets to know him." Henry's eyes rose to the painting over the mantel. The perfect likeness of his dear departed wife and Marcia's beautiful mother. "I grew to love Josephine, and she, I."

"Sometimes it happens that way, dear brother. I could tell how much Josephine adored you and could see the deep affection you felt for her." Dorinda knew the hurt her brother felt whenever his thoughts dwelt on his beloved wife, and he just assumed every arranged marriage would be like theirs. "You were both lucky to find real love, Henry, but you must admit, Krantz Hamish is a strange man. I am not so sure I would choose him for a husband."

"I cannot see why all you women in this household see ill will in Krantz. He is a fine knight, brave and loyal to England."

"To England, or to himself?" she continued, despite her brother's frown. "There has been talk, Henry, of his steaky affairs. I think you close your ears to these mumblings concerning Sir Hamish."

"But are they facts, or just mere gossip, my sharp-tongue sister?" He looked from his sister when the butler opened the door with an announcement. "Frederick, what is it? News of my daughter's where-about?"

"Nay sir, you have visitors. Sir Krantz Hamish and his sister mistress Arabella to see you me lord. Shall I bring them in, sir?"

Henry looked briefly at his sister, looking somewhat forlorn, then back at his faithful servant. "Frederick, tell Sir Hamish and his sister to enter. They must not be kept waiting."

"Very well, me lord." The servant disappeared behind the big door as Dorinda looked up at her brother pleadingly.

"Please Henry, give this marriage some thought before you make anything final. Marcia is your daughter; her happiness should come before anything else, even your beautiful estate."

Henry nodded his head in agreement and turned to see the two visitors coming in the big room. Both brother and sister were decked in fancy traveling clothes. Krantz plastered on a frozen smile as he stepped up to the owner of Karnstein Manor and extended his gloved hand.

"Lord Karnstein, it is so good to see you again."

"It is always a pleasure to be in your company as well, Krantz. I trust the trip to Melbourne was pleasant." Henry reached for Arabella's gloved hand and kissed it. "I have not had the privilege of making your acquaintance, my dear."

"My friend, this is my very lovely sister, Arabella, just two years older than your beautiful daughter." Krantz smiled down at his sister as she placed her own faux smile on her red lips as Henry Karnstein gave her his greetings.

"My dear lord Karnstein, it is a pure honor meeting my dear brother's soon to be father-in-law. I do so look forward to meeting your daughter. My love-struck brother speaks of her constantly." She glanced over at Dorinda and pressed her smile a little bigger, then returned her attention on their host. "As for the trip here, it could not have been nicer." Arabella's tone came out crisp and airy. "The only thing that could have made it more enjoyable would have been to have the company of a handsome gentleman, like yourself, traveling with us."

"You do me much pleasure, my dear Arabella." Henry motioned to the sofa where his sister sat taking in their phony greetings. "This is my sister, Dorinda. I think you have met Krantz before in London, dear sister, have you not?"

"Indeed, I have. It was at the palace, I recall." Dorinda smiled a genuine smile as she waved to the seating. "Please, do sit down and I will ring for tea."

"That would be splendid." Arabella laughed gayly as she joined the older woman on the sofa and glanced down at the empty sherry glass. "It was such a warm, dry ride here and I could not help but notice your empty glass. Perhaps, we all could have a sample of that fine Madeira."

"If you prefer, my dear." Dorinda rang for a maid and ordered four glasses of the rich red wine to be brought in.

While the spoiled sister took a seat next to her host' sister, Krantz stepped up close to lord Henry. "Lord Karnstein, I do not wish to sound pushy, but when will you permit me to marry Marcia? I find with each passing day, I grow more and more impatient to make her my bride." Hearing the man's statement, the maid nervously handed Krantz the glass of Madeira and walked quickly from the room. She did not wish to be in there with this man when her employer informed him about his daughter's leaving. Arabella giggled as she sipped the strong wine.

"Tis true, my lord. My devoted brother is beside himself. If you do not let him marry your daughter soon, I think my love-sick brother should have an attack."

"My sister is a bit absurd over my mental status, but nonetheless, I would feel at ease if I could have your daughter's hand before the twelfth day of the month."

"So soon?" Henry glanced over his glass at his sister, who had sat up to hear clearer what was being said. "I have learned over my years, one who usually gets in a hurry, falls on his face."

"Nay sir, not I! Besides, I have waited long enough, a respectable time for your blessing." Krantz arched his eyebrow and looked up the empty staircase. "By the way, where is my dear lady? Is she napping or strolling about in the rose garden, where I had the great honor of meeting Marcia a few months back?"

"She is neither napping or taking a stroll in the rose garden, Krantz. Marcia is not at Karnstein." Henry looked down at his wine glass to avoid the man's stormy eyes as he stared puzzled.

"Not at Karnstein?"

"Nay, and for that matter, my daughter is not even in Melbourne." Henry casually rolled his eyes over at his confused visitor, waiting for the outburst he knew was sure to come.

"Not here? Not in Melbourne? But I do not understand?" His eyebrow flew up in anger. "Where is she, Lord Karnstein? Where is my betrothed? Where is Marcia?"

"I know not, Krantz." Henry tried to remain calm while the black knight grew more and more angry.

"You know not! What sort or dumb reply you give me! I am no fool! She is your daughter, is she not, sir?"

"Aye, that she is."

"Then why, in God's name, say that you know not her whereabouts'?"

"Because sir, that is the truth of the matter. Marcia was gone when I returned from my visit with you." Henry's voice rose slightly to match his angry visitor. "Marcia decided on her own to run away from this marriage to you. I knew nothing of it until my return from Tilbury, just as I stated, at which time my sister informed me that neither my daughter or her nurse reached London, where she was to go and buy her wedding finery. My men are in search of her at this very moment."

"Can you be sure that she ran away, Lord Karnstein? Perhaps some highway thieves captured them." Arabella stood up to join her brother. "I am certain Marcia had every intention of marring my brother."

"I wish I could agree with you, to save face, but Marcia was dead-set against marrying you Krantz from the moment I mentioned it to her." Henry set his glass on the mantle. "Like I told you, my men are out in search for her now. I am sure I will hear some news soon to her whereabouts'!"

"Then, it is up to you, Lord Karnstein, to inform your daughter that she WILL marry me, whether she approves it or not!" Krantz's anger was clearly visible as he paced the floor.

Watching the man's actions, Henry Karnstein was not so sure of his decision on this man. He joined his sister on the sofa, waiting for the man to settle down and look his way before speaking.

"We shall see, Sir Hamish. I might have to rethink the whole matter over again and decide if you are the right choice for my daughter."

"What the devil do you mean sir? Think the matter over?" Krantz spit out each word as though they had a bitter taste. "You will permit me to marry Marcia, sir, or you will regret it, Karnstein!"

"Is that a threat, Krantz?" Henry stood up in anger, suddenly regretting any dealing with this man. "This is my daughter's life we are talking about! I WILL NOT give her to someone I think unworthy of her!"

The dark knight gritted his teeth as he bawled his fist up, wanting desperately to strike out at Marcia's father but he did not wish to put the final blow to his already failing proposal for fair Marcia's hand. Arabella gently stroked her brother's arm as she whispered softly and seductively.

"There, there Krantz, you must not get upset, my dearest." Arabella moved over toward the sofa and smiled up at the owner of the beautiful manor house. "Lord Karnstein, my brother loves your daughter deeply. It is his concern for her absence and safety that brings out the temper in him. Krantz is truly a decent and honorable man, and if you could only see it in your heart to allow this marriage between my brother and Marcia to take place, then you'll fine he will make her a wonderful husband."

"I think we all could use some time to rest and think more clearly. At least, until all the cobwebs are out of the air." Henry helped Dorinda to her feet and walked her to the stairs. "I will reconsider this marriage, Krantz. In the meantime, my servant will show you and your sister to your rooms. For now, my sister and I bid you goodnight." Henry escorted his sister to her bedchamber, then walked to his, drained from the turn of events.

Safe inside their adjoining rooms, Krantz stared angrily down at his blonde hair sister. Knowing his moods better than anyone else, Arabella shook her blonde curls.

"Stop looking at me that way! It was the only thing I could do, Krantz, to save our plan. You would have spoiled everything with that lose temper of yours, dear brother! You know very well, things will work out easier if you marry that spoiled little bitch!"

"Aye, but we can get the map with or without the permission of Henry Karnstein!" Krantz walked behind a small personal guest bar and opened a bottle of wine, then filled two glasses. Handing a glass to his sister, he turned up his glass and gulped down a mouthful before sinking into a chair. "That man will not stand in my way! He or his precious daughter!"

"But, dear brother, you know we have to have her or we shall never get the damn treasure!" Arabella took the bottle and refilled her brother's glass. "The legend states it clearly. Let me see, how does it go?" she sank down on Krantz's bed. "Oh, yes! 'And bring ye the fair maiden, so rich with beauty and grace, the tenth generation of family Karnstein. Then, and only then, can you find your way to the treasure that lies beyond dangers and demons!"

In his intoxicated state, Krantz gazed over at his sister, lust filling his body as he rose and walked over to join her on the bed. He let his hand run gently over her shapely hip as he whispered.

"Aye, we will take her, you can rest assured, dear sister. We might have to force her to come, but we will get the bitch on that ship if I have to slay everyone here at Karnstein Manor!"

"Aye, my beautiful brother. I know well that you shall not fail. You are much to clever, darling."

She slipped from her dress, revealing a naked body, Krantz took in every detail as he felt his passion grow. Slipping from his own clothing, the dark knight lay down next to his sister and gathered a breast in his hand. Arabella ran her fingers down his chest as she softly spoke. "We will get the treasure, Krantz darling, won't we?"

"Aye, tis my word." His kisses fell on her neck. "Our good fortune will be Marcia's fate. It will be a shame to lose someone so beautiful for all that gold!"

"Quiet your tongue! Talk naught of her!" Arabella pouted and turned her back to him.

"Is my sexy sister jealous of my would-be wife?" Krantz ran his hand slowly over her round buttocks. "It was your idea that it would be better if I were to marry the fair damsel, was it not?"

"Aye, I remember well, brother." Arabella turned over and gazed into his lustful eyes. "And if you must wed her, find some excuse not to bed with her."

"We shall worry about that bridge when we come to it, my sex kitten." His lips folded over hers in a burning kiss. "Nevertheless, the end will be the same for poor Marcia." Krantz laughed lazily as his legs circled Arabella's and they performed an incestuous act.

Chapter Thirteen

Marcia stared at Elizabet as she sat drinking her morning tea. Feeling the girl's burning eyes on her, the nurse looked up from her paper.

"What is it child? Has your old friend and nurse done something to displease my lady?"

"Who did you tell that I had been kidnapped that night Murphy and his men raided Canterbury?" Marcia tilted her head, waiting for a reply.

"Why, tis some man who was at the chapel on the hill." Elizabet tried to picture the young man who had hurried off in the dark to carry news to Agar. "I think I have seen him about Canterbury, perhaps at the chapel the Sunday we attended. Aye, with Father Bellingham, I am sure of it."

"Did he have a stock of thick red hair?" Marcia picked up the teapot and poured herself a steaming cup, then refilled Elizabet's.

"Now that you mention it, tis a big crop of hair he had. A bit untidy but it lay nicely." She chuckled. "I was so worried about you, my lady. I did not really know what was going on."

"Precisely! That is why the Moon Rider is aware of who we are, Lizzie."

Elizabet's eyes grew wide as she stammered. "He knows? But how could he possibly know?"

"You called me Marcia in front Amby, the man with the red hair, and now for some unknown reason Amby told the Moon Rider." Marcia sat the empty teacup down and stood up. "Why did he go to him and not Agar?"

"Perhaps the young priest was out on a mission and could not be reached." The nurse stood up next to her ward and placed a hand on her arm. "So, this Moon Rider knows our name, he cannot know any more, surely." Elizabet thought a minute before adding. "And I am sure I did not tell that young man what my name was."

"Nay, you did not, I did." Marcia looked down with self-discuss. "Rider tricked it out of me. He, is a very clever man, sweet nurse and you are correct. So far, I think the Moon Rider only knows our names, and nothing else about us."

"But, if this man is as clever as you say he is, my dear, he might have ways of finding out." Elizabet looked up at Marcia, questions written on her worried face. "My lady, be honest, you have not seen that masked man since the night he brought you home, have you?"

Marcia bit her lip, knowing she could not hide the truth from this one who had brought her up and whom she loved dearly.

"Aye Lizzie, twice since." She felt herself blush, remembering being in his arms and longing for him to make love to her.

"Twice you say. But, when, dear?" Marcia had walked to the window to avoid eye contact with her lifelong friend. The old nurse walked over next to her, sensing something had brought a change to the girl she had raised and loved as her own. "Please tell me, Marcia."

"Once, the day I went to Collinwood with Agar." Marcia kept her eyes on the street outside the window, too ashamed to look at her best friend. "And once...here, in my room."

"In you room? Your bedchamber?" Lizzie swallowed, afraid at what she might hear but the need to know everything. "But, how...when...what?"

"How? The smooth man came through my window. When? Last night, as you lay sleeping in your chamber. And what?" Marcia glanced down at her wide-eyed nurse. "He made love to me, Lizzie." As the woman's mouth flew open, Marcia could not help the laughter that slipped out and yet at the same time, she felt the hot tears running down her beautiful face. "It is truly alright Lizzie."

"Alright? But, my lady, tis a terrible thing that happened!" Lizzie paced around the room, loud weeping coming from her lips. "It is all my fault! I should have listened to your dear wise father and carted you off to London. None of this would have ever happened and no trouble would we be in."

"Lizzie, we are not in any trouble! I love Rider. It was perfectly natural for me to make love to him." Marcia walked over and poured herself another cup of tea. "The tea has grown cold. I'll make some more."

"How can you think about tea at a time like this, young lady?

I thought your heart belonged to the young priest, not that I was in favor of that set-up." Elizabet was totally confused over Marcia's true feelings.

"My heart does belong to Agar, I love him dearly." Marcia walked over to her bewildered nurse. "Dear, sweet Lizzie, I know it sounds absurd, quite impossible, but the fact is, that I am in love with them both and I do not know what to do about it."

"Your problem is a little more than giant size, Marcia." Elizabet jumped when a heavy knock came on the door. She glanced up at her ward and shook her head. "I hope and pray it is no more bad news." She walked over on wobbly legs to open the door. George Holmes tipped his hat and smiled broadly at the flustered woman.

"Why the long face, Lisa? Tis a beautiful day and all is well, is it not?"

"Nay, not all, Mr. Holmes, but I would rather not discuss it." the heavy nurse stepped aside to let the tavern owner in.

Marcia grabbed her face, feeling it suddenly flush. Due to everything that had been happening with Rider, she had completely forgotten to inform George that she was quitting her job as bar maid in his tavern. Smiling sheepishly, she motioned for him to have a seat.

"George, I must apologize. I am terribly sorry I forgot all about coming down to the tavern."

"Aye. Cia's mind has been preoccupied lately, George." Lizzie walked from the small kitchen with a fresh pot of tea and three cups.

"I was concerned when you did not show up last night for work. I thought you might have taken ill or something, so I came to check on you." George took a sip of the good strong tea. "I was afraid what happened with Murphy might have scared you into quitting."

"I have decided to quit, George, but it is not because I am afraid. Father Bellingham ask me to quit and I just could not say no." Marcia joined her boss on the sofa. "Lisa and I are going into dressmaking, something more suited to me. Father Bellingham said Canterbury could use some good dress makers, and Lisa and I usually make our own clothes. She taught me at a very young age."

"Well, my dear, as bad as I hate to lose you, dressmaking would be a much safer job and you would not be on the streets after dark." George smiled, reassuring Marcia that he understood her decision. "Father Bellingham was right too; we could use some good dressmakers. If you like, you and your aunt can set up a little shop in the empty room next to mine. I have been looking for the right tenant to rent it to."

"That sounds promising George, thank you for the offer. We shall indeed look into it." Marcia was bursting with questions for her old boss and knew he had called Canterbury home for a very long time. "George, what do you know about the master of Collinwood?"

"Lord Collinwood?" his eyebrows lifted in surprise. "Where to begin? I have lived in Canterbury all my life and I have never one time, seen the man."

"Never seen him?" Marcia sat up, confused over her friend's statement. "Never?"

"Do not get me wrong, my dear, I have seen old Lord Collinwood many times. He was a fine, outstanding citizen in Canterbury, but not his son." George shook his head. "I cannot much blame the poor fellow though. After the accident, he did not want to be a public sight for the town folk to stare at and feel sorry for him."

"Accident?" Marcia's heart sank by his revelation. "Please George, tell me everything you know about the young man."

"Well, the story goes, when Lord Collinwood was sixteen, he was trapped inside a burning barn. Those who had found him said he lost a good deal of his face and that is the reason for his staying shut behind those castle walls."

"Good Lord!" Marcia closed her eyes and the masked face came into focus. "That is why he hides his face behind that mask." She spoke softly.

"Mask?" George stared over at the young woman he had grown to love like a daughter. "Marcia, have you seen him?"

"Please George, I think I need some fresh air. Would you excuse me." Marcia ran from the flat, her heart aching for the man she loved. Tears streamed down her cheeks as her footsteps took her up the cobblestone road. When someone touched her shoulder,

Marcia let out a soft scream. Looking around, she saw the loving blue eyes of Agar.

"Cia, what is wrong? Why are you crying so?" his fingers lovingly brushed away the tears. "Did someone do something to you to hurt you? Is your Aunt Lisa alright?"

"Aunt Lisa is healthy as a horse and to answer your other question, nay, no one has hurt me." Marcia looked down, feeling, the great love she had for this man in her heart and here she was thinking about another. "I just heard some disturbing news that tore into my heart and I needed to get away from my aunt and George Holmes. I could feel my tears coming and I did not wish to upset Lisa or make George ask me any more questions."

"What did you hear, Cia?" Agar gently brushed over her hair with his hand.

"George was telling me the story of Lord Collinwood. The accident in the barn, the fire…" Marcia bit her lip. "It's all so sad, dear Agar."

Agar took Marcia into his arms to comfort her, then he led her up the hill to the church gate. His fingers gently squeezed her hand and he locked eyes with her. "How would you like to do me a favor?" She nodded in agreement, feeling somewhat ashamed of her emotional display. "I have a little flower garden in the back, here in the churchyard. Would you pick me some flowers to place in the vase inside the church on the altar? I am not very good at arranging flowers and I feel certain this is something my sweet Cia is good at."

"Agar" Marcia reached up and kissed his lips lightly, then smiled. "I would love to do this for you." She followed him around the church to the flower garden and looked over the pretty colorful flowers. "Oh, I see a basket awaits."

"Aye. I was unhappily prepared to pick them myself after I returned, then I spotted you." The young priest laughed softly. "Saved by an angel!"

Marcia's heart beat wildly just to look into his handsome face. She reached up and touched it before gathering up the basket, then remembered his visit to town. "Agar, after you return from where?"

"I was on my way to a town meeting when I ran into you. I

could not just pass you by in your time of distress." His smile was so brilliant, she laughed softly as he said, "Could I?"

"Nay, I suppose not." Marcia gave him a quick hug, then looked up into his alluring blue eyes as she said seductively. "You, had better run along now or you shall be late. If you do not go soon, I just might decide to keep you here with me."

"Then I had better go while I still have the strength or the will to leave you up here alone." Agar's lips met hers in a lingering kiss. "I will see you when I return, if you are still here."

"I will stay and wait for you, gladly." She blew him a kiss as he walked quickly back around the church and out of sight.

Marcia happily picked the flowers slowly, remembering the kiss Agar had given her before leaving for the meeting in town. She wondered dreamily into the cool church and found the vase waiting on the altar. After arranging the flowers perfectly in the big vase, she stood back to admire the arrangement, when hand clasped over her mouth, startling her. Then her abductor spoke softly in her ear and she felt her pulse beat wildly from the sound of the familiar voice.

"I find you just about everywhere, do I not, Marcia?" releasing her, she turned and looked at the masked man. Every part of him was covered in black except for a white shirt and two openings. for his eyes and his perfect lips. He wore a handsome big black rim hat over the black cover that hid his hair. "I see our young priest has put you to work. Perhaps arranging flowers seem too feminine even for a man who wears a dress."

"First, I would hardly call arranging beautiful flowers, work. I am well trained in flower arranging, having made hundreds for my father's dinner parties." Marcia arched her eyebrow. "Second, Agar does not wear a dress, the young, handsome, and very manly priest, wears a priestly robe!" Marcia stared at his mask, wondering what lay on the other side.

"Why do you stare so, woman?" His voice fell soft upon her ears.

"I am not staring." Marcia looked down, feeling embarrassed from her obvious interest and thought quick to change the subject. "Rider, what are you doing here? A church does not seem to suit you."

"I was looking for you." Rider's hand moved gently over her breast causing her to stepped away, slapping his hand down. A smile crept on his lips as he got in her face. "And, I found you."

"Why? What do you want?" Marcia's body jerked with tension as he continued to smile.

"You Marcia, I want you. I desire you." Rider's white teeth sparkled brightly next to the black mask. "I awoke wanting you, needing you, so, I came to get you, woman."

"Now you listen, Rider, I have no intention of going anywhere with you!" Marcia turn to walk away when he grabbed her. She tried to pull away from his tight grip, but her fight was useless. "I promised Agar I would be here waiting for him and I will be!"

"Nay, wench! You are coming to Collinwood with me." His voice remained calm, which aggravated Marcia even worse. "So, you might as well come peacefully and enjoy the ride, both rides."

"Both rides?" Marcia spit out.

"Aye, my feisty sexy woman. The ride to Collinwood and the personal ride I shall take you on in my bed chamber."

"You beast! I shan't go anywhere with you! Not to Collinwood! Not to Canterbury! Not even an outdoor privy! Absolutely no where!" Marcia's eyes blazed as she took at the man she had actually felt pity for earlier. "I am staying right here, and that is final!"

"Very well, suit yourself!" The masked man sat down in the back pew and pulled her down next to him. "We shall both sit here and wait until that little coward, hiding behind a bible, returns! Then, once and for all, we shall determine who you belong to."

"Nay! You do not own me! I am not some cold treasure you claim by winning a duel! Nor am I land or property you can sell, should you grow tired of owning it!" Marcia shouted. "Just leave! Get out now!"

"Not without you, woman." He smiled and grasped her hand in his. "I guess I am going to have to put an end to this nonsense with the priest once and for all." Rider lend his head back and smiled up at the high ceiling. "Tis a shame to rid the world of such a fine prominent young man, but, I shan't let him keep getting in my way."

Marcia's face grew pale as she looked over at the cool-headed knight. "Surely you do not mean to kill Agar! Please Rider, you cannot!"

"Then, his fate is up to you, Marcia, my love." His eyes remained on the ceiling, showing no concern of his evil intentions just to win fair Marcia's hand. "What say you, woman? We stay here and confront my advisory, or you take me up on my offer? A trip to Collinwood?"

"Very well, Rider." Marcia mumbled with regret, but she would never risk Agar's life. "A trip to Collinwood."

Without delay, the black figure jumped up and led Marcia out the back door where his beautiful black stallion stood waiting while another masked rider held the rein. With ease, Rider lifted Marcia up in his saddle and climbed up behind her. Instead of heading toward the highway that led to the white castle, the two mask men galloped off into the forest, down a winding path, while dodging full grown oak trees. He and the other rider remained silent until they pulled the horses to a stop at the rear of Collinwood Castle, through a massive back entrance. The Moon Rider climbed off then pulled his woman down next to him. Handing the rein to his companion, he waved him off.

"Take care of the horses, friend. My lady and I are going up to bed."

The other mask rider laughed knowingly, waved a hand over his head and rode away, pulling the big black stallion behind him. Marcia stormed angrily after the Lord of Collinwood. She felt certain that she could kill him if she had a weapon handy.

"You, sir, are the least of men!" Marcia spit out each word as the masked man casually shut the door to his bedroom, letting her rage on. "You take to threating a lady to get her to bed with you!" she laughed mockingly. "You call that manly? I call it, a man hard up to get a woman on his own merits!"

Rider's fingers bit into her wrist as he yanked her around to face him. "SILENCE WOMAN! What say you about our love making? Can you stand here and tell me you did not enjoy it? Did I misread the passion between us? The way you moved under me and pulled me closer when you felt your intense desire sweep through your body with total ecstasy? Marcia, can you look into my eyes and say I mean nothing to you? You have no feeling for me at all?"

Marcia looked down and closed her eyes, trying to avoid his penetrating eyes. Her words seemed frozen in her throat. She hated him for making her get so upset and unsure of her own feelings. Tears streamed down her face as she spoke weakly. "Please…don't…"

"Marcia." His voice grew soft as his arms enfolded tenderly around her. "Do not cry, my darling."

She buried her face on his strong chest, his arms tightly surrounding her small waist. Her heart beat wildly as she felt his lips brush upon her hair. Fire swept through her body when he pulled her up close to him and she could feel his erection press tightly against her thigh. Slowly his fingers undid the buttons on her dress and slipped it to the floor. Within seconds, they stood there, completely naked, locked in a fiery embrace. Taking her face gently in his hands, Rider lowered his head and parted his perfect lips over hers, as his tongue found her mouth warm and inviting. With madding slowness, Rider moved his kisses around to her ear and whispered breathlessly.

"Marcia, my woman, my lover." His tongue moved slowly around her dainty ear passionately. "What sort of woman…are you?" his breathing was heavy and deep. "I have never had a woman to fill up my constant thoughts before. Each passing hour, I think of nothing but you. When we are apart, my body aches for you. My loins burst with excitement from the very thought of you. What sort of spell have you cast upon me that I should suffer so when you are not with me?"

"Rider, dear Rider." Marcia let her fingers run down his back, causing him to press in closer. "It is not a spell that taps at your heart. It is my love for you and the reluctance for me to omit it."

"Love? You love me?" Rider's mouth found hers again, then led her to his bed. Stretching across the soft covers, they locked themselves together and tumbled about the bed, their love pouring into one another.

Silently, they lay there, exhausted in each other's arms. The beautiful feeling of their entrancing ecstasy still overpowering them and keeping them spellbound. Rider smiled down warmly into Marcia's eyes as his hand ran lovingly over her bare stomach.

"Stay the night, my love. Lie beside me as I sleep so that I may awaken to your beauty next to me at the break of morn.

"Sounds so tempting, my dearest one, but I dare not." Marcia ran her finger over his lips. "Lizzie will worry if I do not return home. I dashed from the house this morning, with no thought of staying out long. I am sure she will send out a search party to find me and what might she think if she finds me here, with you?"

"I am sure she will turn into bed after speaking with your friend, Agar. I'm certain someone saw you leave with me and has informed him already. He might not approve of my taking you, but he knows he can trust me." His fingers danced over her forehead. "The night is before us, my darling, and we both are weary from our recent activities." Rider's lips were upon hers before he added "Marcia, stay, please stay, my love."

"Aye." She took a deep breath, feeling the need of sleep. "naught could drag me from your bed this night." Wearily, Marcia closed her eyes and fell into a restful sleep.

Chapter Fourteen

Marcia opened her eyes slowly to find the Moon Rider staring loving down at her, head and face still covered with his mask, and dressed in his white shirt and black pants. She sat up quickly, trying to collect her thoughts, remembering falling asleep in Rider's arms.

"Can it truly be morning already?" his words came to her ears soft and romantic. "Did my night with my love pass by so quickly?"

"It did indeed, my lord, for I feel as though I only this moment closed my eyes beside you." Marcia stretched and laughed softly. "Did you sleep well, my lord?"

"Aye, thanks to you being here next to me, for the first night in weeks." Rider gently rubbed his fingers along her beautiful face and across her full lips. "You, belong with me, always, Marcia."

She smiled, then glanced down, her thoughts turning to Agar. What did he think of her? Had she not promised to wait for him? He must think her uncaring and thoughtless. Still smiling, Marcia pointed to her clothes, lying neatly on a chair sitting at the far corner of the dark room.

"Rider, would you please hand me my clothes? I must go home now and try and explain things to Elizabet. She will be beside herself as it is."

"I wished you would stay with me." He got up and went to the chair to gather the garments in his strong arms. "If you would be my wife?"

Marcia looked up, unsure of what to say. What about her feelings for Agar? Where they not as strong as her feeling for Rider? She thought she loved Agar too. The feelings seemed the same, but she wondered. Could Agar give her the love she needed? Would he, being a priest? Marcia knew how she felt when she was in Rider's arms, but then, what about their constant battles? Did she really love him or was it just a physical attraction? Marcia nervously pulled her clothes over her head, then brushed through her hair with her fingers.

"Marcia, you never answered my question." Rider lifted her face in his hand. "Would you consider being my wife?"

"Please Rider, do not ask me?" she read the hurt in his eyes as she reached for his hand. "At least, not yet. I am so confused, so mixed up with my feelings."

"It is the priest, is it not?" There was a hint of anger in his voice, as a cloud covered his beautiful eyes.

"I do not have to tell you that I have a deep feeling for Agar." To avoid his stare, Marcia walked over to the door. "Please, Rider, just take me home. I need time to think."

"Aye, this time you may get away with it, for I have things I must do. But soon, very soon, we must do something about this situation."

"Rider, you must promise me that you will not hurt Agar." She looked up pleadingly. "Please."

"I cannot promise anything Marcia, but for your sake, not his, I will try." He took her hand and led her downstairs where they were fed breakfast. After they had completed the meal of fresh ham, eggs and buttered rolls, Rider took her out to the courtyard in the back of the castle where he had a horse waiting for Marcia. After kissing her goodbye, he ordered one of his men to ride with her, back to Canterbury.

Krantz stared across the table at Henry Karnstein, who was going through a stack of papers after downing the meal prepared for himself, his sister Dorinda, and his house guest. Observing the man closely, he wondered if he had come to a decision about his marriage to Marcia. His fingers gripped the fine table angrily as his attention was drawn to the door opening, and Arabella entering, carrying a sealed letter addressed to her brother.

"Dearest brother, this letter came for you a while ago as I was returning to the table for another glass of wine." Her eyes lit up in mischief. "It is from our dear friend in Canterbury, Vicar Hayworth."

An evil smile invaded Krantz's hard face as he took the letter. "Dear Hayworth, Now, I wonder what the dear chap has to say?"

"May I suggest you open the letter and find out, sir." Henry had been watching the exchange between brother and sister and thought their attraction for each other seemed unnatural. He held up his glass and a servant brought the decanter of wine over and poured it full, then refilled the other two empty glasses. Krantz nodded his head toward the servant, and peered over his glass at his host.

"I intend to do just that, Lord Henry." He smiled over at his sister as he broke open the seal. The dark knight's eyes lit up as he read the contents. "Well now, what a nice little break for me." He slapped the letter lightly in the palm of his hand. "I hope you will not mind, Lord Henry, if I go for a short visit to Canterbury. It is business and it shan't take long." Krantz's smile was so joyful, Henry wondered the reason that brought on the sudden change.

"Of course, I will not mind, Sir Hamish. A man's business is very important and I trust it is something worthwhile." Henry noticed the smile had not faded from his previous serious and angry face. "I mean, you seen to be so overjoyed over your friend's correspondence."

"Indeed! I am frantic with delight over the news!" Krantz walked quickly to the door. "I have not a minute to delay. I trust on my return to Melbourne you will have made up your mind about my proposal of marriage to your daughter."

"Aye, the decision should be made by then."

With Henry's reply, Krantz was gone from the room, Arabella close behind, wine in hand.

"What did Hayworth have to say which was so joyful that you should make with such haste, dear brother?" Arabella clutched his arm tightly.

"Tis good news, beautiful sister." He laughed out. "Hayworth has located Marcia. If I am the one to bring her back to Karnstein, then dear Henry will see no cause but to let me marry her."

"Marcia is in Canterbury? All that distance from here?" Arabella watched her brother as he pulled his traveling bag from the big closet, her eyes regarding him carefully. "Are you sure she is there?"

"She is! The good vicar knows what she and that fat nurse of hers look like. I sent him the sketch drawing I had commissioned when I saw her last." Krantz smiled over at his sister. "The beautiful maiden did not know an artist was drawing her likeness for me. Hayworth will be taking her to me after I arrive." Krantz wrapped a red cape around his shoulders. "The swift little bitch will not know I am there until it is too late."

"What of me, Krantz?" Arabella grew excited. "I come to?"

"Nay, dear sister, you remain here at Karnstein." He patted her flustered face. "This task is mine."

"But, how will I know that you will return for me?" she pouted. "You could well leave from Canterbury to the island with the hidden treasure."

"Dear Arabella, now would I do that to you?" his hand brushed along her hip. "I cannot leave without first getting the map of the island, now, can I?"

"The map? Of course not!" Arabella laughed, feeling relieved. "The map is indeed here someplace, is it not?"

"That is correct, little sister, and that will be your job while I am away getting our bait." Krantz continued to busy himself with getting ready for travel as he glanced at his sister. "Find the map Arabella, so that on my return we can depart, as soon as I am married, for the island."

"And if Karnstein refuses the marriage, dear brother?" Arabella had walked over next to her brother and ran her hand along his arm slowly.

"Should that happen, then we stick to my final plan and leave this manor in a blood bath!" he brushed her hand away and walked quickly to the door. "Just find the map! I will fetch Marcia!"

Elizabet opened the door and caught her breath when Marcia took around her worried nurse.

"Oh, sing praises!" the old companion broke into heavy sobs. "My little dove, I have been worried sick about you. Where on earth have you been?"

"I am so sorry, dear sweet nurse." Marcia kissed her forehead, then shut the door. "I told Rider I should come home, but he insisted it was much to late to travel back to Canterbury."

"You were with him again, my lady?" Elizabet turned and walked on ahead of the girl she had raised, shaking her head in defeat. "Where did I fail you? Where did I go wrong?"

"Lizzie, stop this nonsense. You have been a perfect nanny."

Marcia reached for her hand and clutched it lovingly. "And you have always helped me whenever a problem arrived too big for me to handle."

"If you mean your affair with this mysterious masked man, I am afraid I know not what to say."

"That is just a part of it, Lizzie. How can I be sure which of the two men I truly want? I love them both." Marcia fell on the sofa as tears flooded her eyes. She looked up in desperation. "Dear sweet, nurse, my constant help in time of trouble, tell me how I am to choose? You must, for my heart is torn between the two."

"I may be wrong telling you this, my lady, but tis for your love alone, I say it." Elizabet cleared her throat and sat down next to Marcia. "You have bedded with this Moon Rider. You know his love. The only way to find out for certain is to take yourself to Agar and bed with him."

"Sweet nurse." Marcia hugged her companion's neck lovingly. "I have dwelt on that thought, but was unsure. You have given me my answer."

"Then, my child, on this night you must go to Agar and persuade him to make love to you." She kissed Marcia's head and stood up, crossing herself. "And let us pray that your answer lies in what you do."

Marcia stared at the church door. Her hands were trembling as she folded her right hand into a fist and pounded upon the heavy door. Her waiting seemed endless until the door opened and Agar stood staring down at her.

"Cia, what on earth are you doing here at this time of night?"

"May I come in please?" her voice trembled, both from the cold night air and her reason for being there. Agar reached for her hand and found it cold and trembling. He pulled her inside and shut the door, bolting it secure.

"You are freezing, Cia." Agar led her to his room where a warm fire burned in the big fireplace. "Stand here and warm yourself." He moved over to a cabinet and brought out a blanket and a bottle of wine. "What brings you out on such a cold night?"

"I wanted to apologize for leaving yesterday without a word." She took the glass of wine from his hand and looked down at the rich red color. "I did not want to leave, but I had no other choice."

"I thought perhaps you had to get back home for some reason. The fact that you left your aunt and Mr. Holmes without an explanation perhaps." Agar joined her on the floor by the glowing fire and looked into the flames. "I must admit, I was a bit hurt and disappointed that you were not here when I returned. I had gone by the market on my way home and bought some cheese, bread, and fresh fruit in hopes of us eating together."

Marcia touched his hand. "Dearest Agar, I am deeply sorry, truly." She ran her hand along his cheek. "I would have liked being here with you, all the evening."

"You are here now, Cia. That is all that matters." Agar's lips parted over hers in a passionate kiss. "I love you so much, Cia."

"And I love you, Agar." Her fingers played softly in his blonde hair.

"Cia, you said you came up to apologize. Is that the only reason you came all the way up here tonight?" Agar's hand rested comfortably on her knee as he gazed into her alluring eyes.

"Nay, my love." Marcia lend over and let her tongue play around his ear. His breathing grew heavy as his hand started moving up her leg. She whispered in his ear. "Make love to me, Agar. Give me yourself. Take me."

"Cia, I…" if he had any intentions of stopping, they were quickly gone after Marcia slipped her hand inside his robe and with her other hand, placed his wondering hand between her thighs. Within seconds, Agar had Marcia and himself undressed. Heat flashed through their bodies as Agar pressed deeper and deeper into Marcia. She could feel her heart beating with complete passion as her words flowed from her lips.

"Agar, I love you! I love you!" from deep within her, Marcia felt Agar reach his rapturous ecstasy, then she reached her own.

Afterward, the loving couple lay quietly, neither wanting to pull apart from their warm embrace. Marcia was relaxed and overcome with exhaustion as she closed her eyes dreamingly, aware Elizabet knew where she was. She felt safe here in Agar's strong arms. He was the man she knew he was, capable of giving a woman everything she needed. Marcia's mind drifted lazily until she fell asleep beside the man she loved.

Chapter Fifteen

In a deep sleepy haze, Marcia thought she heard someone knocking from far away. She moved lazily under the warm covers of the soft bed she laid in as she reasoned with herself, Lizzie will get that. Turning on her back, Marcia forced her eyes open when she heard the sound of men's voices just beyond her room. Sitting up, her attention was drawn to the strange surroundings and she shook her head, trying to collect her thoughts as to where she might be. Was she dreaming?

"Agar's room." Marcia smiled, remembering their beautiful night of love and thought, he must have carried her to his bed. The memory of falling asleep in his strong arms next to the warm fire.

Quietly, she climbed from the warm covers and slipped into her clothes, lying neatly on a sofa near the freshly made fire. Marcia reached inside the overnight bag she had brought up that held her personal items. A washcloth, teeth wash and her hairbrush. She was busy combing her hair when Agar and Amby stepped into the room. Her face flushed when the red headed man looked over at her and smiled knowingly. Avoiding his stare, Marcia walked over by the bed and commenced to making it up as she listened to their conversation.

"So, you say you saw Hayworth in the field this morning at first light?" Agar's voice broke the silence.

"Aye, that I did, and he was with a stranger. A dark and moody looking fellow, quite the fancy dresser." Amby glanced over at the girl, then back to his friend. "They were snooping about with lanterns. I am certain they never suspected anyone to be watching that early. The morning fog still clung heavily next to the ground but that did not stop them from their search."

"How long were they there?" Agar walked to the kitchen, Amby following him as far as the door. He propped up to wait.

"My guess would be, a good hour. They were oblivious to the morning chill, so caught up in their frantic search." Amby grew dramatic as he continued. "They were looking for something important, indeed." He moved for Agar, who came back out

96

carrying a tray of tea and cakes.

"I guess they were nosing about the ruins of Helen Karnstein's old place." Agar stopped speaking when Marcia let out a loud gasp and turned to look at her. "Cia, what is it? A spider in the bed?"

"Nay, there is no creepy insect invading your fine bed, Agar. I thought I heard you mention, Karnstein. Did you say Karnstein?" Marcia could not control the shaking in her usually calm voice.

"Aye, Helen Karnstein." Agar set down the tray and handed her a cup of tea, then helped her to the sofa by the fire. The teacup rattled on the saucer and he looked down to see her hand shaking nervously. "Cia, love you are shaking all over. What is it? Does the name Helen Karnstein bother you?"

"Nay, dear Agar. I guess I am a wee bit rattled because your friend caught me inside your bedroom, in the wee hours of the morning." Marcia forced a smile as she sipped the hot tea. "And the morning dampness brought on the chill, but your warm fire and this good hot tea will be just what I need to get warm." She pulled his head down to whisper in his ear. "Had not we company, I would have preferred getting warm in your arms, dearest Agar." Receiving his big smile, she added as she sat back. "Tell me, where is this Helen Karnstein now?"

"Dead, some two-hundred years." Agar took a bite into one of the moist tea cakes and nodded for Amby to join them. "The tale past down goes; Helen and the Lord of Collingwood were madly in love. They had planned to be married when a terrible curse fell on the dear woman. I am not sure about the rest of the story, but poor Helen met with an unusual death." Agar cast his eyes down, his voice fell low, as though somewhere deep within him, he felt a hurt that extended back through generations. "Jason Collinwood took his own life and his body was found next to his beloved Helen's cottage. Helen Karnstein's body was never found. She simply, disappeared."

"You mean, the field behind the church, the spot where you want to build that home for children, was Helen's?" Marcia set down the empty cup and looked from Agar to Amby, suddenly needing answers. "Why would the vicar and a perfect stranger be snooping around old ruins at first light? What could they possibly be looking for?"

"I am not certain of exactly what they are seeking, Cia. At least, not yet, but it has something to do with the Karnstein legend."

"Karnstein legend?" Marcia grew excited and even more confused over this new revelation as she wondered, could we be of some kin to this dear lady? "What sort of legend?"

"It has something to do with a mysterious mystical island, on uncharted seas. The magical place comes replete with demons, dragons, and a treasure of great riches. Most likely gold." Amby sat down his plate and stood up, then wondered to the window and pulled back the heavy curtains. "But he who treads the unknown, can never return without the luck to win the games set before him!"

"You see, dearest Cia, the vicar knows something we do not know and that is why he wants full control over the project. Not to help the orphans build a home, but to have complete control of that land and what he thinks is hidden there." Agar walked over and sat down next to the woman he loved. "Hayworth is an evil man and his purpose for wanting that track of land is strictly for his own selfish greed."

"Then we must stop him Agar." Marcia laid her hand lovely on his "The people of Canterbury must be warned about this man."

"The people of Canterbury trust Hayworth, Cia. They certainly will not listen to me over him and they know you even less. Besides, it is far too dangerous for you to get involved. I fear the vicar will stop at nothing to get what he wants."

"What about the Lord of Collinwood? Could he not convince the people? I am sure the man is greatly admired by all the town citizens. He has helped them time and time again. Without the Moon Rider's help, the town of Canterbury would be bled of all its possessions."

"Their admiration for the Moon Riders heroic actions is without question, dearest one, but the vicar still has a big say in the affairs of Canterbury." Agar squeezed her hand lovingly, obviously unconcerned about his friend's watchful eye. "The people trust him and the vicar knows he has the upper hand. He keeps his deeds swept cleanly under his mat of deceit."

Marcia stood up, hate for this vicar who calls himself a man of God when, in truth, he is a disciple of Lucifer, God's evil enemy. A vicar should be showing the people the right way to live, not leading them astray with lies and thievery. And what about this woman, Helen Karnstein, a possible relative? What could this man be searching for on the property of a woman whose been dead for two-hundred years? Marcia tried to avoid looking directly at Agar when she formed her next question carefully.

"Agar, are there any Karnstein living in Canterbury now?"

"Nay, dear Cia. Helen had only one brother who lived with her until she went missing. After the tragic death of his sister, the young man moved away and was reported to have found a wife and built a grand manor home with the fortune he received from the sale of his sister's large estate, previously owned by Lord Collinwood."

"Do you know where the brother moved to?" Marcia tried not to get too excited, but it could very well be Karnstein Manor that this young man built for his bride.

"Nay, my dearest. I have not the slightest notion." Agar observed her closely before rising to his feet and walking next to her. He put his hand tenderly on the back of her neck and let his fingers move deliberately slow. "You certainly are the inquisitive one, my love."

"It would appear so, but truly, I am just interested in the tragic love story that ended with the loving couple dying instead of getting to live their dreams of marriage and a big family." The statement and reason for her asking so many questions, were only half false. Marcia did wish to know what tragic thing happened to her possible relative, but she sincerely needed to know if Helen's brother built the home she grew up in and if so, that would make him a distant grandfather. Marcia closed her eyes, as Agar kept moving his fingers down her back and could tell she was getting warm from his touch. Hating to break the moment, but knowing she had to leave, Marcia turned around and took his hands. "As much as I would like to stay, I better go home now, darling. Lisa will be wondering about me and I must consider her feelings."

"Aye, love. I understand. Agar lifted her face in his hands as he spoke softly. "Last night, was it good for you?"

"Aye. It shall always be a part of my happier moments, dearest

Agar." Marcia looked from Agar's blue eyes to his waiting lips. She longed for them to kiss her as she said. "And you, did you enjoy last night?"

"As I have never enjoyed anything before." Agar drew her up closer to him. "Cia, my Cia." His lips parted gently over hers as his tongue found her mouth. He slowly let her slide from his arms as a brilliant smile covered his handsome face. "You better run on home now, sweet Cia, before I decide to keep you."

"I shouldn't mind." Marcia laughed softly as she walked to the door. "But then, I suppose you would not get any work finished with me about."

"Nay, none." Agar kissed her lightly on the top of her head as he opened the door. "I need the help of my friend, Amby, but I will call my custodian to see you safely home. Amby, fetch Sash from the back." He helped her with her cape as his worker raced around the church and waited at the gate. "Adieu, my dear."

Farewell, my love." Marcia danced out the door and to the gate. Turned and waved before being escorted to town by Agar's man, Sash.

"Agar, my love-struck friend, your affection for this lady is alright by me and safe within myself but, we would not want this little affair to be spread to the streets below and the wagging tongues of gossiping women." Amby patted Agar's back when he walked back inside and shut the door. "A man who walks the path of a priest, need not show openly his feelings for a woman's tempting feast."

Agar laughed and slapped his friend on his back. "Even a priest is a man, is he not? A man with feelings and desires like any other man, when the right woman comes along."

"And Marcia is this right woman?" Amby smiled broadly. "You might have to fight the great Moon Rider to win the fair maiden's hand. Are you prepared to fight the best?" he said with a twinkle in his eye."

"For the love of Marcia, I would fight the devil himself!" Agar pulled out a coat and cape.

"Just do not let your emotions for her show in public, while wearing that priestly robe. It would give the vicar something to use to turn the town people completely against you, Father

Bellingham. It could undo our cause and we are too close to the truth to find a new identity for you." Amby handed Agar a sword to strap on as they walked to the back of the church.

"You worry much too much, my friend. I shall continue to keep the flock fed and secure. I already have half the citizens of Canterbury believing in me and soon I will find cause to prove their precious vicar is a liar and a thief." Agar went with his friend to the closed stable and collected their horses. "Besides, Amby, you and Cia are the only two people that know we had a one-night affair. I think you know to keep the juicy news to yourself and not share it with any of your friends."

"My lips are sealed! I know who your good friend is. The one who is not afraid to silence me if I should so much as mention Marica's name aloud." Amby waited for Agar to climb on his big horse before he got up in his saddle."

"Good! We understand each other." Agar looked over at his friend, his teasing eyes turning serious. "Amby, I need to know what makes Marcia so interested in the family Karnstein. The very mention of that name caused her to gasp out in shock. Why? This is something I need to get to the bottom of and quickly. She has a strong mind and a determined attitude when she wants to know something. It all frightens me for her safety. We have yet to learn Marcia's full name. You do not suppose she is connected someway to the Karnstein family?"

"If she is, she could be in grave danger if Hayworth finds out."

"Let us make haste to Collinwood. I need a word with my good friend, as you put it. The Moon Rider must be ready to leave at the first sign of danger!" Agar called for the groom. "Markus, saddle up your horse and hide among the shadows of the forest. Keep watch over the field and if you spot anything of interest, bring word to me at once."

"Aye sir, you can count on my watchful eye!" the man raced inside the stable to saddle his horse while Agar and Amby tore off into the woods toward Collinwood Castle.

Chapter Sixteen

"That vicar is a fraud, evil man, Lizzie! I intend to do something about it!" Marcia tried to walk slowly up the narrow street so her old nanny could keep up. Elizabet pulled her wrap up around her neck to ward off the late chill.

"My dear, you best leave well enough alone. We are outsiders, trying to stay hidden. We should not let ourselves get involved. Besides, there is naught that we can do. You know how people take to women who try to speak their opinion on town matters. Especially the men!"

"Elizabet, I think it is high time somebody in this spineless town stood up to that beast and bully!" Marcia focused her attention on the quiet streets as she continued to move forward to the vicar's house. "Agar is the only person who is trying to find out about Hayworth's evil plans and I intend to help him."

"Marcia, I say for all that is best, just stay out of it. Father Bellingham would not want you to stick your neck out! If this man is as bad as you say, then he can be very dangerous to someone who gets in his way, especially a woman!" The dumpy nurse grabbed Marcia's arm when a sudden outburst arose down the street from them. "Ah, now what troubles spoil our silent streets?"

Marcia moved a few steps forward, to see where the voices were coming from. When she noticed that it was the vicar, she realized what the man was doing. Marcia let out a breath of discussed.

"The vicar is at poor Madam Banistry's house causing trouble!" Marcia yanked her hand free from Elizabet's grip. "This is the last straw, Lizzie! I will not stand by and let that overbearing man hurt them! That poor child Nora has had enough to deal with in her short young life without this!"

Marcia stormed down the street until she reached the home of Katherine Banistry, Lizzie struggling to keep up, some distanced behind. Hands firmly placed on her shapely hips, Marcia confronted the arrogant vicar. "Just what are you doing, Vicar Hayworth?"

The angry man slung his head around to face Marcia, his thick fingers still clutching Katherine's arm. Seeing Marcia standing there bold and ready to fight, a sneer fell on his big lips. "Well, well, if it is not the big mouth shrew of Canterbury!"

"I suggest you turn that lady's arm loose right now, Hayworth!" Marcia narrowed her eyes at him in protest. "Someday very soon, this town is going to know what kind of man you really are!"

Elizabet closed her eyes in dread as she crossed herself. The vicar's face grew red with hate as his piercing eyes burned on the brave young woman.

"Little miss smart mouth, you will get your just fruits! Soon, very soon!" he growled.

"Are you threatening me, dear vicar?" Marcia said mockingly. "Dear vicar, have you forgotten the holy lesson of our Lord: Do unto others as you would have them do unto you?" Marcia jumped away when the vicar angrily threw Katherine aside and stepped toward her, hate raging in his eyes. "It is too bad the trusting citizens cannot see their 'wonderful' leader now!" Marcia held her ground.

"I have good reason to be angry with you, dear lady. The council has found this woman to be an unfit mother and I have come to take the child away, by authority given me!" He moved toward the house, but Marcia ran ahead to block the entrance to the door.

"You shall not take Nora, Hayworth! You have no right to judge this woman, nor does your appointed council!"

"The child's welfare is my right! NOW, STEP ASIDE!" His voice grew loud. "I SAID…"

"I heard you, Hayworth, loud and clear. NAY, I WILL NOT STEP ASIDE!" Marcia's voice rose to meet his. "NORA AND HER MOTHER DO NOT BELONG TO YOUR CHURCH VICAR! THEY ARE FATHER BELLINGHAM'S RESPONSIBILTY, NOT YOURS! NOW LEAVE, BEFORE I FETCH AN OFFICER!"

The angry vicar shook his fist in Marcia's face as he lowered his voice menacingly. "You have not seen the last of me, young lady! Take care that your soul is ready for judgement!"

"I trust by that threatening comment, you intend to have me done away with!" Marcia spit out, unafraid of this sick man.

"THE DEVIL TAKES HIS OWN, DEAR LADY!" Hayworth shouted.

Looking into his eyes, she smiled and said mockingly and in a calm voice. "Then, if I were you, vicar, I would be getting prepared for a 'hot' future."

Hayworth turned angrily and stormed across the cobblestone street, disappearing in the shadows. Nora laughed just inside the doorway, where she had been peeking out at the happy turn of events. Marcia got down next to the cripple child and hugged her, laughing herself as she watched the vicar leave with such haste. Elizabet walked over to help Katherine back inside the house. The grateful mother touched Marcia on her arm lightly.

"My dear, I appreciate what you did, but I am afraid you have brought trouble to yourself and your dear aunt."

"I think Cia is wonderful!" Nora burst out. "I think Cia is the bravest and most beautiful woman I have ever seen!"

"Thank you, darling. I think you are pretty brave yourself. I have witnessed your fighting." Marcia gave the sweet girl an extra hug before standing to speak to the girl's mother. "Katherine, I am not sorry I helped you and Nora. It is high time someone told that overbearing man off."

"Cia, I know you meant well by helping us, but Vicar Hayworth will not give up. He will return later with more men to take Nora away from me." Katherine gently hugged her little girl. "I have tried to be the best mother I could for Nora. I am sure there have been times when I could have done better, but I have always loved her as my very own."

"Katherine, do you mean Nora is not your child?" Marcia had witnessed their closeness, read through the actions shared between them and saw the love both held for the other. She had never thought for one minute that Nora was not this lovely woman's daughter.

"Nay, but the child seems as much." Even though Katherine was only in her early thirties, she appeared much older, due to worry, Marcia thought. "Nora is my dead sister's child. I was all the family she had and she was the only family member I had left.

You might say, we adopted one another."

Nora threw her arms loving around her weary aunt's neck and kissed her. "You have always been good to me, Katherine. I have watched you stir the leftover stew and fill up one single bowl, because there wasn't enough for two, then pretend you had already eaten so I could have all we had." Tears filled her young eyes. "I love you, mommy, and I know how much you love me."

"I know Nora darling." Katherine turned to her two visitors and looked up pleadingly. "Would it be too much to ask you to take Nora home with you and keep her for me awhile? I have been a sick woman lately and it gets harder to fight the vicar off, in fear of my heart failing."

"You know Lizzie and I will do anything we can to help you, Katherine." Marcia looked down at her life-long companion to find tears in the dear woman's caring eyes. "There is room for Nora, is there not?"

"We shall find room for the child!" Elizabet found her courage again as she placed a hand on the pale woman. "There is room for you both! That no good scamp will not lay one finger on either of ye!"

"You both are good God-fearing Christian women, to offer so much fortitude, but I will only except your shelter for my daughter. As for myself, it would be better if I remain here. I cannot ask you to risk your own safety for me." Katherine's voice came out weak as she thought to reassure the woman holding her up. "Lizzie, I will be fine here. It is not me the vicar is after; it is the child."

"Nay, I will not be hearing naught of it! That determined jackleg will stop at nothing to find Nora, and that includes beating the truth out of you! You will come with us! Three women are better than one sick lass." Elizabet looked around the tidy little room, furnished with old pieces, most likely family heirlooms. "Now, just gather what personal items you might need and get yourself together for the night chill. We shall pop off to the flat and double lock the doors and windows just in case some skunk comes crawling around in the night."

Marcia laughed at her dear friend's description of the vicar. "Lisa is right, Katherine. You should not be alone. That evil Hayworth will stop at nothing, short of murder." Marcia scooped

Nora up in her arms. "If there is anything I can do about it, that man will never hurt you again."

"Thank you, Cia." Nora laid her head on Marcia's shoulder, feeling safe in her loving arms. "You and Father Bellingham are the only ones that have offered to help us, except, of course..." Nora's eyes reflected in the bright moon shining over the trees behind the hill. "besides him."

"Who, Nora darling?" Marcia walked slowly up the cobblestone hill toward the flat. Her gazed followed the child's transfixed stare. The moon shone big and brightly beyond the small church on the hill, and she knew in her heart what name was to come. "Who, child?"

"The Moon Rider!" her small voice rose with excitement. "He is the bravest man in the entire world!"

Marcia tried to open her heavy eyelids. She had been asleep for almost two hours, according to the chiming mantel clock striking ten. Thinking it was the striking chimes that had awaken her, she closed her eyes until another sound reached her ears. Marcia could sense something moving in the dark room. So, she sat up and looked down at her new bed companion. Elizabet's heavy breathing indicated that she was in a deep sleep. She tried to focus in on the dark room, her ears pealed for any small noise. Once again, the noise came, this time in one corner of the bedchamber. She thought of Rider, but knew he would not hesitate to show himself immediately upon arrival. She quickly dismissed it being her gallant lover but instead a possible intruder, like Vicar Hayworth. Finding her courage, Marcia's feet slipped to the floor, then she felt her way to where she had left the candle stand and the matches. Before she could light the wick, a hand clasped tightly over her mouth, closing in her scream.

"Marcia, my little runaway bride, did you really expect to stay hidden from me?" Krantz whispered mockingly in her ear. "Tis a foolish thing you have done, my dearest Marcia."

She turned to looked up into his mocking eyes, anger clouding her pretty face. He released his hand from her lips, to hear her reply.

"How did you find me, Krantz? We covered our trail well."

"My dear, a man who is important like me, has spies in many places. And these expert spies have ears and eyes." He laughed softly. "Marcia, you must remember that I am the clever one here, not you, darling."

"I would not call a sneaky murderous thief clever, Sir Hamish. On second thought, maybe you are, in your own evil way." Marcia jerked at her arm, trying to pull herself free of his tight grip, but he only smiled, that much bigger. "Turn me loose, Krantz! If not, I will scream!"

"And wake up your house guest, my dear?" he sneered. "That would not be very gracious, now would it, dearest?"

"What do you want, you Black Raven?" she felt her temper growing and tried to move away when his hand moved slowly along her shapely hip.

"I came to take you home to Melbourne. You and I have a wedding to attend, remember?"

"Nay! There is to be no wedding; not with you Krantz!" Marcia sank her teeth in his arm, causing him to jerk away, moaning in pain. Taking the opportunity to flee, Marcia turned and ran. But not seeing the shadow in the far corner, she ran straight into his outstretched arms.

Vicar Hayworth's smile was short of demonic when he stared down at her surprised face. "Going somewhere, mistress Stone? It is, mistress Stone, is it not?"

"You rat! I might have known you were Krantz's bloody spy! The both of you are a perfect match! Evil and cruel!" Marcia did not hold down her voice any longer, for her anger had taken over her control. "How much did that Black Raven pay you, Hayworth? That is what you live for, is it not? The greed of money?"

"I shan't deny I enjoy my wealth, my dear unfortunate stupid girl. And Aye, for this job I will received much from the Black Ravin, and at the appointed time, I shall have more gold than his royal majesty!" Movement from the bed drew the vicar's attention and he clicked his fingers to get Krantz's attention, then pointed to the heavy woman sitting up, looking around confused, calling Marcia's name. The dark eyes of Krantz looked down at the woman he had come after, then at her nurse. The vicar sneered. "I think the old hag has decided to awake."

"She might as well, for it appears sleep cannot help her looks one bit!" he moved just in time before Marcia kicked his shin with her foot. Krantz laughed as he walked over and dragged Elizabet from the warm covers. She let out a gasp when she recognized his mocking face.

"Dear Lord! What in the name of God is going on here?" her voice shook with fear.

"I have come to fetch my bride." Krantz's fingers squeezed Elizabet's fat arms as he pulled her up close to his sneering face. "You never should have led her astray, old bat! You shall pay plenty for all my delay!"

"Let her go Krantz and leave the dear woman alone!" Marcia jerked her arms against the vicar's strong grip. "Leaving was my idea! I had no desire to marry someone like you, then or now! I would rather die a million deaths!"

His eyes lit up as he walked over and touched Marcia's face, still holding on to the scared woman. "Death will come soon enough, my dearest Marcia. You will get your wish, right Hayworth?"

"Aye, indeed! Everything the little bitch deserves." His fingers bit into her flesh, causing her to bite her lip to keep from screaming in pain. "And, it will be a great pleasure to witness it for myself."

"And do you intend to kill me after you marry me, Krantz?" Marcia's eyes shot fire across his smug face. "Aye, you would indeed. That is just the kind of 'loving' husband I expected you to be. What is it you wish to gain from my death? The Karnstein estate is worth a small fortune, but not worth killing someone over. What treasure do you think I possess that will make you and Hayworth richer than our king?"

"It is not anything material that you possess that will bring us these great riches, dear Marcia. Our golden ticket is…you, fair one." Krantz laughed, then felt the heavy foot of Elizabet kick him hard on his shin. He stared down at the angry nurse as she heralded her message clear.

"Ye shan't be taking my lady anywhere, Mr. Hamish! I am certain the master of Karnstein would not like your attitude and cruel threatening words!"

"Like it or not, hag, Lord Karnstein will eventually see things my way!" Krantz slung his hand back and slapped Elizabet across her face. "With or without his approval, with or without force!"

"Why Krantz? I am no more important than your own sister where status is concerned! It is obvious that you are not marrying me for love! Tell me, what it is you seek!"

"I shall, in time." Krantz looked down at her revealing gown, lust growing in his veins. He threw Elizabet to the floor and pulled Marcia away from the vicar. "But you shall know me before we seek our treasure." His hands moved over her buttocks as he watched her closely. "It will give me great pleasure to take you, my little vixen!"

"You shan't have me! My heart belongs to another!" Marcia spit out, getting a smirk from his lips. He shoved her back into the vicar's arms and walked over to the window and waved four more men inside.

"Fetch the woman and child! Bring them in here to me!"

"Leave them alone, Krantz! They have nothing to do with you!" Marcia screamed lightly when she felt a rope being tied around her ankles and hands. She looked to the opening door as one of Krantz's men pulled Katherine into her bedchamber, while another pulled Nora in. When Marcia saw Katherine, she gasped in horror, seeing her face had turned a drab blue and her entire body was trembling uncontrollable. "For God sake, that woman needs help!"

"Someone, fetch a doctor quickly!" Elizabet yelled excitedly as she started over to help the sick woman. Krantz kicked the excited nurse back and she fell hard on the floor. Steering down at her, he forced his black boot on her stomach, causing her to cry out in pain. Marcia tried desperately to free herself from the tight ropes so she could help her old friend. She turned to face Katherine when the pale woman cried out in pain.

"Help me! My heart...help...me..."

Nora gazed down at the loving woman who had raised her, and felt helpless against all the evil men. Tears streamed down her young face as she pleaded with Marcia. "Cia, mommy will die if the doctor does not come now! Please, Cia!"

"My God!" Marcia closed her eyes, trying to fight back her

own tears as her gaze went to the vicar, smiling down at the helpless woman. "Hayworth, have you no part of that which made you become a vicar? If you have an ounce of compassion in your soul, in the name of God, help that woman! Cannot you see she is in great pain?"

"Will you come with us peacefully, Marcia, and not put up a fight?" Krantz knew now was the perfect opportunity to force her to come with them without a fight. He walked slowly by her side and lifted her chin to face him. "It is up to you Marcia. The woman's life for your own?"

"Aye, but just to help her, not because I have a change of heart where you are concern." Marcia looked down at her helpless tied up hands, then back up into his steel eyes. "Just do it now!"

Krantz smiled and took Marcia over by the open window. "I shall take Marcia with me. Vicar, you and the boys will stay here and 'take care' of these three."

"Krantz, you will not hurt them?" Marcia looked helplessly over at her dear friend and nurse. "Please, Krantz, you gave me your word if I came with you without a fight."

"Nay, my loving bride, I shan't hurt them. You were smart enough to come with me peacefully.

One of Krantz's men yanked Elizabet to her feet and held her arms tightly, as she looked sadly at Marcia. "What of this woman, my lord?"

"I go with my lady! You cannot take the girl without me to assist her." The heavy woman tried to break free to run to her ward's side, but the burly man slung her back to the floor.

"Please, Krantz, let her come with us. She is my nurse and aid. "Marcia knew she would feel safer if Elizabet were with her instead of being left behind at the mercy of Vicar Hayworth. "Please Krantz."

His dark steel eyes stared down at the older woman, looking up hopeful. Krantz laughed out mockingly. "The old hag stays here! Men, see to it she cannot follow us!" his attention fell on his beautiful captive. "A married woman has no need of a nurse, my lady."

"My lady!" Elizabet yelled as the dark knight dragged Marcia from the window. Her attention flew to the vicar, staring after his evil friend. "Vicar Hayworth, you promised to help Madam Banistry!"

"And I shall." Hayworth smiled wickedly as he pulled a sword from his belt. "Her suffering shall be relieved very swiftly."

Nora screamed as she arose from the floor and ran over to the shocked vicar, grabbing his obese arm. "No! No...please!"

Katherine stopped moaning as she watched the little girl she loved so much walk for the first time. Tears of joy filled her painful eyes as a peace fell upon her face. Nora knelt down next to her, tears streaming from her eyes at the thought of Katherine dying and leaving her alone.

"Mummy! Mummy! Do not leave me!"

"Baby girl, My dear, dear Nora." Katherine ran her fingers lovingly over the child's face, then touched her leg. "I know there is a heaven now, sweetheart. I am not afraid to die anymore. I have witness the Lord's miracle. Nora, you can walk, you can...walk..." Katherine's hand fell limp from the little girl's wet cheeks as a silent smile fell upon her cold lips. Nora laid down her head across Katherine's dead body and wept.

Elizabet had gotten up and was standing there consumed with both hate and sorrow, yet she also felt joy over Nora's sudden miracle. Before anyone could stop her, the heavy nurse stepped up in front of the vicar and she threw her angry words into his face.

"You were going to kill that poor woman! You had no intention of sending for a doctor! My lady's trust in you was useless and she walked away for naught! You are an evil man! Evil and mean!" The usually quiet and proper woman started striking the vicar, one blow after the next until he retaliated by beating her to a pulp. Elizabet crumbled to the floor, the angry blows coming from all five men. Battered and bruised, she could not move from the great pain, but she managed to get out a few words before passing out. "Nora...run! Run and get help!"

Nora leaped to her feet and raced from the flat and up the cobblestone street, not daring to look back.

CHAPTER Seventeen

Nora banged her small fist heavily on the big church door. Fresh tears stung her red cheeks in the crisp early morning air as her throat grew raw from yelling. The door flung open and Agar stood staring in wonder at his small caller.

"Nora!" he swept the child up in his strong arms. "You are walking, Nora!"

"Aye, Father Bellingham!" her voice shook, both from the early morning chill and the scary scene she just escaped. "Please! Please, you have to help! The mean men, they hit Lisa over and over again until she grew silent. She found the strength to tell me to run for help!" she shook his shoulders with her little hands. "Father, they ...poor Cia!"

"What are you telling me, Nora? What men? What about Cia? Did you recognize any theses thugs?" Agar grabbed his coat and a wrap for the child, then slung them on.

"Some bad man took Cia, out the window! I think he was the leader. I did recognize one of them! The one that was going to kill my mommy...and mommy is...dead! Everything was too much for her weak heart, but...she saw me walked and died peaceful, despite the vicar's mean remarks!" Nora grabbed around Agar's waist and burst into tears as she remembered watching the woman she loved die in front of her.

"So, the vicar has shone his hand and had plans to leave no witnesses. Let us go, sweet one, You, are safe with me." Agar and Nora raced from the churchyard and down the street to the small flat. Bursting down the front door, Agar took in the scene young Nora had describe. Katherine lay silent up against an enter wall, head slightly drooped, and her lips graced a heavenly smile. Feeling her pulse, he knew she was indeed dead, so he walked quickly to where Elizabet lay, bruised and thoroughly beaten. Knelling down, Agar checked her pulse and found a faint heartbeat. Nora had not got out of his sight, for fear the bad men might be hiding inside the house and grab her. Agar gently pulled her into his arms. "

"Nora, do you think you can go get Doctor Ogburn?"

"Aye, father, I will run real fast" Nora rushed out the open door.

Krantz looked please with himself as he lightly brushed his hand over Marcia's shapely hip. Her eyes shot daggers at him as she pulled from his reach. He laughed out and pulled her back in his arms. "Aye! I think I am going to enjoy a spitfire for a change. It can get real boring having someone who is willing to lay with me all the time."

"So, you have another woman." Marcia spit out her words. "What does your little lover think about your plans to marry someone else, Raven?"

"You let me worry about that precious. I have got the broad wrapped around my finger." He looked up when he heard riders coming into the camp. Hayworth climbed down from his horse, glad to have gotten out of Canterbury without being seen. Krantz waited until the vicar grabbed a mug of wine from the servant and fell down in front of the warm fire to warm his big hands. "How did things go back there? Did you have any problems?"

"From two old women and one sick child? Things could not have gone better." The vicar's attention fell on Marcia, who had been listening closely, worried about Lizzie and the Banistry's. "I see you are behaving yourself."

"I trust you kept your part of the bargain!" Marcia was trying to read guilt on the vicar's sneering face. "Did you get help for Katherine? How is she?"

"Dead." The vicar said coldly and without feelings.

"Dead?" Marcia felt a sharp pain of sorrow for this lady she had grown to admire and love. "But, you were supposed to get Katherine help! You kill her, did you not? You murderer!"

"Now, my dear, you are too quick to judge. You have the event all wrong." He took a sip of his red wine, a constant smile on his phony face. "The dear lady just died before we could send for the doctor, that is all."

"You could have helped her sooner! You chose to wait too long" Tears streamed down her face. "You same as killed her! You murderer!"

"How touching. The pretty 'big' mouth lady has a heart." The vicar mocked. "The death of Katherine is really grievous to my heart too. Such a sad ending for such a pathetic life."

"Your phony grief makes me sick!" Marcia cried out. "Well, you shan't get by with it! Elizabet will let everyone of Canterbury know what kind of evil man you really are." Marcia stopped as she watched the vicar's demonic smile fall on his lips. "Lizzie? What have you done to Lizzie?"

"Let us just say, that old hag will not be saying anything to discredit my name to anyone living in or around Canterbury." Hayworth laughed coldly as Marcia stormed out.

"You demon! You, bloody, no account bastard! I hope you rot in hell!"

"Now, is that any way for a lady of your high up-bringing, to say to a man of God." Krantz remarked lightly. "My dear Marcia, you must learn to get along with my friends, now that you belong to me."

"First, I do not belong to you, Krantz Hamish! Second, I have no desires to become friends with a murdering follower of Satan!" she shouted. "Or any of your bloody friends. You are a liar! You promised me no one would be hurt! LIAR!"

"How sweet and touching." Hayworth drank down his wine and stood up stretching. "It is too bad you do not like demons, mistress Karnstein. I am afraid where you are going, you will run into all kinds of demons."

"I can assure you, Hayworth, those demons cannot be any worse than the ones I have already been with!" Marcia did not want to think about what they did to Nora, but she knew she would never rest until she asked. "The child, what did you do with her?"

"Now, what sort of man do you think I am, dear lady? He lay back on his blanket and closed his eyes, but Marcia's scream drove them wide open."

"Vicar Hayworth, did you kill Nora too?" Marcia felt like her insides were pulling apart, worrying over Lizzie and had she suffered a long time while they beat her to death. Poor Katherine, suffering with incredible pain before her heart gave way, right in front of the loving little girl who had trusted her to protect them. "Answer me, Hayworth? If you want any sleep at all!"

"Nay, I did not touch the child. Now, get you some sleep and stopped asking questions. The morning comes early."

"I will stop my questions after this one more. What did you do to Nora? You could not have walked out and left her along with two silent bodies?" Marcia stared over at the vicar as she heard him snore out. She mumbled "Hayworth, you creep!"

"Go to sleep, Marcia." Krantz threw a blanket over her. "And shut up before I gag you. Understand?"

Marcia rolled over on her side and squeezed her eyes closed, to block them out, hate raging within her. Her thoughts went to Agar, bending down to kiss her, so gentle, so loving. Then the masked man was lifting her up into his strong embrace, his head lowering to whisper, "Do not despair, Marcia. I will save you my lady, my dearest love." Marcia opened her eyes, knowing her captors were asleep, she looked up into the star-filled night and whispered.

"Dear God, you must help me. Tell Agar where I am. Tell the Moon Rider to come after me and save me."

Elizabet opened her eyes slowly, her head pounding in pain. She blinked twice, trying to focus on the man standing over her. Her unclear vision caused her to move her hands up to protect herself as she weakly called out.

"No! Please, do not hurt me anymore!"

"Lisa, it is Agar." He spoke calmly as he touched her arms to lower them.

"Agar." A look of relief wreathed her bruised face. "I am glad to see it is you." Her voice came low and barely audible.

"Lisa, save your strength. The doctor said I could not ask you too many questions because you have several blows to your head and you must remain relax." Agar took her hand, to give her the time she needed to answer him, although he was anxious to find Marcia. "I want to know who did this and where they took Cia?"

"It was Krantz Hamish. He and that devil, Vicar Hayworth!" Elizabet coughed as she tried to stand up.

"Calm down, Lisa, and tell me, who is Krantz Hamish? That name is unfamiliar." Agar emotions were filled with deep concern over the woman he loved and he needed answers, but he knew he could not rush Elizabet in her delicate state.

"Krantz is the man Master Karnstein arranged for Marcia to marry. Wanting no part of the marriage to this mean scandal, Marcia fled from his evil clutches."

"Karnstein? Did you say, Marcia?" Agar looked surprised, but the friendly nurse placed a motherly hand on his shoulder and managed a painful smile.

"Aye, Father Bellingham, Cia is really Marcia. My lady's full name is, Marcia Karnstein."

"Marcia Karnstein!" Agar sat down on the side of the bed and looked down at the dear lady, so bruise and beaten, this woman Marcia loved. "No wonder Cia…I mean, Marcia, was so surprised to hear that name, Helen Karnstein."

"What? I do not understand Father." Lizzie looked up confused over the name of a Karnstein she had never heard mentioned."

Agar gently squeezed her hand as he shook his head, knowing he did not have the time to go into poor Helen's life story now. It would have to wait. Marcia needed rescuing from one Krantz Hamish and Vicar Hayworth. "Let us not go into that story right now, Lisa."

"The name is Elizabet." A faint smile came to her swollen mouth. "You will go after Marcia, will you not, Agar? You must! Those men are evil, like I said, and I am certain by what they said, they mean to use her, then get rid of her."

"That may be their feeble plan, but they will soon find out different!" rage swept into Agar's soft blue eyes. "Do you have any idea as to where they might go? I can find out the hard way or you can make it easier and we can track them a whole lot faster if you can help us!"

"My guess is, they are probably headed for Karnstein Estates in Melbourne. That is where we lived before running away to Canterbury." A beefy hand clutched Agar's. "Please, go now! Save Marcia! There is no time to waste!"

"Aye, I agree! But I shan't be the one who goes after Marcia. She will need a fighter. Someone who is unafraid of the unknown, has strength in number and…cares deeply for Marcia!" Tears filled his sad eyes.

"But, Agar, why? Tis you, she loves." Elizabet tried to sit up, but Agar held her down, to keep her still. "You must be the one to go."

"Nay, Elizabet, the Moon Rider is the one who must go. He is her only hope." Agar bit his lip to keep from crying as he took her hand. "God, you know there is naught I would do if it meant helping my Marcia, but we are talking about fighting men with swords for her life. Her 'life' Elizabet! The Moon Rider is the best swordsman in all of England. Big strong men shrink at his silhouette against the moon. Even if I were to take up a sword to defend my dearest, I could never outlast a better opponent. He must go!"

"But, Agar, you know what that might mean?" Elizabet's sadness was written on her face as she touched his tear stain cheek. "Marcia will feel obligated to him. She will have to choose the man who saves her after he risk his life to do so."

"Then, I will take that chance." Agar stood up. "If losing Marcia is the only way to save her life, then it will be so."

"Perhaps, if you go along with him, help him fight. You then might stand a chance to still win her hand. She would never compare the fighting skills between you and this Moon Rider, but she could make her own choice then." Elizabet's eyes lit up with hope for their love.

"Nay, Elizabet. The Moon Rider would never let me go along. He despises me already, because Marcia cares for me." Agar touched her arm lightly and walked over to the door. "I must go to him at once with the news. He will leave with haste, as soon as his men are ready to ride. They can move swiftly when they have a good cause and saving Marcia is the very best cause he has had to fight. I will fight the best way I know how, through constant prayer. My sword and strength are my God and I will pray for a victory!" he moved quickly from the room as Elizabet thought, poor Agar, poor man.

117

Chapter Eighteen

Henry Karnstein stared at Krantz as he stood firm, waiting for a reply. "Well, Lord Henry, what is your answer? Do I have your blessing to marry your daughter, Marcia?"

"My answer must be a firm nay!" the owner of the manor house walked over to his wall cabinet and poured himself a glass of wine to avoid his visitor's angry stare. "I would offer you a glass, sir, but I assume you will want to depart at once. I have thought about this arrangement in depth, and I am certain that marriage between my daughter and yourself was a bad idea."

"Too bad you feel so strongly against it Lord Henry, but I fear there is naught that you can do to stop it!" A cocky sneer came to the man's dark eyes and he threw his head back to announce. "Marcia will be my wife, with or without your approval…sir!"

"Then, if that is the way you feel, it would be best if my men never found Marcia!" Henry set his glass down in a rage and stepped over in front of the arrogant man to confront him. "Dare you speak so bold in my home, Sir Hamish? I suggest that you and your childish sister take your leave at once!"

"Oh, we intend to leave, Henry. As soon as I have gotten the other thing I have come for!" Krantz laughed mockingly as he added. "By the way, Henry, you can call off your men's search for Marcia. I found my runaway bride!"

"And I, dear brother, have found the treasure map!" Arabella danced down the steps, waving a rolled- up map. "Dear sweet Henry, does not care where his guest goes in his quant little house."

"Where is my daughter, Krantz?" Henry demanded. "Where is Marcia?"

"Safe, with my men." He laughed triumphantly. "Now, you really did not expect me to bring her back here until I found out what your decision was, did you, Henry? Do you take me for a fool?"

"Nay sir, I take you for what you are, A stinking dirty swine, Krantz Hamish! What map has your sister stolen? I was a man of the seas, and have many maps, does she even know what to look for?" Henry Karnstein looked from sneering brother to the sick smile of his sister, Arabella. After there was no answer and only silence, Henry ask pleadingly. "What is the real reason you want to marry my daughter?" He noticed movement, and saw his sister walking slowly down the steps, taking in the conversation. When she reached the bottom, she yelled when Arabella grabbed her and held a small dagger under her head.

"Dorinda!" Henry swallowed back his fear, then turned back to the dark knight. "Krantz, what are you trying to do here?"

"Just to let you know, Lord Stupid, that I, the stinking dirty swine, am the one in charge around here, not you! I am the one to give the orders!" Krantz laughed as he grabbed the map from his sister's skirt belt and held it up in Marcia's father's face. "This is our map to great riches! You do as I say and nobody get hurts!"

Karnstein nodded in defense, after the secret alert bell under his table felled to bring in his guards. He assumed Krantz got to them first. "Just take what you want from this house, but leave Marcia here with her family."

"I cannot do that, Henry. Just as the map is the road to great riches, Marcia will be our golden ticket to purchase the gold!" Krantz laughed wickedly, as he waved the map over his head. "With this and your beautiful daughter, whom I shall enjoy first for myself, it is our great fortune to get tons of the finest gold known to man!"

Henry stood straight, sweat beading on his forehead as he stammered out. "My God! Surely, you do not intend to…God, please, nay! Not the legend! The Karnstein Legend!" Henry's face grew pale as he stepped up close to the gawking man. "Please, Krantz, you cannot do this to my baby! You can take everything I own, Sir Hamish, but, please, do not take Marcia to that God-forsaken place! Be a gentleman, anything but this! Marry her, have a big happy family. The right choice will make you a better man!"

"Tempting idea, Henry. To marry Marica and have a big family with her." Krantz closed his eyes and saw her beautiful face. "To be able to make love to my beautiful wife for many fulfilling years." Krantz opened his eyes stun, when he felt Arabella kick his leg with raging jealousy. He narrowed his eyes on her angrily. "You, little bitch! What the hell did you kick me for?"

"You cannot be seriously considering a long happy marriage to…her? Nay! The plan is to get rich, Krantz, you and me! It is the two of us who will live happily ever after, and do not forget that!" Arabella screamed out.

"QUIET WOMAN!" Krantz reached over and slapped her across her jealous face. "I DO NO INTEND TO GIVE UP MY RICHES FOR ANY BROAD, BEAUTIFUL OR NOT!" he smiled when his sister broke into a soft whimpering. "Now, stay quiet Arabella, if you are coming with me."

Dorinda was filled with fear and bewilderment as she searched her brother's eyes for answers. "Henry, What, legend, are you speaking about?" she watched as her brother dropped his head, realizing the worse. "Henry, for God sake, tell me what is going on around here?"

Krantz laughed as he placed the map in his sash. "Family secrets, Henry? I would be happy to tell you all about the legend, mistress Karnstein, but unfortunately, time does not permit it." Krantz clapped his hands and two of his strong men jumped out from hiding and grabbed Henry. "I hate to come and go so fast, Lord Henry, but I am sure, under the circumstances, you understand." He ordered his men to tie them up securely, then said with a smirk. "Do anything that needs doing to slow them down." His eyes fell down on the brother and sister, sitting on the floor, back to back, tied tightly together. "And boys, restrain from killing them. I should not want my in-laws disliking me."

Krantz, darling?" Arabella raced off behind her brother as he made his way quickly from the manor house. "It has been days since I have seen you. Do not you wish to kiss me hello?" she reached him, then touched his strong chest. "I have missed our fun and games, dear Krantz."

"There shall be time for fun and games later, dear sister, but not now. My mine is filled with more important matters."

"More important than I, dearest brother? Surely you cannot mean that woman?" Arabella pouted when he smiled down at her. "Krantz?"

"A little more respect for my new bride, little sister. Her name

120

is Marcia, not 'that woman'! Do we understand each other?" Krantz reached for his horse's reins and turned to the man with him. "Bernard, get her up on your horse. I ride alone! We must leave with haste!" without another word, the riders rode swiftly from the Karnstein courtyard.

The Moon Rider pulled his black stud to a halt in front of the quiet Karnstein Manor. Without hesitation, the black figure jumped from his horse as three of his men burst through the massive front door. Their attention went quickly on the two figures huddled together in a far corner of the great den. With big deliberate steps, Rider stood over the two victims, tied together and bleeding. Dorinda Karnstein looked up wearily as she pleaded.

"Help us. You must cut us free."

Henry gave a helpless laugh. "My dear sister, cannot you see what these men are? They are bandits, mere common highwayman, come to rob us."

"It looks as though you have already been robbed, sir." The Moon Rider pulled his dagger from his wide sash and smiled when the owner of the estate squeezed his eyes shut to block out the fatal blow. "You can relax Lord Karnstein, I have no intention to hurt you or your sister." He slashed through the ropes and nodded for his men to help the couple to their feet. "I am your friend, Lord Karnstein. I have come in search of your daughter."

"Marcia?" Feeling dizzy from the loss of blood, Henry started to fall back down, but the black figure held out his arms to catch him and easily carried him to a long sofa in the room. Henry looked up into the masked face, feeling a ray of hope for his little girl. "Who are you, son?"

"He is the Moon Rider." Rider's good friend helped Dorinda to a chair and smiled at the attractive lady. "Are you alright, madam?"

"Aye, thanks to you fine gentleman for descending upon our dilemma." Dorinda rubbed her sore arms "I shall be forever grateful and even more so when you bring our Marcia home."

Lord Karnstein could not draw his attention off the masked man, who was busy wrapping a tight bandage around the cuts on his legs after applying ointment. "The Moon Rider? We have heard many things of a man called this name, but we thought he was just a legend, a tale made up just for children." The lack of blood had cause Henry's eyes to be hazy so he stared up at another figure holding out something in his hand. When he held it closer, it came into focus, a glass of water.

"Drink this slow sir, you have lost a lot of blood." Amby held the glass for him as he drank. "If anyone can find and rescue your daughter sir, it is the Moon Rider. He is the best!"

"I have done all that I can to help you sir, but my doctor is just outside, I will have him brought in and he can check my bandage and give you some medicine to boost your blood level back up." Rider waved the man standing by the door to fetch their personal doctor. Excepting his orders, the man went quickly out to their horses to collect the doctor who road with the Moon Rider.

Back inside, the Moon Rider had questions of his own for the Lord of Karnstein. "Did Krantz Hamish do this to you?" his voice remained calm and Dorinda could not pull her eyes away from the mysterious masked man with the great manly built. Henry Karnstein nodded a positive as the doctor rushed in with his box of medicines.

"Aye, good sir, Krantz and his cut-throat men who do his bidding." As the doctor checked the expert bandages and saw the tube of relief cream that the masked man used, he pulled out a bottle of dark medicine and ask for a spoon. After taking the healing syrup, Marcia's father touched the Rider's arm. "You, are most thoughtful, Moon Rider."

"Your daughter, did you see her with Hamish?" Rider needed answers.

"Nay, the sly fox left her at his camp!" Lord Henry's eyes grew wide with horror. "Please, you must help my daughter. Marcia is in grave danger as long as Krantz has her! She will surely die if you do not save her from those evil men!"

"I intend to help your daughter, Lord Karnstein, that is the reason I came all the way from Canterbury. Please, you must stay calm and tell me everything you know and make it as fast as possible. There is no time to delay." Rider joined the Lord of Karnstein on the long sofa and gazed down. "Where was Hamish taking Marcia?"

"To the island of great dangers! A small remote island on uncharted seas! The greedy bastards that hold my daughter have no regard for anyone but themselves! My daughter will die a horrendous death and they will walk away with great riches beyond imagination!" Henry covered his face, to blot out the horror he knew she would be facing if not rescued.

"You speak of the Karnstein Legend." Rider's voice came softly from behind his mask.

"Why, yes, but how did you know?" Henry sit up with amazement that someone outside the family Karnstein would know about the ancient legend.

"How I know, is not important, Lord Karnstein. The thing that is most important to me is finding Marcia from this violent fate." Rider stood up, anxious to leave and start his search. "I have no time to lose. Do you have any idea where the mystic island lies?"

"Nay, unfortunately, none." Henry scratched his head as he thought. "The map Krantz took was the only means of knowing the way to this monstrous island."

"There must be something else! This is your family legend, Henry! Think! Think hard, Lord Karnstein! Without any other information it could be hopeless!"

"Wait!" Henry stood up on wobbly legs and Rider jumped up to support him. "There is one possibility, Moon Rider! Help me into the library. If it is still there, then heaven has blessed us with the way!" His hands moved wildly over the books. "It just has to be here!" Henry grew excited as he laughed. "Ha! Here it is, Mystic Landmarks! It has to still be inside this book! It just has to!" Henry flipped through the pages of the old book.

"What is in there? What is it?" Rider grew anxious, hoping it was something to help him find the way to this hidden island.

"A rough copy of the original map. I remember when I was a young lad, about ten, the legend fascinated me!" from the last pages in the back of the old book, a yellow piece of paper slipped from the pages and fell on the floor. "Get it! Open it!"

Rider strong fingers swooped up the yellowed paper and opened it carefully, to keep from tearing the delicate old sheet of paper. It was obvious that young Henry Karnstein had place this sheet of paper over the original map and carefully traced it out, making a perfect copy. With child-like writing and numbers, he copied the wording and the mileage markings perfectly.

"That is my copy! That is the map to" Henry looked over at the islands name "yes, of course, the Island of Mist!" He exclaimed with excitement. "Will it be of any help, Moon Rider?"

"As a young boy of ten, you were quite the expert at copying, Lord Karnstein. This map is as good as the original." Rider gently folded the map and placed it inside his pocket for safe keeping. "Now, I must leave with haste!"

"Take me with you, Moon Rider! I must help my daughter!"

"You are hurt, sir and you will only slow me down." Rider patted Henry on his shoulder. "You can help Marcia better by staying here and getting well. Stay, that is for the best." The Moon Rider dashed from the large house and within seconds, he and his men had disappeared in the growing darkness."

Chapter Nineteen

Marcia looked nervously out over the sea as her heart sank with fear. Where were they taking her and why? They had referred to her as their golden ticket. Marcia's thought wondered back to Canterbury and the ones she had left behind, What, happened to little Nora? And Lizzie, poor dear friend? Tears formed in her beautiful eyes as she remembered the ones she loved so dearly. Agar, her beloved Agar. How she longed to have his strong arms around her, making love, sweet perfect love. And Rider, her thoughts about him made her heart break just the same. Did she really love him too, or was it his mysterious manners? Would she grieve his death, should he get killed?

"Aye, again and again! Oh Rider, I need you, I love you, my darling." Marcia closed the drapes over the port window and fell across her bed crying. "But…tis it not Agar I really love? Tis it not Agar I belong to?" Hearing the door being unlocked, Marcia quickly sat up and stared at the opening door. Krantz smiled as he walked inside, shutting the door behind him.

"Tears?" he walked over and smiled down at her lustfully. "My poor baby."

"Where are you taking me Krantz? I have a right to know!" Marcia tried to control her trembling voice.

"And you shall know, my dearest." Krantz sit down next to her, his eyes taking in her shapely body. "Have you ever perchance heard anything about the Karnstein Legend?"

"Aye, a great tragedy." Marcia's heart sank, recalling the gruesome details Agar had told her about Helen Karnstein and Jason Collinwood. "What has the Karnstein legend got to do with me?"

"My dear, you will play a big part in that little drama." His hand moved along her hip slowly and Marcia shifted quickly to the head of the bed.

"You may take your hands off of me! Tell me, what has Vicar Hayworth got to do with all this?"

"Besides making you my bride, he is the only one trained

enough to read the meaning and warnings of the legend."

"Read from what? What did the thief steal that he should know this legend?" Marcia was feeling very unconvertible from Krantz constant stare.

"A journal he found hidden at the old ruins in Canterbury, if you must know." His eyes roamed over her body.

"So, that is why the vicar was stooping about this morning behind the church." Marcia remembered well the morning she awoke in Agar's bed after they had spent the night making love. Dear Agar. "What was in that journal, Krantz? Who did it belong to?"

"The journal belonged to one Harold Karnstein, Helen's only brother. The Karnstein Legend was written down in it, detailing everything. If you are familiar with legends, then you know they are worded different, almost strangely. Such writings require an expert to decipher its meaning. A man of great knowledge. One who studies ancient books and papers, like a vicar or priest."

"Hayworth." Marcia lowered her eyes, wondering if Agar could have read such writings. Would he understand the meaning? Had he seen the journal and replaced it, to be buried forever under the children home? "But Krantz, how did the vicar recognize me? I went there as Cia Stone. No one knew my real identity. No one, but…"

"The great and wonderful Moon Rider?" Krantz laughed sarcastically. "He knew about you. What your real name was, did he not?" he smiled mockingly and looked unabashed at her bosom, wanting to reach out and claim them for his own. "I would say, the Moon Rider knew a whole lot about you, Marcia. Every beautiful inch."

"What are you implying, Krantz?" Marcia felt as though her heart was breaking into. Could she have misread Rider? Could he have only been using her? Had he been laughing at her inwardly while he held her in his embrace, asking her to marry him?"

"Who do you think Hayworth got all his information from?" Krantz laughed softly, knowing the real reason Hayworth recognized Marcia was not from the great and powerful Moon Rider. Krantz had an artist to sketch the perfect likeness of Marcia for him when he had first gone to see her. In her father's rose

126

garden, the artist stayed well-hidden and was paid well for his excellent work. Sending the drawing to his friend Hayworth turned out to be fulfilling and rewarding. Krantz enjoyed seeing Marcia upset over the man she trusted. He laughed softly. "Poor little Marcia, did I sour your thoughts of your lover?"

"Nay! You blacken not my thoughts, because he whom you speak means naught to me!" She hated Krantz even more for telling her this news. She wanted him to leave, to be rid of his mocking face from her sight. "Get out, Krantz! I care not to talk anymore."

"I too was finished with our talk. I had more pleasant things in mind for us." He laughed between his teeth, almost a hiss, as his hand moved up her leg. "It is time you started playing my wife."

"Nay, I am not your wife, Krantz nor will I ever say those vows for you!" Marcia scrambled as far away from his hands as possible. "Now get out before I scream!"

"And just who do you think will come running to your rescue?" he moved toward her, gloating. My men have their orders and not disturbing me while I am in here with you, is one of them. They try, they die!"

Marcia tried to fight Krantz off as he forced his body across hers and pinned her to the bed. Her kicking and fighting only enhanced his desire for her as the lust drove his hand up between Marcia's thighs.

"My God! Stop!" Marcia managed to pull one hand free and she slung it around, striking him across the face as she yelled. "You bloody bastard!"

Krantz laughed out as he grabbed her hand, pinning it down. "You, my dear, are a high-spirited little wildcat! Taming you will be a pleasure! I will show you what a real man can do. I shall ride your sexy thighs until my loins ache and your body grows sore from all the moving!" Krantz clutched her dress and forced it down over her large breasts as he pulled roughly at one of the nipples. "Admit it, Marcia, you like this!"

"Nay! I hate it as I hate you, Krantz!" Marcia twisted and turned, trying to free herself. She could feel herself growing tired as she said. "Agar will kill you! Do you hear me, Krantz? He will kill you for touching me, you, dirty pig!"

"Now, that really frightens me, Marcia." Krantz laughed mockingly, letting his tongue run lightly over her nipple. "A man who wears women's skirts and carries a bible instead of a sword, really scares me!" Krantz's breathing grew heavier as he moved his hand back and forth between Marcia's legs. "Prepare yourself for entry!"

Without warning, the door was flung open and he jerked his head up angrily and stared at his sister. "Arabella! What the devil are you doing here?"

"I just might ask you the same thing!" her anger coated each word. "Get your ass up and come with me! Now!" she ordered.

"How dare you provoke me, woman!" Hate moved in his eyes, but he stood up and grabbed her wrist tightly. "Arabella, you do not own me! I can do as I damn well choose and no little slut is going to tell me otherwise, understand?"

"I understand one thing! We have a job to do, remember? There will be time for such games later!" she jerked her arm away. "Now, kindly act out your own orders, dear brother!"

Krantz stared down at her briefly, his eyes ablaze, then shoved her out of the way and stormed off, never looking back down on the woman he was about to rape. On the other hand, Arabella gave Marcia a long hard look, throwing invisible daggers down on the beautiful woman who was lying limp from all her defensive fighting to get him from her body.

"Just what did my brother do to you? How far did the little weasel go?"

"Thanks to your interruption Arabella, he was stopped just in time." Marcia forced a smile up to the stone face woman who dripped with venom. "I am truly grateful you stopped him from raping me. Thank you."

"I do not want your thanks, dearie. I just do not like my brother spending his time with the likes of you!" Arabella walked over to the small door. "If it had been one of the ship's crew, I would have gladly let them take you. A little advice, mistress Karnstein, stay away from Krantz! Stop trying to entice him by pretending you do not want him to touch you!"

"It would be my pleasure to stay away from your brother. May

I suggest that it is Krantz you need to tell to keep away from me!" Marcia stood up to fasten her top, feeling instant disgust for this woman.

"Perhaps the other women in his worthless life has to work at turning him own, little sister, but not me! Can I help it if he desires me? I do nothing to lead him on. I just stand, sit, or lay there, saying and doing absolutely nothing and your weak brother cannot keep his dirty hands off me!"

"Well!" Arabella turned up her nose and stormed from the small room. Even with all her distress, Marcia could not help but laugh, knowing that at least she had just won one small battle.

The Moon Rider studied the map carefully in the dimly lit cabin, His thoughts kept wondering to Marcia. Was she alright? She just had to be alright. Surely this Krantz Hamish would not let anything happen to her until they reached the Island of Mist. Poor Marcia, my dearest darling, my love. She must be frightened out of her mind. That devil Hayworth, how I would love to get my hands on that phony.

"Master, I get the impression your mind is not entirely on that map you have been staring at." Rider's companion had been observing him in the stillness, and recognized the symptoms. "You are thinking about your woman, are you not'?"

"Aye, that I am." Rider stood up and slammed his fist in the palm of his hand. "How did I miss the sneaky vicar's friend being the stranger who would kidnapped her? How frightened Marcia must be. I long to take her into my protecting arms and comfort her."

"Aye, with that devil Hayworth, no woman is safe. Look what he did to little Nora's mother, not to mention beating up Marcia's pretend aunt." His friend shook his head in disgust. "That vicar is a disgrace to the brotherhood!"

"If Hayworth survives my sword or that monstrous island, I will see that he is stripped of his vestment and his position as vicar before he is thrown into prison to rot with the other church rats! If anyone hurts Marcia or lays one bloody finger on her, I shall slay him." Rider slapped the ruler in his hand, as he paced the cabin's moving floor. "By all that is Holy in me, naught will stand in the way of getting my woman back! If need be, I will deface anyone who stands in my way!"

"Rider, you sound delirious with revenge over this woman." His masked companion poured out two glasses of rich red wine and handed one to the mysterious man in black. "He who walks in a den of hungry lions is just asking for a bite of trouble."

"Amby, I certainly am glad I brought you along with me and the boys." Rider laughed. "You do make a fellow forget his troubles, if just briefly."

"If my great wisdom is something you can make light of, then by all means, laugh away!" Amby casually took a big gulp of his wine and looked up smiling. "Marcia will be upset because Agar did not come along on our rescue."

"Upset or not, Marcia will have to except the cold hard truth. Agar did what was best for her." The Moon Rider walked back to his small desk and pretended to view the map, although he thoughts kept turning back to Marcia. He glanced over at his smiling companion and made a face of disgust as he said. "Marcia will see that Agar did not stand a chance to bring her back. A priest is not likely to go about killing people, just for getting in his way. Even if the cause should ask for it."

"Maybe, but do not you think for the love of Marcia, Agar would not at least put up a good fight?" Amby smiled over at his frowning companion as he offered him a fresh refill, then filled his own glass, as he continued. "After all, you of all people, must know, the love of a woman can drive a man to do just about anything. Agar might regain the skills at sword fighting he used to enjoy. You have to admit, the good priest put her life first by asking you to come after Marcia, Rider. It is because of the love he has for her that he wanted the best chance in saving her from not only those evil men who captured her, but the monster that waits for her arrival."

"Aye, I am certain that was the young priest's idea. I can give him that much, He put her life in my hands, knowing I was more capable of saving her and she would feel obligated to choose me instead of him. So, he sacrificed any future he might have had with the only woman he loved." Rider laughed to himself. "Women can rule a man's heart and change him forever. The right woman, that is."

"Aye! He who is a man of great strength, can defeat all in a battle, except that with a woman who he loves." Amby lend over and pointed at the map. "Study the map carefully for this is uncharted waters we sail on. We cannot afford to get lost. Time will not allow such failure. The island itself looks extremely difficult and with these strange writings guiding our way, I am glad deciphering them is your responsibility and not mine or the crew." Amby stood up straight and patted Rider on the back as he whispered in his ear. "Remember, I am here in the interest of Agar and I expect a perfect job out of you."

"Aye! Not to worry! I shall get Marcia back. And, although this may be the most dangerous rescue I have ever had to make, for the love of Marcia, it will be worth the dangers and demons!" He glanced up at his companion, his eyes filled with serious emotions. "But you know well that Marcia will choose me to marry after I have rescued her from this island of hell. I see no reason for you to get your hopes up, Amby, and think I may be a true gentleman and let her choose for her own happiness. Like Agar, my life revolves around Marcia and my heart is filled with an overwhelming love. I need her in my life and finally I have the right to claim her for my bride."

"I can see how much you love her, Rider. The exact same way that Agar loves her. I truly feel Marcia has deep feelings for you, and equal is her love for Agar, so, becoming your wife will make her happy in the end. At least Agar still has his church and the work of God." Amby walked over to the cabin door, needing some fresh salty air, and turned around for one last word before stepping out on deck.

"You best study that map and worry about getting her first from those villains, then we shall worry about who 'she' chooses, once you have saved her. Never forget, Marcia has a way of getting what she wants!" Amby smiled mockingly and walked out whistling an old pirate song, 'Give in My Lady and Lay Next to Me…"

Chapter Twenty

The seas were calm until the sailing ship grew nearer to the Island of Mist, where the Karnstein Legend lay. The gruffy loud voice broke through the salty brine air as he yelled from the lookout, Krantz proudly called, the raven's nest: "LAND HO!"

Krantz Hamish laughed loudly. "We have made it! Man, the helm and lower the sails! Make sure we stay at a safe distance, then drop the anchor!" he smiled broadly over at his partner. "Well, Hayworth, if the legend holds everything you said, we both shall be bloody rich soon, old man!"

"Aye, Krantz!" the vicar's eyes scanned the vine-covered island as a misty fog seem to circle around it, giving it a mysterious appearance. He closed his eyes and breathed in the tropical air. "I can almost smell the gold!" Hayworth laughed. "We shall take only the girl, and four other men, of your choosing. The fewer to go ashore the better."

"Aye, smart thinking. Even though we are assured no one can follow us, we still cannot take chances. That masked man you spoke of is very clever and may find a way despite not having a map to guide his way." Krantz yelled to the man he had put in charge of the others. "I will inform my men to be on lookout for another ship, then take immediate action and blast them out of the water!"

"Do whatever you think wise, although I think we outsmarted the great and powerful Moon Rider this time." Hayworth stood aside as the first mate aboard stepped up for his orders.

"Bernard, pick out three good men, brave and unafraid of the unknown. There are things out there we have never seen or imagined, so, the last thing we need is a sissy coward! You, the men, Hayworth and I will get ready to hit the land with the girl. Order a steady watch for any passing vessel and have it disposed."

"Aye-aye, sir! Your orders will be met and delivered then we shall lower a boat." Bernard went about choosing just the right men for this job then lowered the boat and prepared for delivery, two extra men for rowing the boat and staying behind with it."

Arabella had overheard her brother's orders and came up quickly from her cabin and jerked Krantz around to face her. "Make room for one more in your small party, brother! I go with you! You will not leave me behind!"

"Listen Arabella, you are better off here. There are dangers on that island, the likes of which we have never encountered!" Krantz pulled his arm free of her grip. "Now, go below and wait for me!"

"Nay! I go too, or neither one of us goes!" she shouted. "I will not be left behind!"

"Arabella, your brother is right, my dear. The island is too dangerous for a lady." Hayworth took Arabella's hand. "You would make us feel so much better if we knew you were safe here on this ship."

"Aye, safely away from you both, where you could hog up all the treasure for yourselves!" she pouted.

"Arabella, do not be ridiculous! We cannot leave this island any other way but from my ship!" Krantz was growing impatient with his whining sister. "Are you really that stupid?"

"I am not stupid! I do not care what you say or do, Krantz, but I am going with you! Like it or not! You said that bitch was our means to the treasure and nothing would happen to us as long as we had her!" Arabella stomped her foot. "You are wasting time, brother! I will not change my mind! I am going and that is final!"

"ALRIGHT! COME WITH US!" he spoke angrily, feeling the need to strike her. "I have not the time to argue with you, so just listen, little sister, if anything happens to you in that jungle, and you cannot defend yourself, TOUGH!"

"That suits me just fine! Let us go!" she stormed over to the rope latter and started down in the boat.

Krantz watched Arabella disappear over the ship's rail, then called to Bernard. "Bring the girl up and let us depart for the island at once while the day is yet young!"

The strange island lay deathly quiet, stretching its four points into the sea. The rough, rugged mountains loamed up over the jungle below, made up of green trees and a variety of unusual bushes and vines. The new arrivals stared in amazement at what lay in front of them. A land forgotten by time, or perhaps, never inhabited by man, except the Karnstein who happened upon the mysterious island many years ago by accident. Krantz gripped Marcia's hand tightly as his sister watched with hate filled eyes.

Krantz squeezed Marcia's hand as he spoke softly. "Just stay with me, dearest. All will be well." His hand ran along her hip and she jumped back. "Relax, Marcia. You have got to learn to relax to my touch." Laughing, he led the party of eight up through the green curtain of trees and overgrowth.

The Moon Rider stared out at the island his men located a few miles offshore. They pointed out the other ship resting in the waters, cannons aimed out in the open sea. Knowing they were probably not spotted being so far out, Rider waved to the man at the helm.

"Take her around, Scottie, where the island runs its arm out into the sea. Our ship will be well hidden then." He made his way quickly to his cabin and gathered his weapons and supplies. Amby hurried in behind him, strapping on his sword and knife.

"How many go besides the two of us, Rider?"

"We shall pick out four other men to come with us to the island. Two men to stay behind with the boat and the other two will come with us. We shall ask for volunteers this time. This will be no ordinary mission we are taking and I will not ask any man to follow me in this kind of uncertain danger."

"I wonder if Krantz Hamish was just as thoughtful where his men are concerned?" Amby shook his head, as to answer his own question.

"I grant you, the evil hearted raven never considered giving them a choice." Rider walked behind his friend. "Line the men up and I will share all I know with them about the dangers."

Aye, sir!" Amby got all the men aboard the ship to line up, then stood to one side as the Moon Rider stepped forward, dressed ready to fight.

"Men, hear me out. I need four volunteers, who will come with Amby and myself, to the island." Before he could continue, every hand flew up and he laughed softly. "Maybe, you will not be so anxious to follow me inside that jungle after I tell you what you will be facing, gentlemen. Notice I said, 'will' be facing, not 'might' be facing." The men began to grow tense as they looked at one another, trying not to stand out for the sudden fear they were feeling. "I will not hold any man here a coward if he chooses not to come. I cannot say that I blame you, but I really need two men to follow me and Amby and two men to stay with the boat, for a fast get-away if necessary. There are some unusual demons and monsters beyond those trees, and I am not referring to Vicar Hayworth or Krantz Hamish, even though they fit the description. There could be places of illustration, strange and mystifying. This, gentlemen, is a place of great dangers." Rider looked over at Amby as men began to lower their heads, feeling defeated by fear. "Believe me, my good loyal friends, I understand your fear and it does not let me feel less of you. Is there two brave enough to come and two to man the boat?"

"You can count me in Sir!" A big man stepped up as he strapped on his sword. "If my small friend, Amby is going, so will I!"

Thank you Bolt! Do I have one more volunteer to follow me?" Rider looked out over his men as he saw a trusted fighter stepping up from the back of the crowd. "Thank you, McCormick! You can live up to your bragging now!" The stout man laughed, along with the other two men who stepped up, strapping on their swords.

"We know we will be keeping the boat sir, but we shall be prepared if danger should approach us!"

"Sounds good! Let us go, men!" Rider led the fearless group to the island. As they walked toward the forest that waited ahead, the Moon Rider look back to smile at his men. "Well men, this will prove your bravery like never before, as well as my own. Just remember, all our enemies here are not the two-legged manly type."

"No matter, Moon Rider, we are with you all the way!" McCormick yelled. "TO VICTORY!"

"TO VICTORY!" the masked man shouted, as they found the footprints of six men and two women, and followed their path. Being an expert tracker, Rider followed their trail with no trouble and he and his men were use to traveling through thick forest. He whispered to himself. "I am coming Marcia. I have found your beautiful footsteps and I will not let them escape my sight!"

135

Chapter Twenty-One

"We are sure to see a sign soon." Hayworth stared over at Marcia, knowing she would be the first to feel some presence ahead. "All our hopes in finding the treasure lies with Marcia."

Krantz yanked at her slim arm. "Tell us, have you felt anything yet, seen any signs?" she looked up at him confused as he stopped and jerked her around. "Well woman, tell me!"

"I have only felt the fear of the unknown that lies ahead. I have felt naught or neither have I seen any sign." Marcia felt weary from walking the rough path. "Could we please stop and rest? If only for a short time?"

"We can surely." Arabella flopped down on a nearby log, covered with red moss. "I am dead on my feet! This island is nothing but jungle!"

"You are the one who insisted on coming, dear sister! We tried to warn you what it was like, but you would not hear any of it! You and your ridiculous jealousy!" Krantz shot fire down on her and he took hold of her arm and yanked her to her feet. "Get your ass up, Arabella, or We shall leave you right here, alone!" A creepy smile fell on his lips as he added. "But you will not be here alone for very long. Some hungry, slimy creature will have a feast on you!"

"Alright, I am coming! There is no reason for you to be mean to me, dear brother."

"Krantz is right, Arabella, we shall not rest until we find the Karnstein treasure and make it safe off this dangerous island." Hayworth gripped Marcia's face in his hand and said sharply. "Now, get this straight young lady, when you do see something, you be sure and let us know."

"Not if I can help it! I shall never forget what you have done to the people I love after Krantz promised me you would not hurt them!" Marcia took the opportunity to show her discuss for this man by spiting in his face. "I hope you find not the treasure or whatever might lay in your path!"

"Act brave while you can, Marcia, but for now, just move!"

136

Krantz gave her a shove as they continued up the hill.

They had only walked a short distance farther when Marcia stopped cold in her tracks. Her eyes flew open as she let out a gasp. Standing right in front of them was an incredible ugly monster. It appeared to be a green lizard-type man with red eyes and the tongue of a reptile. Her head move up its enormous body and it long sharp pointed tail moved slowly from side to side, blocking their trail completely.

Knowing from her scared expression, Krantz saw Marcia was witnessing something this side of hell. He stared into the empty space ahead of them, then back down at the girl. "Why have you stopped Marcia? What do you see?" Krantz noticed her shaking uncontrollable and he pulled her in his arms as he spoke softly. "What is it? You cannot be left alone out here in this hellish place, Marcia. Please, tell me what you see."

"Surely you can see it, you, stupid bloody bastard!" Marcia started backing back down the hill they had just climbed, needing to get away from the ugly reptile, that seem to mock her with it eyes. "We cannot get through that way! It will destroy us, all of us! Even now, it watches me, knowing I am the only one capable of seeing the ugly beast!"

"It is like the legend states, Krantz. Marcia sees what we cannot." Hayworth suddenly felt helpless from the lack of seeing the danger that lies directly in front of them. He gently pulled Marcia around to face him. "Listen to me, Marcia. Your friend in Canterbury is not dead, we only made sure she could not call for help right away. The child Nora is sad over the loss of her aunt who raised her, but it was the woman's heart that took her life, not us. Believe me, I would never hurt that child." Hayworth would keep the miracle of her walking to himself. It might prove handy later, but for now, they needed Marcia's co-operation if they were to survive. "Marcia, tell me, what does this monster look like?"

Marcia closed her eyes to block out the smiling monster, her body shaking out of control.

Arabella laughed out. "Cannot you see it is just pretense? Just a big show so she can stop to rest! Come on, let us move on while there is still plenty of day left! I, for one, do not wish to be lost on 'this' island after dark!"

137

"Nay! Krantz, stop her!" Marcia grabbed his arm in total fear for her enemies. "It is a horrible giant green lizard, some twenty-foot tall! The creature is part man, with red eyes and the tongue of a snake! His long, pointed tail switches back and forth to block the entire path!"

"Such nonsense!" Arabella laughed as she made her way in front of her brother. "I shall prove she is lying, dear brother. If there were a monster that big standing right in front of us, we would surely see him!"

"There are a great many mysteries on this small island, Arabella. The legend plainly states that only with the tenth generation of a Karnstein maiden, can you find your way to the treasure. As you recall, my dear, the legend states, a treasure lies beyond dangers and demons." Hayworth observed Marcia and knew the young woman really saw something horrifying in front of them. Even the best stage actor could not produce that much fear. "Nay, the girl really does see something; that is plain enough."

"Then, to be certain of her truth, send someone through." Arabella looked at Marcia with hate dripping from her eyes. "I just happen not to believe her."

"We have no men to spare, Arabella!" Krantz looked around for another opening and scratched his head. "Which way to go?"

"Through the path, you fool!" Arabella's voice grew angry. "Cannot you see what she is doing? Mistress Karnstein is using us, making us look stupid!" Her hand flew out as she pointed to the path ahead. "There is NOTHING standing in our way! The path is clear! Now, send a man through this instant, to test that I am right!"

"For God sake, do it Krantz!" Hayworth shook his head in disgust and lend over to whisper, "Pick Roland, he appears the weakest man we have. If there is naught there, then we know that our little Marcia has been lying to us and we shall have to punish her."

"Nay! Krantz, you must not send a man through there! It will be a sure agonizing death for him! He shan't make it! It is not humanly possible!" Marcia heard the lizard man laugh softly and looked over to see his evil, knowing smile. Marcia covered her eyes when Krantz looked around for his unfortunate choice. "Please Krantz, the lizard man is smiling. He has heard all our words and he understands! That evil creature also knows I am the only one that can see him or hear him. My God, it senses a victim!"

"Roland, be a good man. You go, walk up the path." Krantz ordered but the scared man backed away, shaking with fear. As he backed into the vicar, Hayworth jerked him up by the collar and held a dagger next to his throat.

"Roland, you heard our leader! He said, move, you coward! If you do not follow his order, I will personally split your worthless throat!" Hayworth gave him a shove forward as the frighten man stumbled on his feet as he moved slowly up the path until he reached the spot of never turning back.

Marcia screamed as the lizard man moved his hands out slowly and took a firm hold on Roland. The frightened man let out a loud cry as the slimy green claws began disconnecting his body. As the group watched in horror, the lizard slowly became visible to the small group and they slowly began backing up when the monster's great jaws swallowed down the last leg of poor helpless Roland.

Then, a bush started moving apart, revealing another path. Knowing they had a safe way out, the frightened group moved quickly from the horrible scene, the great scrub closing behind them.

The Moon Rider held up his hand for his men to stop. He looked down at the ground then slowly around him. "Something happened here. It seems as if something caused them to stop abruptly." His attention fell on the dandy footprints belonging to the woman he loved. "Look here! Marcia started backing away from something!"

"Perhaps Hamish or Hayworth were threating her, approaching to attack her." Amby examined the footprints.

"Nay, my friend. Marcia is the only one to back before something drove the whole lot backward, minus the one set of man's steps weaving on up the hill, where he simply vanishes." Rider waved his hand over the confusion of footprints and noticed the sudden smooth even steps toward a hedge of large scrubs, then just, disappearing.

Amby had been staring up the hill where the lone man disappeared and noticed some object lying on the torn-up ground. He pulled at the masked man's arm, finger pointing up the hill and on the earth floor.

"There seems to be something lying on the ground up on that hill. Rider, it looks like" Amby stared up at his tall dark leader, disbelieving the words he was about to say. "parts of a man!"

"My Lord! Amby, you are right!" Rider tilted his head and listened to the eyrie stillness. The jungle birds they had heard earlier had grown quiet. He lifted his head to sniff the air, then was drawn back to the spot on the hill. "Men, there is some kind of object standing up on that hill. It is probably one of the dangers or demons the legend spoke of. Whatever it is, this thing is responsible for ripping a man to pieces and devouring him."

"An invisible monster!" Amby swallowed as he stared up the empty hill. "What will we do, Rider. That evil Krantz Hamish sacrificed one of his men to find out! We are better men than that!"

"That we are, my friend. My men will stay safe with me. First, we need to find out the size of our friend up there!" Rider scooped up a handful of stones and threw one up in the open space. An angry roar ripped from the lizard's throat, causing all the men to jump back, except the masked man who toss another stone up in his hand. "He is a big one and strong enough to tear off a man's limbs."

"Sweet Virgin Mary, how do we fight something that huge and that strong?" Amby nervously clutched his sword handle. "Not to mention how invisible the big bully is."

"You must never forget, my friend, David was just a small shepherd boy when he took on the giant Goliath and won, because God was on his side, as he is ours, my loyal one." The Moon Rider reached down for more stones. "Grab some stones men! I think if we make that thing mad enough, he will become visible!" Rider started hurling stones up at the open space as he shouted. "Keep the stones flying fellows! I think, from all the noise he is making, my little trick will work!"

"Just what is your little trick? I cannot possibly see what good throwing stones will do, except make him madder and he might start down the hill after us!" Amby continued to hurl the rocks, each one getting bigger than the last.

The Moon Rider realized the thing on the hill may be able to understand their words, so he turned his back to it and spoke softly. "The monster will no doubt think that he is visible to us since we act as though we can see him. He will then reverse his magic, thinking he has made himself invisible while all the time, we shall see the monster for ourselves."

Amby looked up at the masked man, confused, yet knowing Rider had a reason for speaking softly so he whispered in return. "But, Rider, we cannot see him now."

"He does not know that!" Rider whispered, growing impatient. "That thing sees us throwing stones and looking directly at him! Therefore, the stupid creature 'thinks' we can 'see' him." Rider looked up from Amby and laughed out. "See, what did I tell you? The old lizard has changed to visible, but now, he thinks he is invisible!"

Amby stared up in disbelief at the hideous green lizard-like man, standing a good ten feet tall. "Shit! I wish he was still invisible! He is the ugliest thing I have seen!"

"Aye, but do not say it too loud, my friend. I think he can understand every word we have said, until I turned my back and started speaking softly." Rider looked around and noticed a huge rock hanging out above the green lizard. He smiled to himself and circled the men around him to whisper. "Let us rid the world of this evil lizard-man! Listen fellows, draw that chap's attention as I move around to that ledge hanging out over him to drop him a little message! A message made out of stone!"

"Rider, can you manage that big stone on your own?" Amby pulled his sword out of its case."

"Aye, the stone is already dangling. All it needs is just a little persuasion." He patted the men closest to him on their back. "Now, you fellows would not wish to be up there with me if that ugly lizard happened to look up, would you?" The Moon Rider laughed at his men's expressions of distaste. "Just keep his attention and do not get to close to him. I do not think our old chap can leave his designated spot, This, island, is no ordinary place. He is more than likely some sort of guard and must hold his post at all times." The masked man pulled out his sword and held it up

141

as he shouted: "Action, men!"

Rider rushed off to the ledge that tilted out over the green lizard-man while his men were busy swinging their swords and shouting remarks at the ugly lizard from a safe distance. Rider sat up against the big stone and started pushing his weight against it, where it lay dangerously close to the edge. The large boulder started to move and the earth and small gravel around it sent particles down on the giant lizard's head, causing him to look up and growl. Rider stayed still behind the huge rock, hearing the sound of sliding, he knew the ugly monster had grown curious and was crawling over to check out the rock. Noticing the sudden danger, Amby yelled out and moved in closer to the green lizard-man.

"Hey, you, dumb lizard! Down here!" it slung it angry head around and narrowed its red eyes down on the red-head. "Just because you are big and 'fat' does not make you any better than all the other slimy little lizards I have squashed under my foot!" Amby laughed when the ugly lizard lost all interest in the moving boulder hanging over it grotesque green head and turned around, swinging out his pointed tail. "There is only one difference between you, old chap! Those other lizards were little runts. You are a big overgrown FAT stupid lizard with the brain of a fly!"

The lizard man made a gruesome noise as he flicked his tongue in and out, his anger boiling inside him. Amby backed away as the creature whirled his long huge tail at him while waving his arms wildly. Being careful not to go over with the big stone, the Moon Rider gave one last push that sent the huge boulder hurtling down on the lizard, crushing it to the ground.

"You got him, Rider! The ugly beast is gone!" McCormick yelled up to the ledge. "Victory!"

"Aye, my friends! Victory!" Rider jumped down from the ledge, pointing to the opening bush. "We have found the path! There are the lost footprints! Let us make haste for we must find Marcia!"

The group of brave men made their way quickly through the green gate and followed the newly revealed path.

Chapter Twenty-Two

With each step Marcia took, she felt certain that her passing out was a possibility. As she stumbled along, she could not remember the last meal she had and was almost certain it was the tiny bit she ate in Krantz's camp outside her home. Krantz pulled her along the path, making sure she kept her head up and eyes open for possible danger ahead. The lizard incident still clung in each of their minds as they walked in complete silence. Marcia felt sure that all her hopes of getting out of here alive were gone for good. No one could possibly find her without a map and Krantz had the only one in existence. Marcia had no way of knowing her father had made an exact copy when he was only ten. Her thoughts were suddenly interrupted when Krantz stopped in his tracks. Looking up, all Marcia could see was a very large rock hill in front of her. Their path had just reached another dead end.

"Marcia, tell us what you see? There must be something here." Hayworth had stepped up beside of her when they came to the dead end. "Look Marcia and tell us what lies in this small stone mountain."

"All I see is a mountain, a hill made of rocks." Marcia mumbled, her mind and body filled with fatigue. "I am tired. Sleepy!" she fell limp and her body crumpled into Krantz's arms.

Arabella walked over quickly, ready to claim what she thought was hers. "Brother, what is wrong with her? Is she really sleeping or only playing false?"

"Nay Arabella, the girl has passed out." Hayworth looked around, then slapped Marcia lightly on her face. "Marcia, Marcia, wake up!"

Marcia slowly opened her eyes and stared up at the enormous stone in front of her. She could see a face appearing in the stone. It was a peaceful face, one of calmness and deep caring. Marcia sat up slowly when she thought she heard a voice coming from the loving face, smiling down at her.

"My child" no, Marcia was not imagining the warm voice radiating love in her ears. "Sweet child of Karnstein birth, your destiny lies in joy and mirth. Go very slow to reach your goal, for one follows with love, so strong and bold."

Marcia stepped up close to the comforting voice and whispered. "Dear man of stone." And with those words, she fell softly back to the bed of green. Arabella stared down at her, then looked up at her brother and the vicar.

"What did she mean by man of stone? Speak up Hayworth! Are you not the old man of great wisdom and understanding?"

"The stone must have spoken to Marcia." Hayworth was trying to piece this new mystery together when Arabella laughed in his face.

"A talking stone? Seriously Hayworth, that is totally ridiculous!"

"Then, please explain this?" Hayworth had noticed Marcia was clutching something in her hand. "What have we here?" he reached down and pulled her fingers open and let out a small gasp when he saw the object she was holding. "It is a rose! A perfect red, rose!"

"A rose? In this God forsaken place? Now, where on earth did it come from?" She glanced up at the big stone and laughed. "From this stupid old rock?" Arabella tried to take the rose from Marcia's hand, but the thorns seemed to strike back at her. "Did you see that? It attacked me! The rose…it bit into my hand!" She held out her hand and could plainly see blood sprinkling from the torn tissue.

"Arabella, if you would stay back and act like a lady, you would not get yourself into such a mess!" Krantz pushed her out of his way and stepped up to the vicar. "Explain the rose, Hayworth!"

"This has to be some strange message, but what?" Hayworth stepped up to the rock. "I have never had to deal with rocks that talk or has the magic to give out roses."

"You are the brains of this outfit, Hayworth! You figure it out!" Krantz said angrily. "At this rate, we shall be looking for that damn treasure forever and I want to enjoy it while I am yet young, understand?"

"You must not grow impatient, Krantz. Men slip up when they get in a hurry. The stone will speak to us when it's ready."

144

Hayworth sat down on a dead tree limb and lend back on a live tree. "Just relax, Krantz. Take it easy."

"Relax?" he laughed out sarcastically. "How the hell can I relax when I know there is a lifetime treasure lying somewhere out there and we have to wait here, depending upon a silly rock to make up its mind to speak?"

"He who tries to run ahead of fate, lives in lies of lust and hate!"

Krantz stared up into the face of the stone. In fear, he fell to the ground, his heart beating wildly from the angry stare reflecting in its lavender eyes. Hayworth laughed softly as he pushed himself up and smiled down at Krantz's sudden fright. The vicar stepped up to the face in the stone, and bowled his head in respect.

"Do speak on, great stone of wisdom."

"You cannot seek the treasure more, until the girl has health restored."

"How do we handle this? What must we do?" Hayworth knew to wait patiently for the stone's reply.

"As long as the rose in her hand is red, she will sleep, as though she were dead."

"How can we change the color of the rose, great stone of wisdom?"

"There is a white rose you must find, before you find that appointed time."

"Tell us, where is the white rose you speak of that we might find it?" The vicar tried to keep his voice calm as he felt his body tremble.

"There is a cavern deep in the ground; one room, is huge, its shape is round. The rose you seek is pure and white, lies in the middle, right in sight."

"Sounds easy enough, where is this cavern, how far?" Krantz had overcome his fear and had rose up to speak. The stone face looked down at the brash young man and frowned.

"He who rushes into things, winds up, LOST, where death stings!"

"Krantz, do not be an idiot! Let me handle this!" Hayworth mumbled under his breath, then gave a fake smile to the face in the stone. "Forgive my young friend, mighty one! He is yet young and inexperienced in matters such as these. What more do we need to know, great stone face, to avoid the sting of death?"

"To get the rose, you shall find hard, for it is protected by a very sly guard. Grim, who rules the underworld den, likes to stuff himself with men!"

"What sort of 'thing' is this Grim? Is he as terrible as the green lizard man we encountered some time back?" Krantz tried to remain calm, to keep the rock face from scolding him again.

"Mongol the Lizard man is mean indeed, He rips up his prey, then he will feed. Grim is hideous, a sight to behold, cruel, dangerous, wicked and bold! His bottoms a beast, his top is a man, he has four feet but just one hand."

"I will not set foot in that horrible place!" Arabella flopped down on the ground and looked down at the sleeping young woman and narrowed her eyes. "Not for that bitch!"

"Marcia is our only hope to get to the riches!" Krantz shouted at his sister, causing the jungle birds to squawk out loudly and start flying in all different directions.

"Krantz, let her stay here if she likes. She will just be in our way or cause some sort of trouble for us." Hayworth turned the leader around to see an opening in the left side of the stone. "We will leave one man here to guard the girls. Besides, Marcia is not going anywhere until we find the white rose."

"Aye, you are right. Arabella would just slow us up and I, for one, wish to grab that rose and get out of that devil's den!" Krantz called his first mate. "Bernard, stay with the girls until we return from that damn hole in the earth." Krantz followed Hayworth into the stone's hidden door and headed out to find the cavern with the precious white rose.

Arabella had watched her brother and the vicar disappear inside the big rock, then her attention went on Marcia, sleeping peacefully, her hand clutching the beautiful red rose.

"Little bitch, nothing but trouble! Laying there like some princess in a children's fairy tale!" Krantz's sister looked over at Bernard to make sure he was listening to her ravings. "That poor man got killed by that green lizard and you should have stopped him! It was all your fault he got ripped in threads then swallowed, piece by bloody piece!" Arabella bent down to her face and sneered. "I cannot wait until we are rid of you!"

"Hush, Arabella, that face in the stone might hear you! Now, get some rest." Bernard watched as the opening in the stone closed slowly. "We might have a long wait before anything else happens."

The Moon Rider stared down at the small group below them. He took a breath of relief when he saw Marcia was with them. How still she lay, her hands crossed in front of her like a corpse. The Rider's hope turned to worry and dismay as he spoke softy to the men gathered around him.

"Alright! There is only one man keeping guard. Let us move down quietly, prepare for battle." Rider pulled Amby to one side and whispered. "Something is wrong with Marcia, Amby, I can feel it! My heart is troubled greatly! We have no time to lose!"

Chapter Twenty-Three

The Moon Rider's small group of warriors moved silently up the path where Bernard sat, half asleep, guarding Marcia. Rider motioned for two of his men to slip up on the unsuspecting guard while he signaled for Amby to take care of the woman, arms folded up against the fallen log, fast asleep. Within a flash, the masked men had Bernard tied up to and tree and his mouth thoroughly gagged. The Moon Rider smiled down at the shocked and confused Arabella, as he pressed his sword to her throat.

"Victory!" Rider knelt down next to Marcia and felt her pulse. His attention fell on the red rose clutched in her hand. "Amby, get over here!"

Amby threw his captive over in Doctor Merciton's arms and ran over to where Marcia lay quietly.

"What is wrong with the girl, Rider? Is she not alive?"

"Aye, my love lives, but I do not know for how long." Rider looked around at their surroundings, his eyes stopping at the massive stone. "There is another presence here, I can sense it. But, this one is not evil like the last one."

"What sort of presence?" When Rider was drawn back to the perfect rose, Amby followed his eyes to the rose Marcia clutched tightly in her hands. "Tis a bad omen. The red rose…a symbol of death."

"My thoughts exactly, friend. That is why I must find out the source that is responsible for this!" As the masked man stood up, he looked back at the stone. It was from there he felt the great presence, so he spoke up, in hopes of getting a reply. "If you are there, speak, and tell me what I must do to save this woman."

"Your, heart is true, your heart is pure. So, I shall tell you how to find the cure." The voice from the stone came softly. Amby and the other two warriors had stepped up closer when they heard the voice and shook their heads, disbelieving their own ears. Amby moved up next to the black figure and mumbled.

"Did…did the stone say those words?"

"Aye! It must be the stone of wisdom the legend refers to."

The mysterious knight scooped up Marcia in his arms and carried her in front of the stone, then its face slowly appeared before them and looked down at the Karnstein maiden, lost in sleep. "This woman I hold, I love deeply. Please, there is naught I would do to save my true love. You must tell me how I can help her awake, then get her away from this place!"

"There is a white rose you must find, before you find that appointed time."

"Where can I find this white rose and what must I do to get it?" Rider gently ran his finger over Marcia's lips, wishing his kiss would bring her awake.

"There is a cavern deep in the ground; one room, is huge, its shape is round. The rose that you seek is pure and white. It sits in the middle, right in sight! To get the rose you shall find is hard, for it is protected by a very sly guard. Grim, who rules the underworld den, likes to stuff himself with men."

"I shall fight this foe if I must, for there is naught I would not do for my dearest Marcia." Holding her tightly in one arm, Rider pulled out his sword and held it up. "I go with this sword as my weapon and my God as the shield!"

"There are those that go ahead of you, seeking the rose in the den. They shall find the rose of love will not move for those who drip in evil sin!"

"Then, you sent the others away knowing that they could not possibly get the white rose?" Rider questioned the stone.

"The treasure of Karnstein do they seek to find; I gave her the rose to stall for time. A curse will fall upon her head; if they get the treasure with her, she will be dead!"

"I will not leave her behind! She will go with me! I will take her to the white rose and make her well." Rider turned to face Arabella when she stormed out, remaining quiet long enough.

"You cannot take her! This woman is our golden ticket to great riches!" She narrowed her eyes as she could not resist scanning over his handsome body. "Look, handsome, I am sure we can work something out. I believe my brother will agree to share the treasure with all of you, fine gentlemen!" Arabella could tell from the masked man's constant stare she was not making any lead way with him. "Look, if you are so mad for the girl, I am sure my clever brother can come up with some of his smooth tricks to get the gold and keep the girl in the process!"

"I have no desire to deal with the devil, woman, and you madam are a fool to think I would risk my woman's life for street trash like you nor a scandal like your brother!" Staying calm, the Moon Rider held tight to the woman in his arms. "Miss Hamish, I did not come seeking great riches, I came to rescue my woman from the kidnappers you are! You can give your brother and his crooked friend, Hayworth, my words! Tell them if they seek to stop me from saving my dearest Marcia, The Moon Rider will hit them swiftly and with my sword, I shall slash through their black heart, just like I would a rapid fox!"

As Arabella stood stunned by his outburst, she, soften her approach.

"To find such love would be worth giving up any treasure, fair knight." She looked up helplessly. "Please sir, do not leave me here to face my evil brother and that sick vicar! It is they that seek for great riches, not I. I all but go along with them, because I live in fear of what they might do to me! I begged to be left on the ship but they insisted I come!" Arabella produced tears. "Please, I am frightened, truly. You could not leave a lady in distress, could you?"

The face in the stone rolled his eyes up, knowing the big performance this one was displaying and even though he thought sure the man of honor would see through her charade. The voice came softly, but sternly. "This one who speaks, you cannot trust; Tie her securely, then with haste, take the girl and rush! Then go, go and make her well: but listen to what I must tell. Beware these men, the devil is he; When greed rules the heart, there's danger for thee! With God as your shied and this you have said; Then good shall prevail and evil be dead!"

"I go! I go with wisdom, with love, and most of all, with God!" The Moon Rider gathered Marcia securely in his arms and stood back as the stone door moved open. "Men, we go! Leave them!" he nodded toward their two captives, tied together. "They will not be going anywhere."

The small group moved deep into the cavern, searching for the round room, while keeping their eyes open for Krantz and his men, as well as the monster, Grim. The sound of dripping water was heard throughout the many passages, resembling a maze. Walking just a few steps behind his leader, Amby spoke softly over Rider's shoulder.

"Do you want me to carry Marcia some for you? She must be getting heavy and the footing down here is slimy."

"Thank you but nay, my friend. She is as light as a bird." Rider looked warmly down at Marcia's beautiful peaceful face. "Now that I have found her, I intend to keep her, safe in my arms."

Amby shook his red locks as he pulled the mask off for a clearer watch in the dim light. "I thought as much, but I thought I would offer." Looking down to watch where he was walking, Amby didn't see Rider stop in front of him, causing him to run hard into his back. "He in front who stops too fast, causing the one behind to crash!"

"And if the stone of wisdom were here, he would state: He who looks not where he goes, usually winds up with a bloody nose!" Rider laughed and pointed down to the big open room below them. "There it is! The great stone walls are in a perfect circle."

"Dang, it is the round room alright and down there in the middle is the life rose! The perfect white love rose, lying on twelve smooth round stones! It is just as the face in the big stone stated!" Amby looked for a way down while Rider scanned the room for any sign of Krantz and Hayworth.

"I see no form of life below. I wonder if they tried to get the rose and found they could not retrieve it?"

"Maybe Grim has helped himself to a fine dinner of evil men!" Amby laughed at the idea.

"Aye, that may be their fate!" Rider nodded to the stone steps around the corner from them and started down. "The poor one arm fellow, will probably have heartburn after downing those villains!"

"Aye. I hope he takes long naps after a meal or finds himself too full for another meal so soon, if he happens to show his ugly face." Amby moved quietly behind the masked man. "I really hope he does not pop out from behind some rock. I hate surprises!"

"Aye, the ugly foe may decide to invite us to dinner, his

dinner!" Rider stopped speaking and tilted his head. Amby stared up into his masked face, knowing that the Moon Rider's great senses had felt something nearby. Nervously, Amby gripped his sword's handle in preparation for battle.

"Rider, what is out there? What are you sensing?"

"I hear footsteps, making their way through one of the many passageways." Rider all but ran toward the center of the room where the white rose lay. Amby hurried along behind to keep up with his tall friend, as he looked from side to side for any sign of danger.

"Do you hear 'big' footsteps or little footsteps, Rider?"

"I would guess from the echo each step leaves behind, the thing coming our way is rather large." Rider sat Marcia down as he peered at the white rose, inches away from his grip. Before he could lift the rose from its resting place, he heard a loud roar coming behind him. Quickly the masked man was on his feet, sword in hand as he twisted around to face his dreadful enemy. Never in his lifetime had he witnessed anything that looked like this monstrosity.

Amby made a distasteful face as he moved over next to Rider, and the four men formed an arch. The doctor stood back up on the platform holding his breath as he watched the brave men below him. Amby spoke softly, just under his breath.

"Damn! What on earth is that? He is about the ugliest brute I believe I have ever seen, and I thought that freaky green lizard man was the worse!"

"He seems to sizing us up. I am pretty sure that ugly chap is used to his prey running for cover." Rider chuckled as he said. "I will say one thing for the thing, he does not have the makings of a lady's man, unless there is a female umpacore nearby."

"Umpacore?" Amby looked astonished that his friend might actually know what this mystical beast was.

"Someone had to give him a title. Might as well be me." The moon Rider started walking toward the huge beast. "How else will I know what to put on his gravestone?" The 'umpacore's' four short legs moved from side to side as the fingers on its one hand circled quickly in front of him. Two stony eyes were set far back it its pear shape head with a third, round eye bulging out in the middle of his hairy forehead.

Doctor Merciton had made his way down to where Marcia laid and whispered up to the advancing group of brave men. "Look fellows, old Grim has a spare eye, in case the others go bad." Trying to keep his voice calm, he continued speaking. "Can you not just see the big oath getting fitted for a pair of spectacles made especially for him?"

"Go for the hand, men! That seems to be his main defense!" Rider began swinging his sword toward the monster's hand and his warriors followed his lead. Grim moved his enormous body toward them, his feet moving in all directions like long fingers. "The feet! Watch his feet! He can use them like hands!" As one of the front feet made a swipe at Rider, his swift swinging sword slash the seven moving toes off and sent them flying in the grand musty hall. A horrible scream issued from the monster's throat as he reared up on his hind legs, growing even more angry with the invaders.

"Rider, I think you have made this one mad at us!" Amby's breathing grew heavy from his fighting. "I fear this one is not going to die so easy and we have no dangling rock to hurl down on his ugly head!"

"Aye! This one will be a challenge! I must get near those eyes!" Rider looked around for a possible answer as Amby tried to make light over his comment with a jest.

"I never knew it was this chap's eyes that intrigued you. I would not exactly call them, sexy. Why not just make friends with the beast? I am sure he would feel flattered you liked his weird three eyes."

"I think I shall drop in on dear old Grim!" Rider nodded toward a ridge jutting out over the big monster. "Men, I will take your daggers up with me. I may need all three if in my battle I drop one. As you can witness, I need three good blows!"

Amby stared up at the roaring deformed beast and mumbled to his good friend. "Rider, you...you intend to ride that chap's back and rid him of his eyes? Good Lord! It is a good way to get yourself killed!"

"At the rate we are going, my friend, we will all be killed anyway by our ugly friend if I do not." Rider slapped his friend on the back as he stuck the three daggers in his sash and placed his sword in Amby's hand. "Your job is to get his attention, so here is your time to dance." Rider laughed, joined by the other two fighters as he made his way quickly up the stone steps and out on the rocky ledge. The monster's three eyes followed his movements closely. Amby quickly started singing loudly as he ran back and forth in front of the single hand, drawing Grim's full attention.

"I have a lady, lady lay! Who begs at night, her love to stay! Sing long your song, sweet lady Mae! And bid me ride you all the way"

Rider stood over the rocky ledge, waiting for Grim to make one more step up toward his men and make it easy for him to jump down on his big neck. Smiling at Amby's dance and song, Rider knew his plan was working when the intrigued monsters stepped forward for a better view of this strange intruder in front of him. At that moment, Rider dived perfectly across the beast's hairy neck and plunged the first dagger in the big round bulging eye, causing Amby to jumped back gagging. Grim let out a hideous scream and it filled the four corners of the round room. Throwing his head back wildly, Grim tried to free himself of the black figure. Rider kept a tight grip on the beast's hair as it moved in shock around the room. With panic, the monster tried to reach his attacker with his one hand, but his arm proved to short to reach up that high.

Knowing Grim could not reach him, he pulled another dagger from his sash and began cutting across the deformed monster's neck. The piercing screams created loud echoes that penetrated throughout the entire cavern. Its monstrous body was moving wildly, pressing up upon the rock walls, trying to jar off his executioner. Amby and the other three men ran for cover after retrieving Marcia from where Rider had sat her down, fast asleep and unaware of the nightmare they all were facing.

Rider felt the monster growing weak under him as he continued to slash away at his thick neck. Blood bubbled down Grim's face as he fell limply down on his knees. Rider lifted the dagger up and came down with a fast, sharp blow into the back of its neck and with a few more pitiful moans coming from Grim's dreadful mouth, his big body fell into a heap to the floor.

Removing the daggers, the Moon Rider jumped down,

covered with Grim's blood. Amby and the other men rushed over to check on their leader.

"Are you alright, master? You are covered with blood." Amby needed reassurance that the monster had not got to him when they all ran for cover.'

"Tis the monster's blood you see, my friend. I am fine." Rider looked over at the table where the white rose lay, then search the big room for his woman. He took Amby by the arm and jerked him around. "Where is Marcia?"

Chapter Twenty-Four

"You can relax Rider, we moved Marcia to a safe place when you and Grim were waltzing about the ballroom." Amby brushed his fingers through his red hair, feeling relieved that they had just won another big battle. "There just was not any room left on this big ballroom floor for anyone else, so we had to skedaddle."

"I am glad you can jest, friend." Rider's attention fell on his woman, lying just off the big floor and he moved over quickly to scoop her up into his strong arms. He looked down on her beautiful peaceful face as his words came softly. "Now, my darling, the pure rose will make you well and you shall awaken from this death-like sleep." He carried her to the table of twelve stones and laid her down gently. Taking the white rose carefully in his hand, as not to lose a single pedal, Rider lovingly laid it in her hand. Immediately, the red rose vanished when the rose of life took its place.

Marcia opened her eyes slowly and with the strong arms of the masked man assisting her, she sat up and instantly saw the Moon Rider smiling down at her, as though she was dreaming. Seeing the masked man, Marcia closed her eyes tightly, disbelieving what she saw as her words came out softly.

"My eyes surely deceive me. I thought for a moment I saw..." cracking one eye open, Marcia realized that it really was him and without hesitation, she flung her arms around his neck and burst into tears. "It is you! Oh, thank God, it really is you, Rider!"

"Aye, my love. I have come to take you home." Rider's voice came softly in her ears as his arms protectively embraced the woman he loved so much. "Now come, let us leave this place."

Marcia looked around finally at their gruesome surrounding and smelled the musty air as her ears picked up the dripping water all around them. "What horrible place is this, Rider?'

"This is a cavern deep in the ground and the home of the late monster, Grim." As the Rider answered Marcia's question, his friend Amby looked at him with surprise and pointed to his unstained clothes.

"The creature's blood! It is gone! The pure white rose must

have cleansed you when you lifted it and placed it in Marcia's hand!"

"I am certain, what cleansed me from all that blood stain, had to be something pure and good! Whatever has done it, it is well!" Rider helped Marcia up off the stone table as she looked at him with more questions.

"Did you slay this 'Grim', Rider?"

"Aye, I did!" Moon Rider pointed over to the massive corpse of the creature who ruled the round den. "He stood in the way of my retrieving the love rose of life to make you well."

"You did this for me?" Marcia could not take her eyes off the hideous beast lying in a heap across the room. "Forgive my weakness, but I am glad I slept through the big event."

"We cannot blame you mistress Karnstein. We are grown men, warriors that fight to win, but it was even hard for us to watch our brave master jumping down from that ledge yonder" Bolt shook his head as he recalled the terrible fight. "and he dived down on Grim's big hairy neck with only three daggers to do his battle."

Marcia listened wide-eyed as McCormick picked up Rider's heroic battle. "Our leader is not only brave, missy, he is smart and extremely talented at reading his enemy. In the end, the genius only needed two daggers to kill his prey. One through his big bulgy middle eye and the other to cut through the front of his neck and finish him off with one swift blow in the back of its thick ugly neck!"

"And Rider rode that beast wildly around this room as it tried to knock him off by slamming his body against the wall and raring up, shaking his body." The doctor looked up at his leader with admiration "Rider clutched on to Grim's thick hair and road him like he would a wild horse we choose to break!"

"It would appear, you, sir, live up to your image as a true hero." Marcia smiled up into his mysterious, handsome eyes. "I feel honored that you risk your life, as well as your brave men, to rescue me, Rider."

"It comes easy when the one you are saving is worth the risk, my dearest Marcia." The Moon Rider retrieved his sword from Amby and put it safely away before taking her hand. "Now, no more talk. We must leave with haste just in case Hayworth and

Krantz did not become Grim's last meal and is still here trying to find their way out."

"Krantz? Hayworth?" Marcia wrinkled her brow in thought. The last thing she remembered before the face in the stone sent her into the deep sleep, was, those two evil kidnappers had her, along with three rough men, after losing the forth to the ugly green lizard man. She had assumed Rider and his men overpowered Krantz and his group, then somehow learned about the white rose they needed to wake her up. If Krantz and the vicar were still waiting inside the cavern, could they just be waiting on the Moon Rider to join them and continue to the treasure. Hayworth had told her it was the great Moon Rider who gave him all the information about her. Marcia suddenly pulled free from Rider's grip, anger building in her mind.

"You bloody traitor! How dare you touch me! For a moment there, you had me fooled, until I remembered the back stabber you really are!" as Marcia raved, Rider and his men stared at her, completely confused about her wild accusations toward the man who just risk his life saving her. "There is no need to pretend to me any longer! I know all about you!"

"What manner of talk is this, woman? I have come all this distance to save you and yet, you call me a traitor?" Rider pulled her up to face him, looking deeply in her alluring eyes. "Please tell me what it is I was supposed to have done to make you hate me so?"

"Come now, you know well what!" Marcia stormed. "It was you who supplied Vicar Hayworth with the information they needed about me so he could find out who I really was!"

"Just what information are you referring to, Marcia?" Rider gripped her arms. "Tell me Marcia!"

"You told him who I was! It was obvious, Rider! You were the only one who knew my real name!" she narrowed her eyes at him. "Admit it! The only reason you are here is to get your share of that treasure!"

"Damn you, girl!" Rider angrily pulled her up the stone steps. "Sometimes I wonder why I waste my time on you, Marcia Karnstein!"

"But…that is the reason? Is it not?" Marcia mumbled as he

slung his head around and said loudly.

"Nay! That is not the reason!" Rider stopped at the mouth of the big stone. "Amby, take a look and see if all is clear."

"Aye." Amby stepped up beside of Marcia, and smiled. "Tis true, Marcia. You judge the leader falsely. His mission here is to rescue you and head home. Rider is a man of faith and he would never deal with the likes of Hayworth."

"Amby…" Marcia called after him as he rushed off to do Rider's bidding. Slowly, she looked up at the black figure to find his attention was on the open entrance just ahead of them, as though he chose to avoid looking at her. She reached out and gripped his black cape. "Rider, if what you say is true, then how did Hayworth find out my true identity?"

"You should know better than anyone, Marcia, what a varlet he is." Rider's eyes fell down on her and she felt butterflies floating around inside her stomach. "My guess would be from some of my personal papers getting misplaced for a few days and turning up mysteriously on their own, or so I was told. I am sure you can guess who the thief was that 'borrowed' them, read through them thoroughly, then return them, unseen."

"Vicar Hayworth." Marcia looked down, feeling terrible about accusing Rider after he was risking his life, and the men who followed him, just to save her. "How do you suppose he got inside your castle to get his greedy hands on them? Your place is guarded well. Spies, you think?"

"I can guarantee, there are no spies under my roof, my lady. All there, including the home staff are true and loyal. Hayworth paid me a visit one evening last week. He told me he had come up with some great ideas for the children's home project. One such idea was to permit Father Bellingham to assist him with the planning and programs but finding the right people to oversee the orphanage itself would be solely his decision." I, along with the others present, thought something seemed funny about his ideal, like the man was really not serious about his own statement. I know now he was waiting for his opportunity to go through my personal file and he did so when we were mysterious called away by another visitor, who simply road off when arrived at the gate." Rider remembered back. "I sent a couple of men after him to find out who he was and what he wanted. When the men returned, they informed me the gentleman was a stranger to the area and gotten turned around when he came up on the huge castle. Seeing us approach he grew nervous and decided to return without directions. All assumed it was because of my mysterious appearance, wearing the mask and black outfit." Rider noticed Amby motioning them forward at the opening and waved back at his signal. "All is clear. Let us get out of here."

Marcia took his hand back, squeezing it softly as she said. "Rider? Thank you for coming after me. I was about to lose all hope, thinking I must face some horrible death here."

"Marcia" his fingers ran along her cheeks. "You will never die on this God forsaken island as long as I am alive. It grows late and the island is no place to wonder around in the dark. So, tonight, where we camp, your love is mine. But for now, we move with haste to find safer grounds to pitch our tent."

The small group moved quickly from the large stone opening at the other in, opposite the face of wisdom, where they left Arabella and Bernard tied up and as though guided by a single moonbeam, they found safe ground to set up their camp as the island grew covered in darkness. The only light seen for miles, seemed to be the single moonbeam that kept its constant glow down over their camp.

Chapter Twenty-Five

Marcia stared up at the distant stars and was intrigued by the one bright star that shone overhead, making her feel safe. Or, maybe it was the fact that she was with the Moon Rider that made her feel at ease in her surroundings. Marcia turned to see him speaking to his small group of men and she assumed they were making plans for the following day. Turning her attention back to the stars, her thoughts drifted to Agar. Why had not he come after her, even join forces with Rider? Marcia looked over at the man who helped the young priest every time she was with him. She knew they were the best of friends and Agar trusted him completely. Watching Amby's red hair blowing in the night wind, she smiled and made herself a mental note as she thought. "I will ask Amby tomorrow when the chance arises."

"Oh, Agar." Marcia whispered to herself. "How I long to see him and feel his arms around me. Yet" she turned to gazed upon the handsome dark figure towering up over his trusted men. "I was overjoyed to see his wonderful hidden face. When Rider put his arms around me, I felt so warm and protected." She admired the man who claim to love her so deeply he would risk everything to save her. Marcia could feel her heart beating with total love. How strong and manly he was. It did not really matter to her that she had never seen his face. It is the person inside one falls in love with, that what Lizzie had always taught her.

"Lizzie, dear old Lizzie." A tear ran down Marcia's face as she recalled overhearing the conversation between Hayworth and Krantz about Lizzie's real state. The vicar had convinced her that they did not kill her old nurse, just tie her up so she could not go for help. After Krantz pulled his partner to one side and ordered an explanation for leaving anyone alive to give them away, the lying vicar assured his crooked partner he had indeed saw that the fat bitch was beaten to death before they left. Tears ran down Marcia's beautiful face, grieving the only person she had ever truly felt close to.

Marcia was so caught up in her thoughts that she did not see the dark figure standing over her. He kneeled down and turned her head toward him. Rider immediately noticed that she was crying and he swept her up in his arms.

"Marcia, darling, what is wrong?" his voice was tender and filled with soothing love.

Marcia buried her face in his strong chest as she wept. "Oh, Rider, it is all my fault. If I had not wanted to leave Melbourne, Lizzie would still be alive. Poor, sweet, dear trusting Lizzie."

"Marcia, love" Rider lifted her head up and wiped the tears away with the brush of his fingers. "do not weep, your Lizzie is not dead. She is well and very much alive in Canterbury."

Marcia came quickly to her knees and wrapped her arms around his neck. "Please, say this thing you speak is indeed true, that my adorable nurse is well and alive!"

"Aye, my love. Elizabet was very much alive when last I saw her." Rider laughed along with Marcia. "Tell me, fair maiden, has anyone ever told you how beautiful you are when laughter fills your face?"

"Aye, my father and Lizzie, who states: your frown looks far better turned upside down." Marcia hugged him tightly as she declared. "I love you, dearest Rider! I can never thank you enough for sharing with me this most wonderful, joyful news!"

"And, if some other man had told you, would he have your confession of love?" Rider's hand ran along the back of her neck as he smiled down into her happy face.

"Aye, but I would word it differently." Marcia brushed her lips over his. With passion, Rider drew her in his arms and kissed her, slipping his hand down her dress to claim a perfect firm breast. Marcia's breathing fell heavily on his ear as she whispered. "My love, will not your men make a show of us?"

"Nay, my love. For they have, by my orders, moved themselves inside the tent on the other side of the big rock." The masked man gently undone her bodice as his words flowed from behind the mask. "You are everything to me, Marcia." His lips brushed down her neck. "I love you, Marica. Love you, love you, love you." He repeated over softly as his hands brushed down over her belly, his lips leaving fiery kisses all over her as his sporting continued.

Marcia gripped his back with her fingers as the Rider's naked body moved on top of her. Desire swept through her body as he slid inside her. Within the sweet hush of the mystic night, Rider knew Marcia again.

Dawn fell softly on the quiet grey mountaintops as the wind blew soft fragrant breezes across the island. Hearing an unusual jungle bird call out, Marcia forced her tired eyes open and smiled down at the sleeping form next to her. At some time during the night, Rider had carried her inside his tent for the night. What a joy he had given her the night before and she knew how exhausted he must be from all the fighting that had occurred during the day. Such love and affection that had passed so beautifully between them, brought out her beautiful smile.

She sat up, her thoughts turning to more mundane matters. Marcia felt certain that if she did not find a solitary place where she could relieve herself, her bladder would surely burst. Slowly turning back her side of the covers, she climbed quietly up off the matt on which they lay and gathered up her clothes in her hands. Moving very carefully, so as not to disturb Rider, Marcia made her way into a small grove of trees to relieve herself before getting dressed.

She let out a breath of relief, then to her happy surprise, Marcia's ears caught a familiar sound: Water, rippling over stones. She laughed softly, knowing she was the only one in her party of all men, that was up and awake. Still giggling, she followed the nearby sound.

"A brook! What a lovely idea! I could use a cool bath, even without fine soap!" she continued to move toward the refreshing sound until she spotted the little brook just beyond the trees and to her happy surprise, a gentle waterfall. Marcia gazed out over the clear water and how it ran freely over the smooth rocks lying just below, lining the bottom of the shallow water. "This is a lovely spot for a refreshing bath." She looked around to make sure that no one had followed her before she dropped her clothes on the ground and slid down into the cool water, scooping up a handful to drink.

Marcia knew she could not stay away from the others for long or Rider would grow upset and have his men track her down. One last dip, she climbed out and waited a few moments for the morning's warm sun to dry her body enough to get her clothes back on. Within minutes, Marcia climbed back inside her dress and turned to start back to the camp. She had reached the trees where she had first heard the water, when she thought she heard a limb crack, somewhere close by and stopped quickly to listen. Had her ears started to play tricks on her or did she actually hear footsteps behind her? Before she had time to turn around and find out, a hand clasp over her mouth, startling her.

"So, we meet again, mistress Karnstein." Hayworth jerked her around. "It was not very nice of you leaving us like you did, when you know how much we need you."

"Hayworth, stop gabbing and bring Marcia over here!" Krantz tied a piece of cloth around her mouth and another one around her hands. "I see you cannot be trusted to walk freely, my dear. Now, that we have you, we shall find that damn treasure! I do not fancy staying another sleepless night in the hell of a place!"

Marcia tried to pull herself free from Krantz's grip, but he laughed softly and started pulling her through the tense forest with him.

Amby slapped Rider on his shoulder. "Wake up, Rider! Marcia is gone!"

"Gone!" Rider's dark eyes stared up from his mask, then he scrambled to his feet and quickly got dressed. "Where the devil did that woman go? Does she not know, this is no place to go prancing about?"

"Merciton and I have looked all around for her. She is to be found nowhere."

Rider hurried out the tent and quickly spotted Marcia's footprints and followed them until he came to the grove of trees.

"She relieved herself here." He pointed to a wet spot drying on the ground then noticed her steps followed the running water. "She went for a bath and…" his attention fell to the scuffle of footprints where her kidnappers grabbed her. "Bloody hell! They have got her again!"

Amby stared down at the mess of footprints and scratched his head as he asked. "How many were there?"

"Two came after her! My guess would be Krantz and Hayworth! They left the rest behind with that bitch, Arabella!" His eyes grew dark as he checked for their retreat. "I suppose they finally found their way back to the main entrance where we left their party all tied up and found out who had taken her."

Rider's sharp eyes caught their tracks moving swiftly through the tense forest, where they had made their silent escape.

"Amby, get the things quickly together. We move with haste! There is no time to lose!"

"Aye, master!" Amby shook his head, the dread thought of meeting up with other monsters instead of heading back to the safety of Rider's ship, the Moon Shadow. "I thought for sure that three-eyed Grim had taken care of them for us."

"Well, it is obvious he did not! Now, make ready to depart, immediately!"

Hayworth ripped the cloth from Marcia's mouth when they reached the spot where Arabella, Bernard, and the other three men waited for them. Arabella stood up and brushed off her wrinkled dress.

"It is about time! Let's get that damn treasure and get the hell out of here!" she rubbed her arms briskly with her fingers, to brush away her jitters. "This place is giving me nightmares!"

"I like it no better, dear sister." Krantz said sarcastically as his attention went to Marcia. "It was not easy getting this little damsel away from the Moon Rider."

"Well, I am quite certain that there was no sword fighting between you." Arabella laughed mockingly. "If you had, I am sure he would still have her!"

"We never had to exchange our sword fighting skills, my dear. Marcia decided to take a bath while the Rider and his men slept and that was to our advantage." Hayworth chuckled softly, as his eyes scanned Marcia's body. "Besides not having to match wits with that mask knight, we were treated to a very interesting spectacle."

"Why, you, contemptuous haughty hawk! Some bloody nerve you have! Taking advantage to stare at a lady having a bath!"

Marcia's eyes shot fire "Rider will take you both and cut you into tiny threads!"

"He shall never get that chance! He must have been tired after killing that den monster then making love to you, I am guessing into the wee hours of the morning. Too bad we only arrived this morning and missed all the sporting between the both of you." His knowing smile chill her bones as he chuckled, remembering watching the shapely woman stepping down into the cool stream. "But then, Krantz and I were treated to seeing you in your birthday suit. Quite the looker!" On a dime, the vicar's mood changed as he grabbed her wrist and ordered. "Let us go! We have not any time to lose! Once that wolf has our scent, he will not stop until he has found us!"

"Aye, and who chickened out of steaking inside his tent and killing our foe! Too late now! Let us make haste!" Krantz moved up quickly behind Hayworth and Marcia. He forced his way between them and grabbed Marcia's hand from him. "Just remember Hayworth, Marcia is my territory! She goes with me!"

"Krantz darling!" Arabella ran up beside him, her lip pouting. "Let the vicar bring Marcia! You can take my hand and walk with me."

"Arabella, you are on your own while we are here, or have you forgotten the reason I agreed for you to tag along?" Krantz pushed his sister behind him. "Walk with Hayworth, if he will have you! Just stay away from me before I leave you sitting here!"

"Krantz, Arabella is your sister! I think you owe her better respect!" Marcia never like to see men bully the fairer sex, just because they thought they were dominant. "If not because she is your sister, but because, despite her behavior toward me, she is a lady and should be treated as such!"

"Listen to my precious Marcia defending her arch enemy. I do believe a good Christian girl is turning the other cheek and helping the lost sheep." Hayworth took Arabella by the hand as she continued to stare at the woman she had been treating poorly for days. She sincerely was taking up for her, knowing Krantz felt like slapping her across the mouth. She had seen the look he was giving Marcia as she pleaded her case. To her relief, Krantz simply said.

"Stay out of my family fights, Marcia! What I do or do not do, is strictly my business!" Krantz squeezed her hand. "Now refrain from speaking unless you see, feel, or ear something you need to share with us!"

Hayworth looked up at Krantz, holding Marcia's hand and he felt his anger building, as he pulled Arabella passed the couple ahead, mumbling to himself. Arabella regained her old attitude when she noticed as she walked past her brother, his eyes were wondering down Marcia's dress, a smile on his wicked lips. She whipped her head around to confront him, her temper boiling with jealousy.

"She really has put the poisonous bite on you, has she not, little brother?"

"Knock it off, Arabella and turn around! This is not the time for you to get one of your suspicious tantrums!" Krantz spoke coldly. "Stop thinking every woman I look at is your arrival! Now, stop being so damn watchful of me!"

"I have seen the way you have been looking at her!" Arabella's voice took on a high pitch. "Like that day on the ship! I know what would have happened if I had not come into your cabin! You want her, do you not, Krantz?"

"So, what if I do!" he smiled mockingly back at her angry stare. He shook his head in aggravation, pushed her back around and continued pushing them forward with his wide fast steps. His voice rang in his sister's ears. "Marcia is a challenge, not some little whore who throws herself at me!"

"What?" Arabella slung her whole body around as the vicar struggled to pull her with him. She could feel her face burning red with embarrassment. "Krantz, you dirty rat! See how easy you can get your way with me from now on! You, lousy bloody bastard!"

"The bastard brother of a lustful overbearing sister!" he threw back in her face.

"Would you two cease the constant bickering!" Hayworth, having enough of the sick talk, stopped and turned around to face brother and sister. "Both of you act just like children! All this useless bickering back and forth, is nerve racking and airing out your dirty sex games is in very poor taste! If you were not already headed there, I would say you might be headed for hell by your behavior!" the vicar pointed out the jungle birds, scattering and making loud sounds from their yelling. "Not to mention that you are broadcasting our whereabouts through the air!"

"Then, tell the bitch to leave me alone! Keep her going straight and looking forward! I wish to God we had never brought her with us!" Krantz gritted his teeth as he kicked at a rock. "Why did we not let her walk up that hill she insisted we send someone? We could have used our man rather than her big mouth!"

"She is your sister Krantz! You chose to bring her on this voyage, so she is your problem, not mine!" Hayworth looked over at Arabella. "I am warning you, little girl, any more trouble out of you and we dump you! Understand?"

"I understand Vicar Hayworth." She gave her brother one last strong look, then took the vicar's arm and smiled up at him. "What are we waiting for? Let us find that bloody gold."

"That is the spirit! Aye, now that is more like it!" the vicar laughed and pushed his way through the bush.

They had walked for a few miles then noticed up ahead the path forked off in four different directions. Hayworth studied its formation for several moments before turning to Marcia.

"Alright girl, which is the right path we need to take?"

"How should I know! Just like you, I have never seen this island before, so it's all new to me as well. I know no more than either of you." Marcia stared at him coldly. "It looks like you will have to choose one for yourself."

"That could prove fatal for all of us, Marcia. I am certain you shall see a sign to show us which path to take!" Hayworth pulled her in front of him. "Now, start looking, little lady."

Marcia stared out at the four separate paths. A cold wind kissed her face as she heard a distant hum. Suddenly her body grew cold as she fixed her eyes upon a light blue mist that floated toward her. Within seconds, the mist swirled in front of her like a small whirlwind until it formed itself into a transparent figure. A blue woman with a soft beauty unmatched by a human female. The enchanted beauty spoke softly to Marcia and her magic words flowed from her red lips in rainbow colors.

"I am the keeper of the four paths of truth. No one can see or hear me but you, innocent child."

Marcia tried to speak but her words remained frozen on her lips. The mystic vision smiled.

"Do not try to speak, dear one. Just listen to the words I say." A blue arm lifted to point down each path in turn, her long blue sleeves billowing in the breeze. "Before those who seek the treasure of gold, they must walk down each path with secrets untold. Down each path lies obstacles to hinder the way, their greed will drive them, but they must not stray." The misty figure lifted her arms, her sleeves blowing out gently. "Dear child, if they should reach the last paths end, then greater dangers will be upon you instead of them. Your only hope to survive this day, lies in him who follows, for there are no obstacles too big when love rules the heart!" The blue mist figure stepped closer to Marcia and sprinkled her with blue dust. "This magic dust shall carry you safely through three of the paths, but sure death to those that are careless.

The first path contains the serpent heads. Heads without a body can be even more poisonous when they bite. The second path is strung with fiery holes that can swallow up a man whose footsteps are unsure. The third, great darkness to hide the eyes, the blood red eyes of the reptile men." The beautiful face grew solemn as she reached out toward Marcia, speaking slowly.

"The fourth and last path is the worst of all, for the great blue-green dragon lies beyond the wall. A wall of stone that guard the treasure of pure gold. Standing before it sordid and bold, cunning and strong, lives the one who rules the Island of Mist or Mystic Island, some have called. The great dragon knows no fear and woe to the maiden who drawth near. All his life he sits and waits, for years untold, his appetite growing for a Karnstein damsel for exchange of gold."

Fear running through her veins, Marcia could not control her tears as she thought. "Is there no chance for me? Or will my life end at the hand of a dragon?"

"There is hope! There is love! A love which cometh from God above. Be not afraid, fair maiden, for I will wait invisible at this gate and warn your enchanting young knight, whose heart is true and pure."

Knowing the keeper of the paths can hear her thoughts, Marcia looked into the blue mist and smiled, thinking. "Thank you, warm loving keeper of the four paths."

"My heart goes with you, fair maiden. Tell not what waits on all the paths to these evil ones who lust for gold and you may not have to face the great dragon if they fail to make it to the fourth path." The blue mist twirled once again in front of Marcia, filling her with a gentle peace, then disappeared from her sight. She felt a heavy hand shaking her and she turned to face Hayworth.

"You saw the answer, did you not?"

"Aye, I have seen." Marcia pointed down the left path, the path going east. "We must take each path until we reach the path of gold. That is what the keeper of the path has told me."

"You had better not be lying to us, Marcia!" Hayworth pushed her forward. "Are you absolutely sure we must take all four paths? Would not that be a lot of backtracking to get here to the beginning?"

"Nay! The way the keeper described them, one leads to the other. Why do you not look upon the map you stole from my father. Has it not got a fork beyond the three turns?"

Krantz pulled out the map and studied it briefly, then nodded. "I wondered about those strange markings before. Now, they make perfect sense. The paths just run right into each other, creating the three turns."

"I have not noticed you using the map very often, Krantz." Marcia mocked "If something is worth having, then it is usually worth the trouble of finding and stealing it. Direction, is that not why people need maps?"

"Aye, quite right. You are a pretty remarkable woman, Marcia." Krantz took her hand. "Shall we go together and see what the first path has in store?"

"Aye, Krantz. I am sure if what we have witness so far on this island, could be an indication to what lies ahead, we should be in for one exciting adventure." Marcia smiled slyly and began humming down the path as Krantz ask her.

"Why are you humming? Do you know something you might like to share?"

"Not really Krantz. I hum whenever I am nervous of the unknown and this part of the jungle looks so…" Marcia shivered. "so snaky, don't you think?"

"Did you have to mention snakes? I forgot my boots!"

Arabella looked nervously around as Krantz's laughed.

"Not to worry, Marcia. I will not let anything happen to you."
She looked straight ahead, and said,

"Of course not. Then you would not have your Karnstein maiden to get all that rotten gold!"

Chapter Twenty-Six

The group slowed their pace as the underbrush made it more difficult to walk. Marcia knew what to expect any time now, and although she knew she was safe from the deadly heads, the very thought of them gave her the real shivers. She cleared her throat to break through the silence and her train of dreadful thoughts. Glancing up at Krantz, who was casing out the area, she asked.

"Tell me fellows, what happened to you back there in that cavern?"

"Now, that is quite a story!" Arabella laughed, recalling their frightening experience. "The whole thing is really humorous."

"Stop it, Arabella!" Krantz narrowed his eyes at his sister. "If you do not mind, my dearest Marcia, I would just as soon forget that little incident."

"Aye, I just bet you would, you, coward!" Arabella laughed mockingly "Do you know what four great big strong men did in that cavern? Would you like to hear?"

"Aye." Marcia turned to face Arabella who was walking near her. "It might help take my mind off this gruesome place. What happen?"

"The fearless group made their way through the musty cavern and eventually found the round, room, just as old stone face had said. They could see the white rose lying on the table in the center of the huge room and were about to run out and get it when they heard this huge noise." Arabella giggled, recalling how one of the brave men told her their experience after she had begged him to share what happen with her and Bernard. "Well, they knew they had to get that rose or else little bitty you would never wake up. Big brave Krantz decided he would be the one to make the big sacrifice."

Marcia smiled up at his blushing face. "Did you do that, just for me, Krantz? How heroic."

"Oh indeed, so brave and heroic. When he finally reached the white rose, it would not budge for him. He pulled and tugged, but all he got was lots of scratches from the attacking thorns."

172

Arabella bent over laughing. "That is when all the fun begun. I am really sorry I was not there to see it for myself!"

"There was nothing funny about a big ugly monster with three eyes coming towards you with the intention of eating you!" Krantz stared at his sister, hate raging in his eyes. "Anyone in their right mind, would have been scared!" His attention went to the soldier who told his sister about their adventure. "You louse, I told you not to tell that bitch anything!"

"Poor brother, scared he was, when he started crying and screaming for help. He should have known with his group of cowards, he was on his on." Arabella pointed to the vicar and laughed out. "Mr. Wizard kept yelling for him to get the rose!"

"That is all he cared about! That damn white rose!" Krantz stormed out at Hayworth. "He could have cared less if I became old Grim's next meal!"

"Look, Krantz, you got out. What are complaining about?" Hayworth mumbled, more concerned over what the path had hidden. "If the shoe were on the other foot, I am certain you would have not lifted a finger to help me."

"Well, Marcia, as I was telling you, the stupid group got lost in the passageways and could not find their way out until after dark. They came stumbling back, blaming each other for getting lost. Is that not funny?" Arabella stopped suddenly when she heard a piercing cry behind her.

They all turned around to see one of Krantz's men shaking his arm violently, trying to knock off three attached heads that clung tight with their teeth. Within seconds, they could hear hissing all around them and the morbid sound grew louder until it became deafening to their ears. Arabella began screaming as she threw herself in her brother's arms. He gave her a push backward then grabbed Marcia's arm.

"Let us get the hell out of here!" making out the path, Krantz turned and started to run when the man attacked pleaded for help.

"Please, do not leave me!" he yelled when he felt himself falling to the covered ground. Snake heads dived from the heavy grass all over his face and neck. The man's screams tore above that of the hissing snakes until finally they died away.

Hayworth stared wildly at the jumping heads around them,

their forked tongues shooting in and out and their strange un-natural teeth protruding from the mouth. "Let us move!" Their feet moved swiftly along the path. Arabella let out a horrified scream.

"I have been bitten!" They turned to see Arabella shaking her hand, trying to rid herself of the ugly head. She looked up pleading. "Please, somebody, help me!"

Marcia could not take the cold neglect that all the men were showing the frighten young woman. She jerked herself free from Krantz and ran back to Arabella. Clamping her teeth together to help calm her nerves, Marcia took a firm hold on the head and pulled it free. She quickly threw it down and stomped it under her foot. The hissing immediately stopped and the end of the path became visible.

Arabella took a relieved breath as she whispered, "Thank God!" her face grew distorted as she felt the sharp pain run through her red hand. She looked at Marcia, tears running down her face. "Please, do something. My hand is in terrible pain!"

Marcia stared over at Krantz, who was busy checking the map. She grabbed his arm and spoke angrily. "Help her Krantz! She is your sister! I know you brought medicines and ointments in case someone got hurt!"

"Help her? How, may I help cure a snake bite I know knowing about?" His words came cold and by his dull expression, Krantz was clearly not interested in his sister trouble.

"You have a knife! Cut open the snake bite and suck out the deadly poison before it kills her!"

Krantz only sneered at Marcia. "After what she has said about me? She deserves to die!"

"You, vindictive bastard!" Marcia stared over at the vicar angrily as he talked casually with the other men. "Either you do it, Hayworth, or give me your knife now!" Marcia heard Arabella panting for breath. "But, for God sakes, do whatever you are going to do now, vicar?"

Hayworth pulled the knife from his pocket and walked over to the two women. He smiled down at Marcia as he cut through the already swollen hand. Marcia quickly lifted her hand and sucked out the poison. Arabella watched as Marcia spit out the deadly liquid and ripped off the end of her petticoat to die around her hand.

"How…how can I ever thank you enough, Marcia?"

"You just did." Marcia squeezed Arabella's good hand and smiled. Krantz jerked Marcia's arm around.

"How touching, the both of you becoming friends. Tis bad it will be a short friendship!" He smiled. "Let us move on, and Marcia, if you know anything about what lies beyond this path, you had better tell us if you want your new friend to survive."

"I told you Krantz, I know naught!" Marcia spit out, hoping the overbearing man would be the one to fall in one of the fiery holes.

"Alright, but you had better be telling the truth because you are leading the way!" Krantz gave her a push down the second path and the others reluctantly followed.

"The tracks end here! Now what?" Amby looked at the four paths, going north, south, east, and west. "How do we know which to take since there appear to be no tracks going down either?"

"Look around and see if they left any clues. A dropped object, perhaps." Rider scanned the ground around them, trying to find anything to lead them on. "There is naught to be found. It is as you have said, my friend. Their tracks just seemed to stop here. We must wait for a sign."

"A sign? Suppose there is no sign, Rider. There is no speaking mountain around. Just four empty paths leading to God knows what." Amby looked around in discuss. "He who waits for fate to move can become stale with age."

"Do not be so down, my friend. This is no ordinary place, remember?" Rider walked over and gazed down one of the long paths. "He who has patience usually wins the race."

"Usually wins the race, that is not saying 'always', besides…" the red headed mate caught sight of the blue cloud dust floating toward them in a humming wind. "Rider, are you seeing what I am?"

"Aye." Rider watched the whirlwind of blue mist swirl in front of them. "It must be the messenger we wait for."

The mist formed once again into the beautiful blue maiden, her arms waving in welcome.

"I have stood in wait for you, young knight. Listen, and take heed to what I have to say."

Amby lend over to his friend and whispered. "Not so bad looking for vapor, aye master? Perhaps, just a little on the blue side."

"Stay still, Amby, before you hurt her feelings and she changes her mine about helping us." Rider flashed a handsome smile for the vision before them. "Please tell us what we must do to find Marcia Karnstein."

"I am the keeper of the four paths. I know each path well so please pay close attention to my words. Each path you go down is ruled by some vile serpent. Beware them all!" the keeper pointed to the first path. "The east path is the first to tread. What lies hidden in the tall under grass are the serpent heads, deadly and looking for a prey to bite. They lie in wait, unseen before it is to late. They find it easy to hide in the tall grass because they do not have a body. Do not pause to listen to the loud hissing call, for it will paralyze your movements. If you can avoid stopping to look, they will not bite you at all."

Amby punched Rider's arm and mumbled. "In other words, if we hang around and pay the heads a little visit, the evil residence will put the bite on us!"

"Amby, if you do not keep quiet, I am going to put the bite on you, myself." Rider spoke from the corner of his mouth, then nodded a positive with his head. "We understand, wise keeper, continue."

"The second path going west, is the path of fiery holes. This path is very tricky and may betray the eye. There is one way and one way only to make it out safely. Focus on the middle and walk straight. A line you shall see, a line of blue to guide you where you might hesitate by what you see, but do not let your eye betray your faith and keep straight with the line made by me, for it will help guide thee."

"I understand. What we can see is not always real. Just keep our eyes on the blue line, straight in the middle." Rider nodded his head. "Please continue."

"The third path, that which is north, is home for the reptile men. Their bodies are that of a standing snake, their heads are oversized and eyes like a human. Make ready your swords, for that is their weapon. With scaly strong arms and sharp pointed fingers and toes, the reptile man can grip his sword and swing to kill." The lady of mist stepped closer to give a warning. "Now, this is very important, so listen carefully. If one of their swords strike you and even if you bleed and feel severe pain, it is just your imagination. Beware, if you give in to it, you shall surely die."

"Imagination. A rare un-explained occurrence that seems real but it fact, is not! Aye, I understand." Rider looked thoughtful, worry mounting for the woman he loved. "Tell me, what does the last path hold in store?"

"I am afraid the other three paths will seem simple compared to the last." The keeper of the path said sorrowful.

"Seems simple? I almost hate to hear it!" Amby forced out a weak laugh. "One cannot say, this trip has been boring."

"At least, I can truthfully say, my men are earning their pay this go-around!" Rider winked at his longtime friend. "Now, get quiet and listen."

The keeper of the four paths seemed to smile, listening to the two friends, then regained her serious expression. "The south path itself has nothing in store. It is what lives at the end, a dragon named Gore. The dragon is sneaky clever, a giant with three heads. Its long teeth and claws will tear men to shreds. Karnstein blood is what he lusted for, a maiden, poor Marcia, next victim of Gore."

"There must be something I can do to save her!" Rider pleaded.

"Is thy love true?" the blue keeper stared upon the Moon Rider, standing tall and strong above his loyal men.

"Aye! There is no love greater than the love I hold for Marcia. I have asked her to be my wife!" Rider's words were soft and true. "I will do anything to save my love's life, even if it should mean losing my own."

"Thy love is indeed true, young Rider. I will tell you what to do." She raised her blue arms high above her head, the sleeves billowing gently in the breeze. "If things look grim, I shall stall for time, but you must be fast what ere you do, and find the golden tablet of love. Gore guards it closely, it's always in his sight so it should not be hard to spot. His robust presence is easy to see and the golden tablet is a good twelve-inch square. But, when the stone touches your hand, grab on to your lady and run with haste! All

177

who are with you must flea off the land, for its time has reversed and is ticking away. For as soon as the tablet has been set free, my power will increase. I shall put an end to this horror and this island will 'decease'!

"That means, when I grab the golden tablet, we will be running out of time. We must find our way back to the ship and we shall have to go back down each of the four paths, through the forest, to the mountain and continued to retrace our steps until we wind up on the beach."

"Be at peace, beloved. I would not leave you without a way out!" the keeper said softly. "After you have safely escaped this evil place, it will be destroyed completely."

"But, what about you and the face in the stone? Neither of you deserve to perish with those things that are evil in the sight of God." Rider grieved to think that these two must lose their existence if he and his men could win. "Is there no other way, good keeper of the paths?"

"You have a kind and generous heart, Moon Rider. Be at peace and know, the destruction of the island cannot destroy me or the face in the stone. No more than the destruction of Sodom and Gamora had in taking the angels sent by God! We shall return to the land of bright gold, called Eternity!" The blue figure began to turn back to mist as it whispered. "Remember, all that I have told you. Go now with God!" The mist vanished in whirlwind and all that remain were five startled men.

"Come, my friends, we have no time to lose! Watched where you step and remember, no stopping to hear the hissing concert! We have got a job to do!" Rider led the way into the first path.

Chapter Twenty-Seven

"What…what are they?" Arabella's voice shook as she stared in disbelief at the ground before them, puffing green smoke up into their faces. Fires crackled in the holes surrounding the small group. The frightened young woman gripped Marcia's arm and drew in closer to her. "That horrible smell! My God, Krantz, this has got to be hell! Let us turn back before we all are consumed."

"Shut up, Arabella! I told you to keep your damn mouth shut! Now, stop your useless wining!" he looked nervously at the fires, shooting up out of their deadly traps.

"Aye, your brother is right, missy! Remember we said we would dump you if you started to give us trouble?" Hayworth gave the girl a satanic wicked smiled as he added. "I cannot think of a better place to throw you than right here!"

Arabella burst into tears and Marcia reached back and took her hand, then whispered. "Arabella, just stay with me and you shall be alright."

"Let us go!" Krantz started through the smoke. It stung his eyes and made seeing the path difficult, so he waved one of his men up. "Carter, move ahead and find a way out of this hell hole!"

"Why me, sir? I am no tracker!" the nervous man began to back away, shaking his head. "You want me to go first! If I fall…then you will know…the way is wrong!"

Carter started to run to the back when Hayworth grabbed him around the neck, where he held his sharp dagger. "Carter, you heard Krantz give you an order! Move!"

Carter made his way slowly up the smoky path and found himself surrounded by fiery holes, flames lapping at his feet. His eyes froze to the large smoking hole directly in front of him, in the middle of the path. His feet stood only inches away from the fiery gaping furnace. Carter tried to speak up, but his words came out in a tremble.

"Sir, there is a big hole right in the middle of the path. We must go around it and the ground on the side appears solid."

"Then go around the damn thing, Carter!" Krantz yelled as he tried to see his man through the tense smoke. "I said, move your sorry ass, Carter! Now!"

Carter moved slowly off the path, keeping his eyes on the large hole in the middle. Thinking the ground was solid, Carter stepped forward and fell head on into the fiery pit below him. A loud yell ripped from the man's throat as the flames sucked him under, Then, there was silence.

"My God! He fell into one of the fiery holes!" Marcia screamed. "I cannot take this anymore!" she started running straight down the path, staying in the middle. With the blue dust protecting her, the path was the safest way to get out. Arabella ran with her, still clutching her hand.

"Hayworth stared over at Krantz. "Did you see that? The path must be a trick to the eye and that giant hole we see in the middle is really not there! The middle must be the only safe way out of here!"

"Aye, but…" Krantz stared down into the fiery pit, flames reaching up to claim them. "It looks so bloody real!"

"There are many things on this mysterious island I cannot explain, Krantz! But it only makes sense! Carter stepped over there on what looks like solid ground, even now, and we both watched him fall through!" Hayworth got up next to the leader. "Marcia and your sister ran right over that hole! You witness it too!"

"Then, you go first Hayworth!" Krantz moved behind him carefully, as not to get off the path.

"Like I said, I would not call this island a normal place." The vicar took a step forward and the elusion disappeared. He turned around and laughed out. "See! What did I tell you? Completely fake! Let us move! Time is ticking on and who knows if that Moon Rider has picked up our trail or not."

"Well, when the great and mighty warrior arrives at the four paths, he will be on his on! We have Marcia!" Krantz quickly followed behind the vicar and the remaining men ran frantically to catch up with their leader.

The hissing sound rose around Rider and his band of warriors. Without hesitation, their legs carried them quickly through the high grass as the ear-piercing sound grew louder. Their fearless leader called over his shoulder as he continued to run.

"No matter what you do, men, DO NOT STOP! Cover your ears with your hands and just keep running!"

Within minutes the hissing noise stopped and the end of the path came into view. Amby shook his head free of the hissing echoes.

"That neighborhood was a bit noisy for my liking. I do not think I would like living in that grasses area!"

"Aye, England will look good to the eye. Let us hurry and get out task over with so we can sail back to friendlier waters." Rider moved quickly down the second path.

The silent group ahead on the third path walked with caution along the overgrown path. The trees hung heavy on this part of the island and heavy moss hung down the massive limbs, cascading almost to the grassy ground below. Again, no jungle birds could be heard down the dreary path and the thick canopy overhead kept the sunlight from shining through. The deeper they walked in the forest, the darker it became. Arabella moved even closer to Marcia, her body shivering uncontrollable. She whispered, not wishing her brother or the evil vicar to hear her.

"Marcia, we are going to die, I just know it."

"You must not think like that, Arabella. There is hope we can all survive this nightmare. There is always hope!" Marcia's voice came soothing and comforting to the weary girl.

"There is no hope for me, Marcia." Arabella wiped the tears from her face, and suddenly stopped, freezing in her footsteps. An eerie cry was coming out of the dark forest and Arabella's first reaction was to scream and cover her ears. "What is it?"

"Hell, if I know!" Krantz strained his eyes to make out any movement coming from the horrible noise. "It sounds like some sort of demon!"

Chills ran down Marcia's back, remembering the words of the keeper of the paths. She let out a gasp when she saw shadows moving all around them. Slowly their forms became visible to the frightened group. They had arms and legs like a man, but a heavy tail swung loose at their back. Their skin resembled that of a crocodile and their oversize head looked like a snake, with the eyes of a human. Sharp black claws clung tightly to bright shiny swords as they circled their prey. The irritating noise they had heard, gurgled from their oval shape mouth.

"Bernard, Hayworth! Draw your swords! We must fight them or they will slay all of us!" Krantz gripped his sword nervously. "Then the first chance we see, we must make a run for it!"

"Such horrible monsters! We shall never escape them! How can we make it out alive!" Arabella screamed as they drew nearer.

"Marcia, keep that bitch quiet or I will!" Krantz yelled, as he made ready his sword.

Marcia gently put her arm around the frightened girl and spoke softly. "Arabella, listen to me. Just stay with me and those reptile men cannot harm you. I have been sprinkled with a dust shield to help me safely through the first three paths."

"And…those creatures cannot harm anyone who touches you?" Arabella smiled hopefully through her tears. "So, if you make it, I make it! Marcia, then we must turn back and not go to the forth path. I have learned whom I can truly trust and it is not my selfish brother. Losing a true friend like you is not worth all the gold in the world."

Marcia smiled, happy at last to have won Arabella over. Not only on her side, but on the side of good, but Krantz's smile was for something far more sinister,

"How lucky for me." He thought, after overhearing the conversation between Marcia and his sister. His smirk went to the vicar, fear dripping down his face as he held his sword in his shaky sweaty palms, "Too bad you did not hear Marcia's good news for safe passage. Now the beautiful treasure will be all mine and I will not need to share it with anyone." Krantz grabbed Marcia's arm as she and his sister were about to sneak back down the path.

"Going somewhere ladies?" he smiled mockingly. "Not just yet. I want to see Hayworth wallow in his own blood. It would appear he is not the only one to read or hear signs."

"You heard our conversation?" Marcia looked down at her wrist and it was obvious from his tight grip he had no intention of letting it go. "You bloody freak! You do not give a damn about anyone but yourself!"

"That is right, sweetheart. Krantz comes first, now and always!" he laughed out as the reptile men passed them by and surrounded Bernard, Hayworth. Krantz called out "Aye! Kill them! Kill them both!"

"Krantz, are you mad! Get back down here and help us, you fool!" Hayworth yelled as he tried to fight off the ugly invaders with his sword.

"I am not the fool, Hayworth!" Krantz smiled, please with himself. "The fact that I live and the two of you die, is proof!"

"Do something!" the vicar's breathing grew heavy as he body grew weaker. "Die, you, ugly serpent! Do you never grow tired?" he glanced up at the smiling man who had betrayed him. "In God's name, Help us!"

"In God's name? Hayworth, you were never a faithful vicar, so why start pretending now? Now that you face death?" Krantz chuckled, enjoying the fight. "My need for you is complete. I leave you to the hand of your new acquaintances! Happy death, old man!"

Bernard, his best man, fell at the feet of the retile men. They lifted the swords above his head in unison, gave a hissing cry, and thrust them down on him. Shrieks tore from the man's throat as blood gushed from the holes in his head and neck. The cries continued for several minutes, then died away. Marcia and Arabella screamed as they watched in disbelief at how long it took Bernard to die.

"It is a trick! Somehow, a trick!" Hayworth yelled and threw down his sword, causing the reptile men to back away from him. "I knew it! Without a sword, they move away!" Hayworth started back up the hill as Krantz grew aggravated and yelled.

"Do not be a fool, old man! Bernard is dead! Too bad too, he was a good man. Those creatures are just waiting and now with your back turned, they will get you!"

"Nay! You are lying Krantz! They have all but gone!"

Krantz drew the dagger from his belt and gave an evil smile. "To be on the safe side, just in case you are right, this dagger brings forth real blood!" Krantz threw the sharp dagger into the vicar's chest. Hitting his mark, Hayworth screamed, grabbed his chest and fell to his knees. The reptile men moved back in on him, their swords swinging to finish him off. The army of reptiles surrounded the wounded vicar, lifted their swords and came down in unison, bringing forth many cries and lots of blood.

Marcia, out of compassion for her enemy took the dagger Arabella had showed her and aimed for the suffering man, making a perfect pitch. Vicar Hayworth fell over, no more in earthly pain.

Krantz laughed as he smiled down at his captive, and started pulling her and Arabella to the end of the path. "Well ladies, looks like we made it."

"You are crazy, Krantz Hamish! A bloody murderer! You mar the very ground you walk on! Too bad there is not a fifth path on this miserable island so you could terrorize innocent people!" tears flooded down Marcia's cheeks "This island suits you! You are just another dangerous monster!"

"Krantz, you have gone mad! Has our treasure disrupted your mind?" Arabella cover her face in her hands. "I cannot believe this person is my brother."

"Then, do not think of me at all!" Krantz pushed the two young women down the fourth path. "After I have collected my treasure; did you here me, Arabella, MY TREASURE, I shall not be bothered with you ever again."

Arabella, in a panic, grabbed his arm. "You do not intend to leave me alone here on the horrible island? Do you Krantz? After all we have meant to each other."

"Arabella, do not flatter yourself. You mean absolutely 'nothing' to me. You never have. I just used you to get what I wanted and now, I have finished with you." Krantz smiled down at his sister mockingly. I do not need you anymore, dear sister. Now that I am richer than God, women will come to me and I can choose among them whom I desire. Now I can 'make love' and enjoy it!" he pushed her forward. "Now, shut up and start walking!"

"No! I will not go another step with you!" Arabella let out a soft scream when Krantz pulled a spare dagger from his belt and slashed her arm.

"The next outburst from you, I will gladly slash through your vocal cord to silence you, permanently! Now, unless you want your throat cut, move your sorry ass!"

Turning slowly, to begin the fourth and final path, Arabella felt Marcia take her hand and walk along beside her, toward the dragon at the far end.

Chapter Twenty-Eight

Rider and his men formed a straight line as they traversed the path of fire. Amby grabbed his arm when they came to the large fiery pit in the middle of their path. The belching flames leaped up at their feet and the heat was felt all the way to the last man in line.

"Master, this mammoth hole is going to be impossible to jump! We shall have to go around, less we fall in!"

"Nay, have you forgotten so quickly, my friend. The keeper of the four paths told us to stay on the blue line. Look close in the middle of the smoke. See, there it is, just as she has promised!" Rider pointed out the faint blue line he had been following.

"Aye, but what about the pit of fire?" Amby looked nervously down at the lapping flames. "The land beside the pit looks solid. See, it grows grass!"

"And it can be only deceiving to the eye! The fiery pit you can see clearly, yet it is a trick to the eye, nothing more!" Rider slapped Amby on the back and laughed. "Stand back and watch! I will show you!" Before Amby could stop the masked man, Rider had made it safely through the tense smoke. "See, just a trick! Now, come on!"

Closing his eyes, Amby began walking through the smoke and mumbling. "He who walks in smoke-filled places usually get burnt." He cracked his eyes open and saw Rider standing in front of him smiling, so he added. "But, he who does not try, usually never finds out."

"Did it help to close your eyes, my friend?" Rider pulled him the rest of the way and tossed a large stone on the 'solid' ground to prove his point to Amby. As soon as the stone hit what looked like grass, the large flaming pit appeared and swallowed it up, causing the red head to gasp loudly. "That is what the keeper warned us about and look…" Rider pointed to the end of the trail. "The third path lies just beyond and we must make haste! Time is running out for Marcia! Are you ready men?"

"Why not?" Amby shifted his sword to another position. "If I even thought about stopping to rest and having time to think things over, I might not come!"

Rider laughed and began walking quickly down the path of the Reptile men.

Krantz pointed at the red stones lining the path as they neared the end. They were perfectly round, except for their level tops. "This must be the old demon's wall, see how it builds the closer we get to what appears to be a high entranced." Krantz barely got the remark from his mouth when a giant rodent ran through their feet and up the path, carrying what appeared to be a dead swollen lizard in its sharp teeth. "Now, where do you think that little varmint is heading in such a hurry?"

"It looks as those he has found himself a fine meal to share among friends." Marcia watched the rat scurry around the high entrance and out of sight.

When they reached the entrance, the small group noticed the strange stones had become redder, as though painted. "These double red rocks must be the demons main gate!" Krantz laughed, thinking such poor construction for a demon, worth millions in pure gold. "At least the color suits him."

"You should know." Marcia said mockingly. "Being his blood brother, you both choose Satan's favorite color as well."

"Enjoy your pitiful criticism while you can, dearest. I will not have to put up with you much longer." Krantz snarled as he gripped her arm tightly. "Your fate is in my hands."

"Then I would just as soon be with the dragon!" Marcia spat back.

"Dragon?" his eyes grew wide, along with his sister's. He had expected another big lizard, but never a dragon.

Marcia gazed down, disgusted for letting it slip, even though she was aware he would soon find out. Angrily, he shook her. "If you know the one on the fourth path is a dragon, then you had to know what to expect down all the paths, did you not?"

"Aye! Too bad one of those bad things did not get you!" Fire shot from her eyes. "But as dear old Hayworth used to say: 'the devil takes care of his own!'"

"Shut it up right now!" Krantz was too busy staring at the woman aggravating him to notice he had reached the dragon's lair until he heard its loud roar. Krantz's quick reflects jerked him and

Marcia around to face the dragon, sitting casually upon a huge rock. Krantz and the two frightened women all stood frozen, unsure as to what the incredible giant monster was. By his appearance, it was obvious to all three, the twenty-foot-tall blue-green beast with a long tail was indeed a dragon, The, obvious difference was his three large heads, each with two eyes. The six eyes moved back and forth on the newcomers below him. His husky voice roared out at them, shooting out a small flame.

"WHO DARES TO COME IN MY PRESENCE UN-ANNOUCED? SPEAK!"

Krantz took one step up in front of the big dragon and bowed his head in respect, then spoke out. "I have come as your friend, great and powerful dragon."

"'MY NAME IS 'GORE'!" Krantz jumped back shaking when the dragon yelled back. "THAT IS HOW YOU MUST ADDRESS ME!"

"Gore, of course." Krantz swallowed back his incredible fear and continued. "Forgive me, great Gore. Perhaps you will except my apologies when I tell you I have brought you the Karnstein maiden. I am told, for the exchange of gold."

"THE KARNSTEIN MAIDEN, YOU SAY?" Gore's eyes lit up. "For exchange of some gold?"

"Aye! The legend states: He who brings one fair maiden of the tenth generation of Karnstein, will in return receive a wealth of pure gold!" Krantz feeling a little braver, pointed at his two female companions, clinging to each other. "As you can see, I have brought her."

The dragon's three heads bent forward to take in the two young women shaking in front of him. He smiled his approval and lend back.

"That is true what you have said, for the KARNSTEIN MAIDEN stands before me. Both, lovely and delectable." His six eyes rolled on Krantz. "I will give you GOLD for the maiden of KARNSTEIN BLOOD." Gore grinned slyly from all three lips. "My legion has brought me a small morsel or as you mortals call it, an appetizer to begin my long-awaited feast. A nice dead lizard, swollen with maggots and worms."

Marcia whispered in Arabella's ear. "The grouse lizard that

rodent was carrying!" looking up, she noticed the dragon smiling at her, giving her the shivers.

"So, you have been preparing for a feast with the Karnstein maiden, in hopes someone would bring one?" Krantz noticed an army of rodents scurried out from openings in the big throne rock and raced back and forth in front of the huge dragon. He started reaching down to pick up three by their tails, popping one in each mouth. Krantz looked away, feeling like gagging, as he waited for the three lips to stop chomping. "Where…where you hoping…?"

"I COULD SMELL THE BLOOD OF KARNSTEIN ON MY ISLAND1 SHE IS HERE!" Gore's head came forward. "SEND HER TO ME!"

"Not until I have my gold." Krantz ordered.

"NOT UNTIL I SEE THE WOMAN YOU HAVE BROUGHT ME!" the blue-green dragon roared loudly, fire shooting from his center mouth near Krantz's feet. "NOW, SEND HER TO ME BEFORE I DEVOUR ALL THREE OF YOU!"

"Aye! She comes!" Krantz grabbed Arabella and pulled her kicking and screaming along with him.

"Krantz, what are you doing? Please! It's not me the dragon wants!" she screamed louder the closer she came to the horrible stench. Tiring of her struggles and her loud screams, Krantz slapped her hard against her mouth. The scared sister broke down in silent sobs as she whispered. "Krantz, Krantz, Krantz!"

"Take her!" Krantz waited for the dragon to reach down before pushing his sister into its outstretched arms and stepping away. "Take her and give me my gold."

The dragon's six eyes stared down at the frighten girl below him, where he had laid her gently on his fat stomach. Arabella started screaming again when his long fingers scooped her up and moved the shapely woman by each head in turn. Arabella fainted after seeing her reflection in his red eyes and knew it could not be just a bad nightmare. The dragon licked his three lips.

"She looks good enough to eat."

"Nay!" Marcia screamed and started to run up in hopes of helping Arabella, not thinking there was not much she could do except tell the dragon that she was the real Karnstein, and Gore would end up eating both of them anyway. Krantz grabbed Marcia and clamped his hand over her mouth.

"Shut up Marcia, if you want to live." He whispered as the wily dragon slanted his eyes at the two waiting below and gave them a knowing smile as he smacked his lips in unison.

Watching below in horrified belief, Marcia felt as though she was going to faint as well. She closed her eyes tight and prayed under her breath, "Please God, do not let that poor girl regain consciousness. Let her stay asleep until this nightmare is over. And please Lord, forgive her." Marcia's prayer was interrupted when the dragon chuckled.

"I cannot stand a sleeping meal." The cunning dragon smiled down at Marcia and winked with all six eyes. She felt sure Gore had read her mind and the thoughts filled her heart with horror at what else he had been able to read or hear spoken in a whisper. "Wake up, my little morsel." The giant dragon lightly spit in her face, causing Arabella to open her eyes. Instantly, she began screaming again, and knowing the deadly outcome, she lifted up her voice.

"Jesus! Forgive me, a sinner! I believe in you Lord, because my friend has shone me your light through her face! Make my death swift and forgive my weakness if I scream one last time, out of fear from this monster! Be with my friend and keep her safe!" Arabella faced the dragon. "You can kill my body, great Gore, but you will never take my soul."

"Then, I will let this JE-SUS have your unseen soul, while I enjoy a tasty treat!" the dragon lifted her to his mouth and as he opened it wide, Arabella screamed one last time, when he stuck her head and shoulders in his middle mouth a crunched down. The screams from Arabella were cut off, but the piercing screams from Marcia's throat echoed through the open air and was carried downwind toward the third path by a light blue mist.

Chapter Twenty-Nine

"My God! What was that?" Amby tried to focus his eyes along the dark path. "It sounded like a woman!"

"It was Marcia!" Rider stopped and clutched his chest. "Dear keeper, tell me I am not too late! Give me a sign, anything!" he waited in the stillness for a brief moment and began again. "I beg you, Marcia is my life and my life is about to die, I can feel it! Everything I have and love in this world will be gone forever if I do not save Marcia!"

The blue mist floated above the Moon Rider's head as the keeper of the four paths became visible. "Make haste, my friend, to fight the reptile men and remember what I told you about the wounds they make being your imagination, how much it hurts. DO NOT GIVE IN TO THE PAIN OR YOU WILL DIE! One usually does not take up his sword to fight them, for they will not attack but still try and block your way. This time, knowing your skills for fighting, meet them head on with your swords and fight them quickly, then the last path will reveal itself to you. Marcia is yet still safe and I will stall for time. She is a strong-willed young lady and will also stall immediate death by charming the dragon." This made Rider and his men smiled, knowing how head-strong his lady could be. "Yes, I see you know her well. But, nevertheless, this Gore is steadfast in his mission to eat a Karnstein maiden before the setting of the sun, so hurry, only hurry, hurry! You MUST HURRY!" the mist faded and in her place, there stood ten hideous reptile men, sword drawn for battle.

Without hesitation, Rider and his brave band of warriors began fighting the beast of prey. Within seconds, Rider dropped four of the attackers while his men easily took care of all but the one fighting the doctor, not as advanced in his skill for sword fighting. Merciton let out a scream as the last attacker cut him through the chest. Rider was on the Reptile man in a flash and killed him on the spot. Then he bent down to Merciton who was bleeding badly.

"It is over for me, Rider. He got me in the heart, I am dying!" he mumbled in pain.

"Nay, my friend, it is only your imagination, as the keeper has said. You must not give in to it!" Rider lifted his head in his arms. "Let me help you up and you shall see."

"Nay, Rider! I am a physician and I know what a mortal wound looks like! My imagination could never hurt like this. Face it I am dying master, but I have fought hard and even though I lost, you still have a chance to save your woman." The doctor coughed. "Leave me and go!"

"Rider, we cannot leave him." Amby watched as Rider stood up and walked back to the path. "You must convince him." The red head watched as their leader knelt back down to the scared doctor.

"Look Doc, the keeper said..." the doctor took Rider's hand weakly. "There is no time for me. God speed you! Now, go...go find Marcia!"

Amby cleared his throat and pulled Rider to his feet, then winked at him before smiling down at the doctor. "Old doc here is right, master. Well, Merciton, now that you are dying, I might as well confess what your wife and I have been up to." The doctor's eyes flew open. "I feel, the need to confess and tell you everything I have been doing so I can live with myself. I cannot let you die without getting it off my chest."

"What are you talking about?" the doctor sat up and stared angrily at Amby. "Go ahead! How long have you and Breanna been having an affair?"

"An affair? Oh, you miss understood my confession. She and I have been meeting in secret to plan a big 50th birthday party for you." Amby jumped back behind the black figure when Merciton took to his feet to grab him.

"Why you, little red-headed...I ought to..." the doctor looked down at his chest and saw all the blood had vanished, and laughed out. "Well, what do you know, I think I will live after all!"

"Aye!" Rider laughed and slapped Amby on his back. "Thanks to quick thinking! Let us go!"

"Aye, we have a lady to save!" the doctor laughed and hugged Amby. "You are a crazy proverb-speaking bastard, but, I love you!"

"He who has a friend that cares are better off than a rich man with none." Amby raced off after Rider.

The dragon licked his fingers and smiled at the two waiting below him. "Now, I suppose you want me to give you your gold." His sly smile sent goosebumps up Marcia's neck.

"Aye! Then we will be on our way and never bother you again." Krantz held tight to Marcia's hand and stepped back when Gore rolled his eyes at him in a strange slant. "YOU …LIED…TO…ME!"

"Lied?" a lump formed back in Krantz's throat as he struggled to speak. "Lied about…what?"

"The KARNSTEIN MAIDEN!" the cunning dragon pointed his long sharp finger down at Marcia. "SHE IS THE KARNSTEIN MAIDEN!" He spit fire near Krantz's feet. "IS SHE NOT?"

"Alright! Aye, aye!" Krantz shook from the dragon's angry stare. "I merely jest, wise one. Gore is far too clever for me!" Krantz pulled Marcia forward. "Here she is! You may have her! Just give me the gold!"

"You tried to test me and yet, you still scream for gold?" the old dragon chuckled as he gazed down at the beautiful fair young maiden beyond his reach. "Not that I blame you none, Krantz!" he snickered at the man's obvious surprise for knowing his name. "Aye, my hearing is as keen as my mind reading! I too would have lied to save this delicate rose for myself. You may not have both! The woman or the gold? Choose?"

Krantz looked down at Marcia and ran his finger over her lips. "Oh, to have had both! Sorry dearest, but I came a long way for this gold and I will not leave without it!" Krantz turned back to the dragon. "The legend promised gold in exchange of a Karnstein maiden! I have brought her! I made my way through hell on this island bringing her and have loss everyone who was with me!" his face grew sweaty. "Now, give it to me!"

"BEEN THROUGH HELL, HAVE YOU?" The dragon squinted his eyes and laughed sarcastically. "Krantz Hamish, you might as well get use to it, since you will be a permanent resident there soon!"

"Do I get the gold or…do I take mistress Karnstein back with me, now? Krantz started backing up slowly, prepared to make a run for it as he gripped Marcia's hand.

"You are a man of greed, are you not?" the dragon laughed out. "Give me the girl and you shall have your gold."

"The gold first this time, Gore!" Krantz gripped Marcia's hand tightly. "I am waiting!"

The dragon's big heads dropped down toward Krantz and demanded: "THE GIRL...THEN THE GOLD!"

"Very well, Gore. But, at least permit me to see my gold first! How do I know if it even existed!"

"WART!" the dragon summoned and the rock under him moved back like a door as a giant humpback rat ran out and bowed down in front of the ugly dragon. Gore reached down and picked him up by the tail and held him close to one eye. "Wart, this man wishes to see the gold he shall receive for this fair maiden."

The deformed rodent looked down at the humans standing below them and squeaked out. "A lovely fair maiden she is too, your mighty one. Well worth the going price of 50,000 stark stones!"

"My thoughts exactly, wart!" the dragon turned the squirming rodent around and licked his lip. "Wart, why have I not eaten you? You are so...ugly and old! Perhaps I need a younger, faster leader, for my legion army."

The big rat dripped sweat as he forced a chuckle. "Younger perhaps, old brave leader, but not wise with age and my leadership is without blemish." Wart nodded his head up and down nervously. "I am the only rat that can talk and it took you years to train me! Please...great Gore! Let me show this one the gold!"

"Very well, Wart." The dragon smiled and lowered the rat back on the ground where he started running back and forth, screaming out orders. Two rats pushed out a cart holding a 50lb. gold bar, shaped like a river stone, then rolled it in front of Krantz. The rat looked up and pointed at the shiny rock. A huge wart set visible on his long nose.

"One solid gold stark stone!" he jumped back when Krantz picked it up and turned it around in his hand, smiling. "You said, 50,000 stark stones? How can I get them all back to my ship? And who will lead me there safely?"

"Why, I will personally take you to your ship, which is closer than you think!" the rodent laughed, revealing protruding yellow teeth. "Gore's legion army will cart the rest to your ship and hope it stays afloat!" Wart snickered.

"It is a big strong ship, Wart!" Krantz felt stupid talking to a dirty rodent, so he pulled Marcia up toward the dragon. "Here, the Karnstein maiden!"

"Your gold awaits you!" Gore pointed to the army of rats marching out with carts of 'stark stones' and heading down a new path. The long line stretched out for a mile. "Take it and leave!"

"I go then." He reached down and kissed Marcia. "Goodbye my love! I am truly sorry it did not work out as I planned."

"I am certain you must be heartbroken to leave me and have only cold rocks to keep you warm at night, you murderer!" Marcia's eyes shot fire. "Just go and take your precious gold and enjoy it while you can! Soon, you will face a devil far worse than this three-headed dragon!" she wiped off her lips and slapped her hand on his sneering face. "Keep your kiss, Judas! Gore and I would like to see the back side of you walking away!"

"Here1 Here!" Gore clapped his hands. "You heard the lady, Krantz, GO! NO ONE WANTS YOU HERE!"

Krantz laughed, as he ran his hand over the gold bar and looked up at the large gold tablet hanging over the dragon's head. "Before I depart, what about that gold tablet above your head?"

"You have your gold! Now take it and go!"

"What is the tablet? It appears to have exquisite jewels all around it? Diamonds, rubies, emeralds! Why it so special, Gore?" Krantz looked up greedy, needing to have more. "Does it hold some sort of magic?"

"The tablet belongs to ME! NOW LEAVE BEFORE YOU PROVOKE ME!" the dragon spit fire toward Krantz. "NO MAN WILL TOUCH IT OR HE WILL SURELY DIE! THE NEXT TIME I SPIT FIRE, I WILL STRIKE YOU DOWN!"

Krantz tucked the heavy bar of gold tight to his chest, and left poor Marcia at the mercy of the mighty dragon. She shook when he gazed down at her, just as he had Arabella earlier. Despite her fear, she managed to speak up.

"Gore, I know that it is your intention to eat me, but would you not rather have a friend who can communicate with you with the intelligence you deserve?" Marcia waved her hand at the line of rats racing after their leader, Wart, pushing heavy carts of stark stones. "It must get lonely and sometimes trying when Wart is the only one you have to talk with."

"Dear Marcia, you make an excellent point, although I do not think my choice of food would suit a fair damsel like yourself." Gore tilted his head, taking in her ideal. "Dead lizards and squirming rats seem to turn your stomach and I know an occasional live human is out of the question, not to mention your ear-piercing screams when I chomp down on one."

Marcia swallowed back her sudden nausea as she tried to smile. "Great Gore, I would leave those fine dishes for you to enjoy. I can live on fresh fruit and spring water."

Gore made a distasteful face. "Fresh fruit? Spring water?" he closed his eyes and shook his head. "Yuk! But, should I have chosen to keep you for my companion, which sounds very tempting, I would see that your needs were met." Marcia thought she saw sadness come over the big dragon's face. "But my need for revenge is so much greater, beautiful girl. To remain happy, I MUST eat a Karnstein maiden this day!"

"Then, old friend, can I first know why you only desire the blood of Karnstein maidens over any other name?" Marcia took a deep breath, hoping for a little more time in case Rider was on his way.

"I cannot see the harm in telling you." Gore reached down and lifted her up and sat her on the rock near his three heads. "You see, my dear, my great appetite used to be satisfied by anyone or anything that passed my path, even necessitous people. I was never choosy. Then one day, your ancient ancestor came to my peaceful little island seeking to steal all its wealth. This small island contains millions of tons of stark stones. That evil Krantz got just a small amount but had he have asked for more, his great ship would surely sink to the bottom of the sea. Norwood Karnstein, your ancestor, had brought his wife along with him, for he was a lustful man and needed her quite regularly." The dragon's long finger pointed to the golden tablet above his head, directly behind him. "Karnstein and his beautiful wife, Sarah, had even stole the tablet of love from the temple of truth. Perhaps you spoke with the face inside the sacred temple."

"Aye, a wise and good being." Marcia remembered the face in the stone, putting her into a deep sleep to stall for time.

"Until your ancestor moved the tablet, the powers within the temple ruled this island. Your ancestor stole it, and that is how I came by it and now rule the island!"

"Gore, did my evil ancestor do more than just steal the riches off your island?" Marcia asked softly. "I cannot believe you are greedy enough to choose that reason for revenge."

"And you would be right, my child. Norwood Karnstein was not only a thief, he was a coldblooded murderer, just like that evil Krantz!" hate came to the dragon's three faces. "After throwing a sword in my lady dragon's neck, he set her on fire and burned her while she yet lived. I can still hear her screams as the flames fried her!"

"Gore, old friend, I am truly sorry. It must have hurt you deeply and it has left you so alone and lonely all these many years." Marcia could not help but feel some pity for the big dragon. "Did you take revenge on Norwood and his wife, Sarah?"

"In my great anger, I caught the couple and while I held Karnstein down with my foot, I ate his wife in front of him, then swore my revenge, to eat a Karnstein maiden, every tenth generation. Then I sat down the murderer and torched him with my flames, laughing at his screams, as he burned alive!"

"Even though I know revenge is wrong, Gore, I can understand why you hated these two people who killed your mate, but why do you wait ten generations to have a Karnstein maiden?"

"Because my loneness is so great, I have found a way to ease the pain." He rolled his eyes at Marcia. "You are an understanding girl, Marcia. The first to actually speak to me instead of constant screaming. You have a good heart and I know your after life will be rewarded." He smiled slyly. "Even though eating you will leave me lonely once more, it shall be a privilege having one so thoughtful and who will not, hopefully, scream right in my face."

"I hope you do not mind if I see it differently." She swallowed at the thought of being stuck inside his big mouth. "I am probably not as good as I look and you might end up spitting me out."

The large dragon chuckled at the thought of something as

tender as this one being nasty. "Sweet Marcia, it does my heart good to laugh and to find a human who can make jest, even at such a crucial time." The two heads flanking the middle one, began yawning, perhaps getting bored by all the chatter.

"Dear Gore, it appears we have bored your right and left heads, for they seem to grow weary." Marcia had hoped this could buy her a little more time as she added. "I have noticed your head is the only one that can speak. Is there some reason why your other two heads cannot talk?"

"The golden tablet holds magic, but only the strongest can contain its powerful force. That would be me, my dear." Gore yawned loudly and quickly covered his mouth. "Forgive me, my dear, for I suddenly grow tired. I do not worry about how tasty you will be, for I can see you are sweet and tender." Another yawn as the blue mist continued to sprinkle sleeping dust down over the dragon's heads. "I think I shall take a little nap before I dine on you, my dear."

"Aye, that is a wonderful idea, Gore, but first, you never told me why you wait ten generations to have a Karnstein maiden." Marcia thought the sleepier he became, the longer he would nap, and besides, she really needed to know why he waited just in time for her to be born.

"That is what I meant by easing the pain. I sleep for ten generations between meals." Gore stretched his four arms, the two middle and one on either end. "I think I will take that little rest before eating you. I will enjoy it better if I am wide awake." The dragon placed his long finger across her. "Just lock you up tight and close my eyes." He mumbled a few more scrambled words, then drifted off to sleep.

Chapter Thirty

The Moon Rider looked out from the forest that grew next to the fourth path and noticed the scene before him. His heart beat wildly watching the deadly dragon place what appeared to be a long finger over Marcia, to hold her down. He and his men had quietly witnessed the conversation going on between the very small and petite Marcia and the twenty-foot three headed dragon. Seeing the monster fall asleep, Rider turned to Amby and his other three men, then whispered.

"Listen and listen well. We only have one chance to get Marcia and make it safe out of here. Are you ready, gentlemen?"

"Aye master!" they answered quietly in unison, all eyes on the deadly dragon.

"Amby and I will go up to Marcia, hoping not to startle her, so she cannot give us away. She is already on edge and the slightest touch could frighten her. After speaking with her, I will climb up to get the tablet of love, as was instructed by the keeper of the four paths. The dragon is sure to awaken when it is lifted from its stand. If he does, I will hold his attention long enough for Amby to snatch Marcia and make a clean break, replacing her with a rolled-up cloth. If he should remember to hold her back down, the cloth might fool him for a while until you, Amby get her safely down with the men."

"Sounds like a good plan." Amby answered, but his attention was on the rats pouring out from under the rock in a straight line, pushing what looked like a cart of some kind. Rider looked down at him and slapped his arm to get his attention.

"Are you listen to my orders, Amby? Your mind seems to be on those stupid rats!" Rider pulled him around. "Do you know what to do?"

"Aye! We go up there with Marcia!" Amby looked up at the situation. "We go…up there…with that…sleeping dragon?"

"Now I have your attention!" Rider looked down serious. "I will tell Marcia what to do and you be ready to snatch her, replace her with the cloth, then get the hell back down for a fast get-away!

I will keep that monster's attention to give you time."

"Aye, I can do this! We will save Marcia, then get our butts off this island!"

"My plans exactly!" Rider turned when he heard the doctor say his name.

"What about us, master?" Merciton put his fingers tightly around his sword handle.

"Just stay hidden in the forest and be on standby. If you see I can use some help getting that three headed things attention, start acting up, but stay clear of his flames." Rider slapped the doctor lightly on his back. "Otherwise, you three just keep your eyes open for the escape path. I am sure the keeper of the paths will have one standing ready for us."

"Aye! Good luck sir. It seems to be with you." McCormick pointed to the evening sky, revealing a big new moon rising above the hilltop. "Victory!"

"Aye, victory!" Rider took Amby's arm and led him quietly up past the trailing rodents, the end of the long train. "They are just an army of slaves, Amby, probably delivering the last of Krantz's big treasure."

"I never knew rats could be slaves or do manual labor?" Amby whispered as he followed Rider up the step rock.

"Then I suppose you knew, faces in rocks could talk, lizards could resemble men, snakes could live without bodies, pits of fire could appear real, when they were not or a giant named Grim could have three eyes! And a lady made of mist could be blue."

"I get your point." Amby forced a smile "This is no ordinary place."

"Correct, now stay quiet." Rider slipped up behind Marcia and covered her mouth. She closed her eyes and smiled. Turning her face slowly, she looked up into Rider's loving eyes. She let out a long sigh of relief, then whispered.

"Thank God, It's you! You came!"

"We are going to get you out of here, Marcia. Now listen. Amby will pull you out from the dragon's finger when I draw his attention away from you."

"Rider, please! I do not want to live if something happens to you!" Marcia wanted to hug him, but her arms were locked down firmly by the sleeping dragon.

"You, just do as I say." His words fell softly around her ears as his lips covered her in a kiss. "A kiss for luck. Now, get ready."

"I will." Marcia gave him a real smile, finally feeling hope. "Be careful."

"Aye." He patted her head. "That is my brave girl." Rider walked over on the ledge just under the gold tablet, then climbed up the stones to reach the top. He looked over the edge and gave Amby their signal, then carefully lifted the heavy tablet from its resting place. The wind began to blow wildly when his fingers touched it, placing its power inside of him.

At that instant, the dragon opened his eyes and twirled his three heads around to see what had disturbed the sacred tablet. The dragon opened his mouth to speak, never thinking the power he had was now in the one holding the golden tablet. "WH…WH..AT..GROWL!"the roar grew louder and louder!

The Moon Rider stood boldly against the big red moon as he waved the gold tablet in his left hand and held his sword up toward the sky and gave his triumphant cry! The dragon lifted his arms and roared angrily. Amby grabbed Marcia, threw down the cloth, then started running quickly from the rock and made a run for the forest.

The angry dragon was so mad over the loss of his magic, he stood up and waved his four hands toward Rider. The far end hand came within inches, but the great swordsman, slash it off and sent it flying through the air as he yelled over the cries of the wounded dragon, "VICTORY!" and raced off the hill, across the opening, then into the tree lined path, into Marcia's arms.

The angry dragon shot fire toward the small group and began making his way off the rock. Amby grabbed Rider's arm and pointed to the large stone behind them opening, their escape door. Rider pulled Marcia through as his men quickly followed and before Gore could reach it, the stone slammed shut.

Rider led the group quickly across the soft sand on the beach toward the waiting boat. The blue lady had brought them straight down the four deadly paths, which led back across the small island to where they started out.

They could hear Gore pounding his way through the stone

when they ran up to the boat, the waiting men, jumping up when they saw them and heard the horrible loud noise coming from the other side of the big stone in front of them.

"You fellows, and…" one of the rowers tilted his hat at Marcia. "you, madam, act as though the devil were after you." Rider pushed him out of the way and helped Marcia on, then waited for his helpers to get aboard. "Look fellows, we do not have time to explain why we need to get out butts off this island, but get in now and grab those ores!"

"What on earth is that loud noise?" The other rower mumbled as he took his seat. "It sounds horrible!"

"It's just a twenty-foot dragon that shoots fire and is mad as hell at us!" Amby chuckled at the man's shocked face and slapped his back. "So, when Rider climbs aboard, you had better start rowing."

"Just…a dragon?" his rowing partner swallowed.

"Aye, so let's get this baby moving before it breaks through. He might have lost his power to talk but he is still a twenty-foot, fire-breathing, dragon. Once he is free, it will take him only six giant steps to make it here to us." Rider gave the boat a shove and the tiny craft began to float out in the harbor toward The Moon Rider's ship.

The boat was a safe distance when the dragon broke free and came through the stone, fire spraying from his mouths. The island began to shake and tremble as loud explosions were heard all over the small island. The lady of mist had started the destruction of the Island of Mist and the jungle birds took off across the sea, sensing its great demise. Once a good, peaceful island, it had become overcome by the evils of the underworld and the angel of the mist and the face of wisdom, had orders by its creator, to destroy it, completely.

Rider, Marcia, and all the crew, watched as the dragon fought to stand upright when the ground began to crack open in a great earthquake and the island began sinking into the sea. The dragon let out a mournful cry as the sea covered him up. When the mountains went under, fire shot up from the sea with a loud ear-breaking explosion, then all grew quiet.

Marcia could not help but feel a little sad for her old friend,

Gore. Of course, she knew he was bad, and did have a big apatite, for humans, especially Karnstein maidens. But he was a dragon, after all, and she had seen a different side of him that was almost charming.

"Marcia, my love, you seem to be sad." Rider pulled her into his strong protecting arms. "If you are thinking about the lady of mist or the face of wisdom, they will be fine. It was they who destroyed the island."

"I knew God, in His mercy, would spare them, Rider." Marcia lend her head over on his shoulder. "Call me crazy, but my heart is sad over poor lonely Gore having to die like that. For a dragon, he was really quite intelligent."

"Perhaps it was the golden tablet that made him more human, my darling. I know you got to know him better than anyone else. I really believe the old fellow liked you, darling." His hand caressed her hair. "I can see how anyone or anything would fall in love with you, Marcia. But, nevertheless, he still was a dragon and would have killed us all if he had that chance."

"And I appreciate you saving me from a sure death. The big tease was going to eat me as soon as he woke up." Marcia watched as the blue mist blew gently by the boat, then swirled around them. A soft voice fell from the mist on them, saying:

"Love and peace to him who is true."

Then another familiar voice was heard above the sea breeze. "All is well, love wins the test. Now, we go to find peace and rest."

"The one with the black heart is traveling before you, thinking he has won with riches untold." The blue mist followed them safely to the ship then floated up and up as Rider called after them.

"Our thanks to you both! Farewell dear friends! We shall meet again in Heaven!"

Then the blue mist floated out of sight as it completely disappeared in the open firmament.

Chapter Thirty-One

The huge sails set out across the open sea toward England. Settled back in his cabin, Rider gently hugged the woman he loved, grateful the terrible ordeal was behind them. "Finally, the ship seems to have picked up her speed. The wind has caught the sails and now we shall make quick time of it."

"It will be good getting back to the homeland. I know Lizzie has been worried sick over me, not knowing if you arrived in time to save me from that dragon."

"I serious doubt your Lizzie expected a dragon would be the one waiting for you, although I cannot imagine what the dear lady thought." Rider got two glasses and poured rich red wine for them and handed one to Marcia. "This should help you relax, my dearest one." Rider sat down and took a big sip, then looked thoughtful. "I wonder if those poor rats got back to the island just in time to sink down with it?"

"You know, I never considered how those rats got that gold to Krantz's ship! They rolled the stark stone, their name for gold bar, in some sort of cart. I suppose to the beach, then I am lost as to what those rodents did."

"This is my guess. When the rats reached the water, they rolled the 'stark stone' off the cart into the water and swam it out to the ship." Rider smiled at Marcia taking in his explanation. "How they got on Krantz's ship with them, is anyone's guess."

"Maybe they found a little trap door on the side of the ship or rolled it up a gang blank." Marcia laughed. "Ask Krantz before you kill the heartless bastard!"

"Aye! I will make him squeal like the rat he is." Rider sat up and turned his head to listen. "The ship has slowed down. I will go up on deck and see why we are slowing." Rider reached down and kissed her. "You may enjoy more wine and rest from your trying day."

"Be careful Rider." Marcia touched his face lovingly. "I will wait for you on that second glass. I will just lie down and rest until you return."

203

"I shan't be long, Marcia, darling." He raced up to the ship captain and looked out into the starry sky. "I never grow tired of this view.

"Aye, tis a beautiful sight sir and very peaceful out here tonight. There is a clam on the sea and until the wind picks back up, we will be drifting ahead." The captain reassured his leader. "Be at rest sir. You look tired and there are many miles to go until we reach the homeland. I will inform you if we spot the Ravin."

"Good man, thank you Conns." Rider padded his back. "Just keep her headed straight. We should overtake Krantz near the British shore. He can move only so fast with all those stark stones and possible castaways."

"Aye, heavy gold can hold you back, sir, but I am not following the castaways you are referring to."

"The ones that loaded all that gold for him from the island." Rider laughed. "I would bet the old Ravin is overrun right now with island rats!"

"Rats?" Captain Conns titled his head. "I believe you really need to get some sleep, Rider. I will wake you if I see the Ravin."

"Thank you." Rider chuckled and went back down to his cabin. Marcia had stretched out on his bed and was fast asleep. He tiptoed over and covered her up, poured himself another glass of wine, and settled in his soft chair, to sleep until morning.

The morning sun was breaking in the eastern sky over the glistening water. The ship's lookout spotted Krantz's ship, the Ravin, making its way slowly toward England's coast. Land could be plainly seen in the distanced as the captain sent a runner down to inform their leader. The lookout cupped his hand around his mouth as he called out "SHIP AHOY!"

Rider stepped out into the fresh morning air, the sails bellowing out as the wind drove them forward. The lookout race up and pointed out toward the horizon at the vessel in front of them.

"Look sir, it is Krantz's ship, headed for home."

"Aye, so it is. I thought he might have sank in the deep waters with all that gold aboard the Ravin." Rider's eyes lit up. "He actually thought he would get away with his treasure."

"Aye, the black hearted villain!" Amby stared out angrily at the black sails on the Ravin as it moved toward the inland. "He certainly proved to be the biggest monster of all. I asked Marcia what had happened to Vicar Haywood when we were waiting for you to join us in the woods and she said Krantz threw his dagger in the man's heart when Hayworth realized the Lizard men could not really kill him. Of course, after being fatally wounded in the chest, the lizard men came down with their swords. Marcia, feeling sorry for his long suffering, threw Arabella's dagger in Hayworth to finish him off. She said Krantz just made fun of her and pulled her on toward the fourth path." Amby looked once again at the dark ship and mumbled. "He who walks the evil trail will get his pay, and get it well!"

"Aye!" Rider smiled down at his friend. "Wake the men up and get them ready for battle. Have a light breakfast, for we shall be drawing close to the Ravin in about one hour." His eyes fell toward his cabin. "Tell cook to prepare a pot of tea for me and Marcia, along with some warm scones and have them delivered to my cabin as soon as possible. I will dine with my lady and prepare for battle! Off with you!"

Rider watched his friend race off quickly to alert the cook, then went down to the crew quarters to prepare the men.

"Rider." Marcia sat bushing her long chestnut hair when he stepped back through the door. He walked over to her, bent down and kissed her sweet lips. "Mum, you found my mint roots. I would ask if you slept well, my love, but by the blush in your beautiful cheeks, I would say you are ready to witness my revenge on Krantz for kidnapping my woman!"

"I would not miss a single detail of his demise." Marcia smiled as she watched him put on his black coat and hat. "Has his ship been spotted already?"

"Marcia, you slept all the night and a good part of the morning, so the wind did catch our sails and without a heavy load of gold to hold us back, such as was Krantz's dilemma, we have all but caught up with the Ravin." A knock came on the door and Rider smiled at Marcia as he went to open it. "You have to be as hungry as I, sweet one." Rider took the tray and shut the door, setting it down on his desk. Marcia got up to pour the tea.

"Permit me, sir knight. You need to save all your strength for the upcoming battle." Marcia remembered Rider taking two lumps of sugar and a heavy pour of cream, from her morning breakfast at his castle. "I hope it is to your liking."

"It looks perfect, darling, just like you." Rider took a sip as he watched her happily place two scones on his plate with fresh butter and jelly. "I could get used to you doing this for me every morning, Marcia."

"I would like nothing more." She smiled down, shyly. "Well, maybe I can think of one thing I would like better."

"Oh?" Rider's eyes lit up. "And what might that me, my little spitfire?"

"You tease and yet you know I speak of our sporting in bed."

"Mumm! I prefer that above everything we do together, pretty woman!" he began eating, while she joined him in tea and scones. After eating, he got up to strap on his sword, then he pulled her in his embrace. "Soon, it will be over."

"Rider, be careful. I cannot lose you now."

"You shan't lose me, my dearest." His lips parted over hers in a passionate kiss. He knew his men were waiting, but they would not interrupt his time with Marcia. "When we return to Canterbury, you will become my wife."

"Aye, I will gladly become your wife, Rider." She gave him a brilliant smile. "Where shall I watch the battle?"

"From this cabin, through the port window. I will have the ship stop for your viewing, although you might not see all of it if we move from place to place. Just know, no matter how anxious you become, do not leave this room! Do I have your word?"

"Aye, I give you my word. I shall stay put!" Marcia followed him to the door. "Can I not come up with you for a few minutes before the ship pulls alongside of the Ravin?"

Rider took her hand and led her up on deck. The ocean breezes blew through her long hair as she looked at Rider's ship drawing closer to Krantz's. Rider took the captains view glass and looked at the men on Raven's deck. One tall man stood out above the rest and he recognized the kidnapper immediately.

"Well now, there's our man, standing right in plain sight." Rider looked closer and laughed "I think he found one of his stowaways! Krantz seems to be fussing with one of the rats that delivered his gold."

"Let me see!" Marcia took the glass and focused in on the big rat with a humped back and one huge wart sitting right at the end of his long stout. "Oh, dear! Poor Wart! He never got back to the island."

"Wart?" Rider laughed.

"Wart was Gore's head rat. He had trained him how to talk and lead the other rats." Marcia handed the glass back so Rider could look again. "Wart had two distinctive marking, a humped back and a big wart on his nose, the source of his name."

"Maybe it is a good thing old Wart could not get back. He would have gone under like his slave master." Amby had been listening. "I do not know who is worse to work for, Gore or Krantz!"

"I know what you mean, Amby. Gore threatened to eat him and it appears mean old heartless Krantz is dangling him over the ship's rail."

"I hope the little varmint can swim the distance to England's shore." Rider handed the glass back to the captain. "Prepare to pull the Moon Shadow up next to the Ravin, Conns! Marcia, down in our cabin!" The Moon Rider pulled out his sword, held it in front of him as he bowed toward the woman he loved. "For my lady! I will gladly slay this villain, Krantz Hamish, and in thy name, Marcia Karnstein, it shall be done!"

"My heart will go with you in battle, brave knight!" Marcia reached up and kissed his lips. "For luck, my darling! Now go and slay the Ravin and this dove will be yours!"

"Aye, it shall be finished!" Rider smiled brightly. "Now, you below and stay put!"

When the two ships met side by side, the battle was on. They had taken them by surprise for their attention was on the port just a few miles away. Rider and his men swung aboard the black ship, swords drawn to fight.

Krantz ran in the middle of his men and started shouting out orders. "Men, kill the invaders! They are after our gold! Focus on the man with the mask, take him! Kill him!"

"Hide yourself among your men, Krantz?" The Moon Rider's

voice rang out over the noise of the war cries. "You cannot hide from me! It is you I have come after! Step forward and feel my cold steel!"

"Get him men! Cannot you see he is a thief! Stop him and I will reward you!"

As Krantz's men surrounded Rider, the power given him by the golden tablet helped him quickly take down every man around him. Krantz, backed away and started running to his cabin and locked himself inside.

Making a clear path for himself, the Moon Rider ran down the steps to find Krantz. Marcia had been watching with anxiety and drew closer to the port window when Rider followed after Krantz, going out of her view.

"Please Lord, be with the right! Let the Moon Rider destroy thine enemy!"

Meanwhile, Rider stood just outside Krantz's cabin and could hear heavy breathing just inside. Rider smiled to himself, knowing the coward had locked himself in.

"Hiding behind the door, Krantz, you cowardly chap!" Using his newfound strength, Rider burst the door open, jumping clear of the dagger in Krantz's hand. Twirling around in the air, Rider easily kicked the knife away and smiled down at his enemy. "Did I not tell you I came after you? It is your time to die now, Krantz!"

"Listen, I tried to save Marcia from that three-headed dragon, but he was one step ahead of me! He knew Arabella was not Marcia, but ate her anyway!" Krantz started to sweat when Rider stepped forward angrily. "Look, I am sorry Marcia had to die, but I could not outwit that dragon!"

"You sent your own sister to her horrible death! You, slimy devil!"

"Neither of us can have Marcia now! Listen to me, I have got enough gold for both of us! The children's home, you can easily build it now!" he begged. "Just do not make me fight you! I would hate to kill the legend of the Moon Rider, forever!"

"You, idiot! Do you think I would ever share your blood money! Look at all the lives you have wasted just for the lust of wealth!" Moon Rider laughed. "I shall have a good life with my own treasure, Hamish! I will have a full enjoyable life with my new bride! Marcia is very much alive, Krantz! She was a little wiser than the old dragon and had him chatting like an old friend. My sweet and beautiful Marcia even felt pity for old Gore when his island was being sucked under the sea. Aye, everyone you left behind is now buried beneath the sea. Marcia's smarts bought her the time I needed to arrive and save her and the sacred Tablet of Good!"

"You have got Marcia and the golden tablet?" Krantz's eyes grew wide as a new greed took over his senses, "How did you managed to get away with the dragon's two prize treasures? You too are only a mere man, like myself. The people have built you up to something you cannot retain! You will bleed just like every other man I have killed with my deadly sword!"

"Your new brave words do not frighten me, Hamish! And even if I did not have the power of the tablet, I could easily beat you!" Rider chuckled. "My quick thinking and swift actions are what saved my lady from the dragon. After I lifted the golden tablet off its stand, I received the power and the sleeping dragon awoke to nothing, his intelligence and his speech was taking away!"

"How did you escape the first three paths and why could you lift the white rose from its resting place, when I could not get it to budge?" Krantz was trying to buy himself time to plan his attack.

"The keeper of the four paths helped us because she could read our hearts, much like she read yours and refused to speak to you. Instead she warned Marcia and gave her a safe path through, which you later discovered, then killed your partner."

"Hayworth was of no value to me anymore. Why split the gold with him?"

"Why did you drop Wart into the ocean?" Rider smiled, knowing Krantz realized how long they had been observing him. "Was you afraid old Wart was going to squeal on you for all those murders?"

"He was just a stupid rat! He kept laughing and saying, I was worthless!"

"Smart Rat!" Rider knew Krantz was trying to sort out his defense. "About the rose, it only moved for someone with a good heart. Once again, the wise face in the rock, did not tell you that little part, giving me time to arrive and take Marcia away."

"I got her back then, Rider, and I will get her again, after I have cut your heart out!" Krantz lifted his sword and laughed. "Nay, Moon Rider, it is you who will die this day! Luck has been with me all the way! It will not abandon me now!"

"That is were you are wrong! Your so-called luck has run out, Krantz Hamish! It ran out the minute you took my woman! That was your big mistake, chap! No man messes with my woman and gets by with it! Ask all of those cold bastards in the ground!" Rider shifted his sword from hand to hand. "Get ready!"

"Ready!" Krantz jumped forward, slashing at the Moon Rider. Their sword clashed for several minutes before Rider made his victory shout.

"This is it, Krantz! I give you my blade..." his sword flew around, cutting Krantz across his chest. "That is for Marcia! That is for my love!" Krantz fell dead at Rider's feet, knocking over a stand of candles. The room immediately went up in flames, as Rider grabbed the one stark stone Krantz had brought aboard and dashed from the burning ship, along with his men. The battle was over.

Chapter Thirty-Two

As the people aboard the Moon Shadow watched the Ravin burning, the cook raced over to his leader, face a flushed with excitement. "Sir, I think I have found the reason for the Moon Shadows slow start! You have to see it to believe it, sir!"

"What has got you so excited Epperson? Did you find another stash of grub below deck?" Amby laughed at the robust man's red face. "Perhaps, tons of fresh potatoes or hard rolls to hold the ship down?"

"Nay! Jest if you will, Amby! Thar are thousands of bright stones lying thick on the lower deck, where we store the gun powder and cannons, I have never seen that many stones together in one place before, except perhaps, the King's palace!" Epperson nodded to Rider. "Nay, naught even Collinwood castle has that many stones."

"How on earth did those stark stones get on my ship?" Rider knew that could be the only explanation for thousands of bright stones to be lying in the bottom of the Moon Shadow, "And if we have the gold, what was slowing Krantz down?"

"Where is Wart when you need him?" Marcia looked up at Rider, puzzled as well. "Do you suppose the rats got the wrong ship to unload the stark stones?"

"Is it gold bars or stark stones?" the cook scratched his bald head.

"It is all the same, Epperson. Marcia, now that you mention Wart, I ask Hamish before I took his life, why he drowned Wart. He claimed the rat was laughing at him and calling him worthless. If he knew Krantz did not have the gold, that would make sense. Without the gold, he was same as worthless and he went through all that for nothing, because of one smart rat."

"So, Wart could still talk?" Marcia looked out at the coast growing nearer. "Wart is our only hope of finding out what really happened. How did they get the gold on your ship and what did they substitute it with on the Ravin?"

"If that rat drowned, we shall never know!" Rider waved at

211

the man on the pier as the ship pulled in to the harbor and dropped anchor.

"Darling, what are you going to do with all that gold?" Marcia put her arms around his neck as his crew hustled to tie down the Moon Shadow.

"I will give some to my brave men, build that children's home, help wherever needs real help and stash the rest away for me and my bride." Rider smiled and shouted orders to his men, then helped Marcia off the ship. "I know you will want to look in on Elizabet and get a good bath. I will plan a quick wedding for us, as soon as your father and aunt have arrived to attend it from Melbourne." Rider gather her up into his arms and kissed her with burning passion. "I would take you myself, but I have to get this ship unloaded and take care of business at Collinwood. I will send Amby with you, then he can come straight way and check on his friend, the young priest."

"Of course, Agar, must be worried sick as well." Marcia felt her heart sink as her thoughts turned to the handsome priest she had grown to love. "You have a good heart, Rider, despite your rough exterior." She touched his face. "Go on in peace and know I am yours."

"Aye! You belong to me now! I love you, Marcia." He kissed her one last time and called Amby to take her to the town flat. "I shall see you on our wedding day. Adieu."

Marcia took Amby's hand and walked down the cobblestone street, away from the piers and the smell of fish and saltwater.

Marcia's eyes grew misty when she saw the little flat she and Lizzie shared. She turned to hug the shaggy red head with green eyes. "Thank you, Amby. I hope you find Agar fairing well. Tell him…tell him I hope to see him very soon. I must see him before…" tears rolled down her cheeks. "Oh, Amby, why did I have to fall in love with two men? I do love Rider, with all my heart! But, I feel the exact love for Agar! I do not wish to hurt him!"

"There, there Marcia, things will work out, they always seem to find a way." Amby touched her face gently. "Agar is an understanding man and he will see what is the right thing for you.

Yes, he loves you, very much, I am afraid, but common sense will prevail. After all, the man who chooses to walk with the Lord, must learn to give up the luxuries of this world and pardon my boldness, but that definitely means s-e-x!"

"I hope I did not make the righteous man fall from grace, Amby." Marcia smiled. "Please tell Agar I will be up soon to see him."

"I will tell him, and Marcia, you did not exactly make the priest fall from grace, I do believe Agar had a big hand in your affair." Amby gave her a quick hug. "Now, stop your worry and go make your old friend happy."

Marcia watched the friend of both Agar and Rider, walked on up the path toward the white church on the hill, then lifted her knuckled hand to knock on the front door. When Elizabet opened the door, she let out a happy laugh and grabbed her young ward.

"Thank God! Sweet Lord Jesus be praised!" she squeezed her in her soft loving arms. "Marcia! You are safe, at last."

"Aye, thanks to the Moon Rider and his brave loyal men!" Marcia laughed through her mixed emotions. "What do you hear of Agar?"

"Agar has supported you with his prayers." The old nurse ran her hand through Marcia wind-swept hair. "A sea voyage can prove challenging for a lady's hair."

"I must look a mess! Although, Rider did not seem to mind my messy hair style."

"Men rarely notice such things, my lady. I dare say, they can aid in messing up a lady's hair when it comes to sporting." Lizzie blushed, never having known a man's love before.

"I can assure you, Lizzie, Rider treats me like a real lady." Marcia walked around the small room, seeming cramped after sailing on the Moon Shadow. "You spoke of Agar. How does he fare, Lizzie?" her heart grew sad, knowing she would have to confront Agar, sooner or later.

"I can honestly say, I know not how the young priest fares. Only one man, another brother of the clergy, has been with Agar ever since your kidnapping. Agar has been locked away up there, inside that chapel, praying day in and day out, non-stop, except to excuse himself. Then the clergy will pray until he returns to resume his praying." The old woman pulled a handkerchief from the apron pocket and blew her nose. "Agar wanted to come after you, my lady, but he feared he would be no match with the demons."

"And he let Rider go, knowing what I must do." Marcia spoke softly, her heart breaking for the man she loved. "Agar knew, he must have known."

"Aye, he knew, child, if you speak of marriage to the Moon Rider." Elizabet continued to weep.

"Aye, I speak thus! Rider saved my life Lizzie, from many dangerous obstacles and the three-headed dragon that wanted to eat me, because I was born a Karnstein maiden. And Rider saved me from the evil Krantz Hamish, who had left my father and my aunt for dead or dying, then offered me to that dragon for gold!" Marcia buried her head in her nurse's lap as she spoke between sobs, "Tis only fair to marry Rider, Lizzie and I do love him. But how can I break Agar's heart? He sent Rider for me, because he loved me so much. Agar knew he would lose me, but…he did it anyway."

"Aye, the man loves you with a real true heart, my lady. I know I was against it from the beginning, but now that it is over, my heart is sad for the love you both will never know." Nurse and ward cried in each other's arms for some time before Lizzie lifted the girl's face and smiled. "But, we must cheer up. When is the wedding to be, dear girl?"

"In one short week and would have been much sooner if father and auntie were here already. I do not think Rider can wait much longer and I am busting to tell Agar before he hears it from an outsider. I owe him that and so much more. I must tell him tomorrow."

"Good! It is for the best that you get a warm bath and into your gown this night. You are in much need of rest." Elizabet blew her nose. "If you need to talk about what happen on your adventure, my ears are yours. My poor child, this has been a sad time for you. Worrying about me and your parents, poor Agar, and having to break his heart. God knows what horrible things you witness while away."

"Aye, Lizzie, a lot of mixed emotions. Watching people die

such terrible, painful ways, seeing Krantz's sister, Arabella, eaten by that same dragon he gave me to, holding my breath when Rider fought Krantz on the Ravin, knowing it would be a fight till the last man was left standing. Even though I knew the Moon Rider was the best swordsman in all of England, I could not help but fear for his life! I do love him, truly, with all my heart, as well." Marcia stood up and walked to the window, gazing up at the white church, fading with the evening sun. "Aye Lizzie, both sad and yet joyful too!" she turned to face her nurse and friend, "I shall be happy with Rider and honored to be his wife. I only wished I did not have to destroy Agar."

"Oh child, I can see you love young Agar deeply. Do you not, sweet Maria?"

Marcia ran over in Elizabet's soft arms for comfort. "Aye! Oh Lizzie, he is in my heart so deeply, I think I shall never be able to forget him. I love him, sweet darling Agar."

"There, there." Elizabet sniffed. "What is done is done. We must not weep for what is lost, but rejoice in that which we have gained. A find man, respectable and admired by all the town people. A man of great wealth, who can take care of you properly. You will never go for want nor for the lack of love. If what you say is true, Rider loves you with his whole heart and is very devoted to you. To take one's life and put it out there to save the one he loves is the best kind of love."

"Aye, I must try and be a happy joyful bride." Marcia forced a smile.

"It shall indeed be a beautiful wedding, the bride all in white and the groom all in black. Will he get rid of the mask and head cover for your special day?" Elizabet was glad the subject had changed to a happier topic.

"Nay, the accident left him scarred and I do not think he wishes for anyone to see his face or hair after the fire."

"Well, the groom will have a mysterious look about him and keep everyone wondering." Elizabet laughed, suddenly feeling giddy. "I shall get some help from the village ladies and we shall spend what time we need to sew you a beautiful wedding dress and a veil of which to hide your face behind, until the big kiss."

"You are a love!" Marcia hugged her nurse. "And while you

spend your time sewing my perfect dress, I shall spend my time breaking Agar's heart."

"You must not torture yourself so, my dear." Lizzie looked up when the door opened and Nora ran in. "Come in child and see who is home."

Marcia looked over to see the little girl standing just inside the door, checking her out. She smiled and held out her arms to see the miracle for herself. "Come here sweetheart!" Nora laughed and ran over to hugged Marcia. "Nora, I was so happy to hear about you walking."

"Oh, Marcia! You had us scared to death! Poor Father Bellingham has not been out of the chapel the entire time you have been gone. I have been up to visit and bring him and Father Mason some food, but there was a sign on the big doors asking that the congregation leave him in solitude. I put my ear up at the door and could hear him praying, so I did not wish to bother him."

"Then, I shall go up tonight." Marcia held her hand up for Elizabet's rebuttal and got her wrap and draped it around her. She rubbed her hand through Nora's hair. "I am so glad you are walking! It does my heart good. I am going right by your house; I will walk you there then on my way up the hill."

"Marcia, I think you had better wait until morning, child." Elizabet followed her to the door.

"I cannot wait, Lizzie. I wanted to go to him first, even before coming here, but I just could not find the strength." Marcia hugged her old nurse. "I owe him something Lizzie. He needs to see that I am alright. I must go now."

"Alright, me darling girl. Just be careful out there in the growing darkness." Elizabet smiled reassuringly and patted her head.

"After what I have been through, dear Lizzie, Canterbury will seem like walking through the golden paths of Heaven." Marcia winked and taking Nora by her hand, went out the door and took her to the two matrons' sister's home, where she now lived, happy and loved.

Chapter Thirty-Three

After taking a deep breath to calm her nerves, Marcia knocked on the big double doors. Amby opened it and smiled down at her.

"I thought you were waiting until tomorrow." His voice came out loudly, to warn Agar of her arrival. "Please step inside out of the night air, Marcia."

"I could not wait until tomorrow, Amby. Little Nora came by and told me how he had shut himself away to pray constantly for me and my safety. I knew you would let him know I was back and safe, but if it were me, I would be anxious to see his face." Marcia looked up at him sadly. "You did not say anything about the wedding, did you?"

"You ask me not to, on the way from the docks, sweet one. Although Agar ask me many questions, I did not betray a trust." Amby took her hand and led her through the church to Agar's small rooms.

Agar looked up from the sofa, his blue eyes moist with fresh tears. Standing quickly, Agar made his way to Marcia and took her into his arms. She burst into tears as her arms clung around his neck.

"You must not cry, my love. You are safe and unhurt; that is what makes me happy." Agar spoke softly in her ear. "I have longed to see you again."

"Oh, dearest Agar, I have missed you with all my heart." Marcia looked around at Amby with pleading eyes. "Could we have this night alone, dear friend. Please! And, say naught to no one."

Amby's eyes met Agar's and got the signal to leave. "Aye, sweet girl. But just because my heart bleeds for my friend Agar. He deserves something." Amby bent down and kissed Marcia on the cheek then disappeared out through the church. The couple set quietly to listen for the church door to shut, then Agar passionately embraced Marcia as his hungry lips melted over hers.

"Sweet my love, speak not of what you came here to tell me, for I already know." Agar's kisses clung to her waiting lips. "Just be mine tonight Marcia. Let the world outside not exist, just this

217

once. Let there just be you and me, bound together as one."

"Aye, my love. Take me, make love to me, for I am truly thine." Marcia stood up and removed her wrinkle dress, never having the time for that bath or change of clothes. If he had noticed, he never let on as he removed the priestly robe over his head and led her over to his bed. He gently lay her down on it, then stretched out next to the woman he loved. His fingers tenderly ran down between her breast and down her belly. Their breathing rose together in heated passion.

"Marcia" he whispered. "you are my life. I searched for hope and I did find it. I searched for peace, and it too I found, moving and alive. But then I searched for love and I could not find it, until I found it in you, my darling."

"Oh, Agar, I was not really looking for love, only an escape from a bad marriage proposal, then I came to this town and nearly killed the one I fell madly in love with, even knowing you were a priest." Marcia pulled him closer into her arms. "Love me, dear Agar. Love me, all through the night and let not the morn arise without our love reaching to great heights together!" her lips ran down his neck and on his bare chest. "Sleep awaits those who cannot love. I need not sleep, only your love." Her lips sent fire through his body as her lips moved gently down his stomach. "And I only need you, this night, my darling Agar."

"And I you, dearest one. I love you Marcia." Agar moved over her then laid down as he connected them as one. Softly, tenderly, Marcia and Agar made love until dawn kissed the dew on the windowpane.

Marcia looked over at Agar and saw him watching her, then he slowly rubbed his hand along her shapely hips, his voice coming softly to her ears.

"The morning has come to fast. I know not what took the night."

"Could it have been all the love we tried to steal and store away in our hearts as a beautiful memory? Time has a way of slipping through our fingers, my darling." Marcia reached over to kiss him, knowing they must last a lifetime. "I wished I did not have to say farewell, dear Agar."

"But, we must, my love. You are engaged to another and he risk his life to save you when I could not." Agar slid from the bed and pulled his robe over his head. "Be off now before he grows suspicious. Rider is a just man unless you mess with his woman, then all bets are out the window." With steady fingers, he helped Marcia fasten her dress. "This dress has seen a lot of action." Agar turned his head to smile when Marcia's eyes flew open, wondering what he had meant. Surely, he did not know she had made love to Rider on that island.

"Action?" Marcia forced a laugh. "It is a bit dirty, isn't it?"

"I am referring to the ordeal on that island and all that time you have been gone, darling." Agar helped her with her rap. "I know you have a wedding to prepare for, so I want hold you up any longer."

"I shall always love you, Agar." Marcia ran over into his waiting arms. "I know you are trying to be strong for me, my darling. You will love me always too, won't you?"

"Oh Marcia, I should not, for you belong to another and I should not covet another man's wife." His lips brushed across her hair. "And you should forget me too."

"I...I could never forget you nor stop the love I have for you!" a tear fell down her cheek. "Agar?"

"Have you any doubts to my love, dearest Marcia?" Agar hugged her tightly. "Even though I know I should forget, I could sooner forget my own life as to forget you. I love you Marcia and I shall always have you in my heart!"

"I am sorry, my love, that I caused you so much hurt and grief." Tears flowed from the eyes. "Can you ever forgive me?"

"Marcia, there is naught to forgive." Agar lifted her face in his hands. "You have not cause me any pain, only joy and happiness. The greatest happiness I have ever known. It will last me a lifetime and I shall always remember my happier days with you and be grateful for the chance to love such a beautiful special woman."

"Agar...sweet loving Agar," Marcia clung to him, not wanting to leave his arms. Agar gently reached down to take her hand and lead her to the double doors.

"Go, dearest one, while I have the strength to send you away into another man's arms. Your husband awaits his bride."

"Agar...I..."

"Shhh." Agar gently pressed his finger to her lips. "Go, my angel and have a good life." He kissed her forehead. "Adieu."

"Oh!" Marcia picked up her skirt tails and ran across the courtyard and through the open gate without turning around. Agar brushed the tears away from his face, then walked silently into the church.

"Rider, you have got to see this!" Amby had gone down to the cellar to help the wine steward pick out the wine to bring up for the wedding that evening. Noticing movement in the wine cellar, he bent down for closer observation and saw a rat staring up at him, with a big wart on his nose.

"You mean to tell me, Wart is down in my wine cellar?" Rider was trying to button his shirt and his fingers kept shaking.

"Here Rider, permit me to help you." Amby chuckled. "Not to worry Rider, every groom gets nervous on his wedding day or is it the rat that has you upset?"

"Where is Wart now? Did he get away?" Rider brushed Amby's hands away and fastened each button, then checked himself out in the mirror. Something in the mirror behind his friend dash past him and into his wardrobe. Rider walked over and yanked the door open and demanded. "Alright Wart, get yourself out here this instant!"

"Rider, what are you doing? That rat is down in the cellar somewhere." Amby stopped short when he noticed the humped back rat slink out and look up shyly. "Wart?"

"That right! I am Wart. I...I guess you are wondering what I am doing in your castle, sir knight?" the nervous rat gave Rider a shaky smile. "I sorta snuck on your wagon when those gents were loading up all those stark stones I hid away in your fine ship. I never really trusted that Krantz fellow, making a deal with Gore. Gold for that pretty little lady. The mean man had already served the old boss the little nervous, screaming, blonde lady and he chomped her up in three bites."

"Is all this gory information necessary, Wart?" Amby felt like gagging. "Why did you give us the gold and not the devil Krantz?"

"Like I told you, young man, I did not like that shifty eyed

Krantz from the moment I set my tiny eyes on him." The humped back rat looked back up at Rider. "Then I saw you in action at the sacred rock after the face in the stone spoke to you. I could tell you loved that pretty little girl, cause you went to the cavern of the Grim, a buddy of my old boss, Gore."

"You saw me?" Rider knew he must have witness seeing him at the stone face. "You certainly get around for a slave."

"I was a slave, sir knight, but now that my island home is buried beneath the deep sea, I am a free rat and with the aid of your find ship, I hope you will take me and the entire legion to our old home."

"Is this the reason you gave me the stark stones, Wart? You wish my crew to take you and all your friends to another island?"

"Not just another island, sir knight, but Rat Island. It sits sorta between here and the Island of mist. Many years ago, some pirates landed on Rat Island just to check it out. We, being rats and all, smelled cheese on their ship, anchored just a few yards out, and swam out to steal some, then return before the pirates returned. Unfortunately, the pirates set sail and we were still munching on cheese when we realized we were out at sea. They landed on Island of mist and having found us aboard, ran us off their ship. End of story!"

"Not quite. Wart. What did you substitute the stark stones for on Krantz's ship?" Rider placed the cover over his head, then looked down. "You wish to go home?"

"Ah, yes! It took two rats to push each cart to the beach, but only one rat to swim it out to the waiting ship. There were 50,000 stark stone, so that required 100,000 rats to cart to the beach. The 50,000 bars of fool's gold were already hidden on the beach. As 50,000 rats swam the stork stones out, the other 50,000 rats took the fool's gold out to the Ravin. Each ship had another 50,000 rats waiting to help load the stones on each ship." Wart smiled broadly, showing a missing tooth. "The entire rat population is accounted for, all 201,000 rats. We planned to stay aboard your ship and leave the island of Mist and slavery behind. I was planning my escape off the Ravin when Krantz caught me and threw me overboard. The rats aboard the Moon Shadow helped get me on."

"So, the only real gold bar Krantz had was the one in his

office." The Moon Rider laughed, then saw Wart shaking his head, a negative. "What, did he have more?"

"Nope! The gold bar you took from his office was fool's gold. I deliberately gave it to him in front of Gore, who cannot tell the difference either." Wart chuckled. "Looks like it fooled you too."

"That it did, Wart." Rider checked the time and pulled his mask and hat on. "I would love to chat more, Wart. But I am getting married in one hour and I hear the guest arriving."

"A real wedding! You are marring that pretty little lady. May I be the ring barrier? I am really good at carrying things bright." Wart put his paws together to beg. "Please! I think she liked me, a little."

"Marcia was sad when she thought Wart had drowned." Amby looked thoughtful.

"On one condition Wart, you cannot scare the guest. You must come out with me and Amby and stay quiet during the ceremony." Rider took the rings from his pocket and laid them on a small pillar. "Can you handle this?"

"Are you kidding? I will be doing this as a friend, not a slave." Wart blushed "Ah shucks, getting hitched!"

"My brides, awaits! Let us do this!" The Moon Rider stepped from his room, Amby and Wart right behind.

Chapter Thirty-Four

Marcia smiled at herself in the big mirror in Rider's guest suite. She could not believe that she was the beautiful bride on the other side. As Elizabet helped her with her hair, she blew her nose. "I promise myself I would not get sloppy." She sniffed. "Oh, Marcia, you are the loveliest bride I have ever seen!"

"Oh, Lizzie, you are just partial. I must admit, the gown you made me so lovingly is the prettiest I have ever seen, even the one the princess wore when she got married in the palace, two years back." When her old nurse laid down the brush, Marcia got up and danced around the room. "What do you say, honest words Lizzie, do you think Rider will like it?"

"He will adore it! Any man who did not would be completely out of his head!" Elizabet laughed and walked over to see who had knocked at the door. "Come in Dorinda, and feast your eyes on your beautiful niece. Marcia could put our princess to shame."

Dorinda smiled over at the lovely bride, then walked over to hug her. "Oh Marcia, your mother would be so proud of you, my dear. Not only marrying a man of great means, but a man that you love with a whole heart." With care she took the wedding veil and placed it over Marcia's head. "The guest is waiting. The happy groom is waiting with his best man and..." Dorinda shrug her shoulders. "A strange, humped back rat is carrying the rings on a pillow."

"Wart?" Marcia laughed. "Wart is alive! He did not drown!"

"Apparently not, my dear." Dorinda tried to smile. "He just stands there and...smiles."

"He has not said anything?" Marcia checked her reflection one last time. "Wart was chatting away on the island."

"A...ah...talking rat?" Elizabet swallowed.

"I shall tell you all about it one day, when I do not have an anxious groom waiting." Marcia swallowed and took a big breath. "Oh, I am so nervous." Another big breath and then she smiled. "Alright, take me to my knight."

223

Rider looked from the mask and smiled broadly when he finally saw Marcia walking toward him. He took her hand the moment she stepped beside him and whispered in her ear.

"Ah, how delicious you look, my dearest. I cannot wait to get you into my bed."

"Do not you mean, our bed, sir knight?" Marcia whispered back, and peeked around him to see Wart smiling up at her. "It is good to see you alive and well, Wart."

"My congratulations my dear." Wart took a formal bow. "I would sing at your wedding, but, alas, I cannot carry a decent tune."

"Just having you here is a special gift, Wart," Marcia turned to Rider and whispered. "I see he can still talk."

"That is because, my inquisitive bride, he was taught to speak, Gore had speech through the power of the golden tablet." Rider squeezed her hand.

"You shall not be using any of that power on me this night, will you?" Marcia smiled at the minister, waiting for the couple to begin.

"Nay, I shall rely on my own skills and talents, my dear." He turned her to face the preacher. "You may begin, Reverend Tanner."

The service went quickly, as the Moon Rider had instructed. After several, guest gave a toast, congratulating the married couple, Rider bid his guest to enjoy the food and wine, said his farewells, then led Marcia up to their bedchamber. She could hear the men guest laughing loudly and clinking their glasses with each other as they made their way up the steps. She thought she had heard Wart say, "How rude!" and she could not help but laugh softly as he opened the door.

"Happy hunting, Rider!" Doctor Merciton called out.

"Such a happy couple, hey Wart?" Amby smiled broadly and poured a little of his wine in a small dish for the weeping rat. Amby walked over to the staircase and gazed up toward the door. "And the happy thing about it, 'everyone' will be happy."

Elizabet had overheard the redhead and tapped him on the back. "Excuse me, young man, did you forget about poor Agar? I am certain he cannot never be happy."

"Nay, madam. Agar had his good times." Amby smiled up the steps. "But I did always warn him, he who tangles with the feeling of a woman, will feel the tangles she will give him in return."

Rider smiled down at Marcia as he scooped her up into his strong arms and carried her in the doorway. "Well, my little bride, at long last you are mine!"

"Aye, that I am!" Marcia smiled and looked around to find candles burning softly on the bedside table and the mantel. A bottle of expensive wine and two glasses set waiting on a tray with one long stem white rose. The smell of roses filled the room from the big vase filled with three dozen white roses and the bed was scattered with fresh red rose pedals. "Oh, Rider! Everything smells so lovely."

He buried his face in her neck and softly said. "Aye, but my favorite smell is my woman's sweet fragrant."

"Now, I know why you insisted on having the wedding here at Collinwood, Rider." Marcia looped her arms around his neck. "You did not have far to go for our first night as husband and wife."

"Aye, but then, can I help it if my woman just happens to make me hunger after her, all the time?" he laughed softly and pulled her back in his arms. "You look so beautiful right now, darling." Rider smiled slyly. "I think I am getting hungry for your love, my dearest."

"You beast! You just think, you want me?" Marcia smiled and started unbuttoning his shirt. "You really want me, do you not?"

"Aye, Marcia, all the time!" Rider grew serious as his lips parted over hers. His fingers glided down her dress, unbuttoning each button on her dress. She jumped away, holding the dress pressed tightly against her body. "What is wrong, my love? Have I done anything to offend you?"

"Nay, naught! Now that you are my husband, dear Rider, I want to see your face. You cannot hide from your wife forever." Marcia tilted her head, determined to wait until he complied to her wishes. "Take away the mask and let me see you, my darling."

"Nay! I cannot grant you this wish, Marcia. I…I feel that you will grow sick and not love me any longer." Rider turned his back to her and walked over by the window. Marcia followed him and gently placed her hand on his shoulder.

"My dearest love, I love you for what is inside you. A good loving man who sincerely cares about his fellow man and the man who has sworn his love to me. Rider, I know the real person you are and I think you are beautiful no matter what you look like."

His hand clutched her face as his lips parted over hers, then he gave her his radiant smile and nodded his head.

"Then, if I am loved so deeply and completely, regardless to my appearance, I should trust you and show you what lies on the other side of this mask." Rider turned his back to her as his fingers slowly removed the mask over his head, then the black cover from his hair and dropped them on the floor at his feet.

Marcia stared at the blonde hair, her heart began beating wildly as she grabbed her chest, her eyes wide in shock. She swallowed as she took a big breath and spoke softly.

"Rider, turn around, please."

As the Moon Rider turned slowly around, Marcia let out a soft cry. Those same alluring blue eyes, that had looked at her so often. The same nose and perfect lips. She stood frozen, not knowing what to say or do. Rider smiled brightly and cleared his throat.

"I thought it might be quite a shock, my love."

"A shock?" Marcia ran over and threw her arms around his neck, then kissed his lips thankfully. "Agar, why did you not tell me it was you all along? All this time I have been thinking that I have been in love with two men, a priest and a mysterious knight! Two completely different personalities! One, a true gentleman, soft spoken and gentle, the other, outgoing, sometimes a little overbearing, even conceded, but always very romantic!" she stepped back and paused. He came forward to take her in his arms and she pushed him away, then frowned up into his smiling face. "That was a mean, nasty trick, Agar! Or is it Rider? How dare you use me to play a personal joke with!"

"Ah! Come on, sweet one, it was all harmless." Rider tried once again to pull her into his embrace, but she would have no part of it, and turned and stormed across the room. "Oh, Marcia, you have got both the men you love. This should make you happy."

"I AM HAPPY!" she yelled. "It is just the way you managed to fool me!"

"Well, if you must know, I could not tell you who the Moon Rider was until I was sure it was safe." Rider looked at her imploringly. "Come on, sweetheart, I love you."

"I love you too, Agar. Or, again, I ask, is it Rider?" Marcia turned her back to him, arms folded stubbornly. "Some jest!"

"My full name is Agar Bellingham Collinwood. The name I go by to fight those who wrong others is, the Moon Rider, a hero and legend from the moment I returned to Collinwood Castle and put on that mask." Agar walked over and placed his hand lovingly on her shoulder. "Marcia, love?"

"What about the priestly role? What purpose was that for?" Marcia remained cold, needing answers.

"I had to get near the people, so, I would know what Hayworth and his cohorts were up too."

"And what about the priest Nora heard praying in the church when the Moon Rider, you, came after me?"

"Nora heard the real priest praying in the chapel, along with a fellow clergyman. The priest stationed there was good enough to let me pretend to be the new priest until I showed the citizens of Canterbury what a villain their loving vicar was." Agar's fingers moved up her silky neck. "Marcia."

"I guess you and Amby got many a chuckle from me, running from Agar's arms to yours and afraid of hurting either one of you!" Marcia grew warm to his constant touching.

"Well, it did get a bit funny at times, I must admit." He chuckled and Marcia started to pull away when he grabbed her and turned her around to face him. "But, through it all, my love for you continued to grow as I have never loved before. The most important thing is that I love you, Marcia. I need you forever by my side! I have loved you from the first moment you nearly ran me down and I dived out of the way."

Marcia looked down and laughed softly. "I never did get to fix you that dinner for your near tragedy, did I?" she was growing hot under his heavy embrace.

"Nay, you did not. But I shall be more than glad to have you now, my darling." Agar's lips parted passionately over hers as their love blossomed forth from Collinwood Castle.

A soft blue mist floated around the castle and drifted near the master bedchamber as it seemed to whisper in the soft evening breezes:

"Love on, dear lovers! Thy joys to begin! For love always conquers! Love, always wins!"

At the first rays of light, a voice could be heard calling out at the full moon while it still graced the dawning sky. From the master bedchamber came the war cry, the cry of victory. The Moon Rider won his battle to win the fair maiden of Karnstein, and live happier ever after!

The End

www.ingramcontent.com/pod-product-compliance
Lightning Source LLC
Chambersburg PA
CBHW060428180626
46817CB00007B/2720